Storm of Ecstasy

Other Titles by Setta Jay:

The Guardians of the Realms Series:

Hidden Ecstasy

Ecstasy Unbound

Ecstasy Claimed

Denying Ecstasy

Tempting Ecstasy

Piercing Ecstasy

Binding Ecstasy

Searing Ecstasy

Divine Ecstasy

Storm of Ecstasy

Setta Jay

A Guardians of the Realms Novel

Copyright:

Disclaimer:

This book is a work of fiction. Any resemblance to any person living or dead is purely coincidental. The characters and places are products of the author's imagination and used fictitiously.

Warning: Gods gone crazy, bad language, dirty talk, and explicit scenes meant for mature audiences.

Contributors:

Editor: BookBlinders

Proofreader: Pauline Nolet

Cover Image: Fotolia

Acknowledgements:

As always, I'd like to send out a huge thank you to my editor and proofreader, Lindy and Pauline, for helping make these books the best they can be.

Tons of love to my husband for just being amazing throughout the process.

Thank you to all the Book Bloggers who have given me immeasurable support and guidance. Sending out big hugs to you all!

I also want to thank those of you in the Setta's Sexies fan groups on Facebook and Goodreads. You make me smile every day! I love you all!

Thank you to all who post, engage or just watch the craziness from the sidelines in all my social media outlets.

And lastly, a MASSIVE thank you to all of the fans for reading. I wouldn't be able to do what I love without your support.

Storm of Ecstasy – Book Nine (The Guardians of the Realms)

As the son of Hades and a Guardian of the Realms, Pothos has been gifted with immense power to protect the inhabitants of the four Realms of Earth. When the evil God Apollo is stolen and the Guardians are forced to wake Hades from his sleeping confinement, P is faced with a long held dangerous secret; that he was born of two worlds. Learning that his mother was a Priestess from the unknown world of Thule, Hades also confesses that P has been kept hidden from all who dwell there as his very life is in danger the moment their Gods learn of his existence. As P struggles to make sense of the life he has lived and what this means for his future he finds himself forcibly pulled into Thule by an unstoppable divine force. Bracing for attack, he instead finds himself faced with a threat of a different sort, a beautiful golden Goddess who calls to the very depths of his soul.

Gefn is a Goddess of Thule, dedicated to the preservation of her world. A world constantly faced with wildly shifting energy left behind in the wake of warring Gods. Haunted after witnessing the brutal murders of her closest friends, her Priestesses, she has lived a life of relative loneliness but for her few remaining siblings and her pair of giant, magical lynx gifted to her at birth. They are Guardians of Thule and her most trusted companions. When they lead her to a hidden garden outside her missing sister's palace she is shocked to find a winged male who calls to her most primal desires, unleashing her power in a way that sweeps her into a passion she's never known. His sudden disappearance leads her and her brothers into a tense and deadly standoff in another world.

As both worlds collide will Pothos and Gefn's unique mating end in his death? Or will the strength of their love help them survive a storm of ecstasy as they uncover more secrets that could save them all?

Author's Note—Starting the Series with this Title (Contains Some Spoilers to Earlier Books):

We've always done our best to make the Guardians of the Realms series as standalone as possible, but I do not recommend starting with book nine. If you decide to try it anyway, this is a little background that may help:

The twelve Guardians of the Realms were gifted with immense power and responsibility to watch over the four Realms: Earth (the Realm of humanity), Heaven (Realm of pure souls), Hell (Realm of tainted souls), and Tetartos (Realm of beasts and Immortals). They were also charged by the Creators with watching over the sleeping Gods, who would "one day be needed on Earth." The nine male and three female Guardians represent the strongest and most powerful of the Immortal races, and all are telepathically linked along with their various other gifts.

Of the twelve sleeping Gods, only Hades, Athena and Aphrodite were good, the others were tainted with evil. Yet all were sent into sleeping chambers that were meant to purge the bad Gods of all the dark energies they'd consumed while feeding off the suffering of humans and Immortals instead of the pure energy of the Earth, which was the sustenance of Immortals and Gods alike.

Unfortunately the Creators hadn't sent Ares and Artemis' evil triplets, the spawn of a dark incestuous coupling, to sleep. They'd left them restrained to their prison in Hell Realm, not realizing that one day the evil beings would be able to cause chaos from their cage. So for centuries the Guardians have battled against demon souls the evil three send out to possess humans while at the same time continuously dispatching hell beasts into Heaven and Tetartos

Realms.

As for the Immortal races, Apollo and Hermes, two of the worst Gods, experimented on, imprisoned and then callously bred any they could find before being sent to sleep. Their goal had been to create a powerful army, so they infused the races with animal DNA to give them added strength and instincts.

One of the tormented Immortal breeders, Charybdis, eventually cast a spell using a portion of her own life force in the ultimate sacrifice. The spell ensured that the Gods could no longer force them to breed and take their young to warrior camps. Immortals could no longer produce young with one who wasn't their fated mate. After the Immortals were freed by the Creators and exiled to Tetartos, finding a mate had turned into an exceedingly rare and beautiful occurrence. An event that made the pair more powerful and allowed for the possibility of children a decade after their souls had connected.

And so it had always been until something changed. Suddenly Guardians were finding their fated mates. The added power that came from the pairings was making already powerful beings as strong as the Gods themselves.

A couple of months ago Apollo was freed from his sleeping unit by a now dead enemy of the Guardians. Before the Guardians could recapture him, the Deity was abducted by unknown warriors. Without a clue as to the God's whereabouts, the Guardians were forced to awaken Hades, the strongest of the Gods, in the hope that he could telepathically track his brother.

He hadn't been able to find Apollo, but he did have knowledge they needed, including the fact that they were dealing with a previously unknown ancient world... Thule.

Hades had once held a secret allegiance with the Thulian God Agnarr. The Deity told no one of the other world or of his ally as a way to ensure neither world learned of his son, Pothos' birth to a priestess of Thule. The long-dead female had warned Hades that the Gods of Thule would demand Pothos' death if they ever became aware of his existence.

With Apollo gone, Hades was forced to share the hidden information before attempting to contact his old Thulian ally using drops from a powerful blue stone into a mist-shrouded lake on a hidden northern island of Earth. Unfortunately, instead of Agnarr, a female Goddess, Kara, came through a portal from Thule instead and attempted to forcibly take Hades back with her.

Now Kara lay unconscious in a Guardian holding cell, still recovering from her attempt at abducting the powerful God.

Pothos, struggling with the knowledge of being of two worlds, found himself gazing into the mystical lake where his father had nearly been taken. When something magical and blue rose to the surface, he found himself pulled into the world he was never supposed to see. Into the path of a golden Goddess that called to his soul. After an interruption to the brief but passionate interlude, Pothos was uncontrollably drawn back to Earth.

Chapter 1

Hroarr's Palace, World of Thule – Fifteen Minutes Ago

"Are you well, my Goddess?" Laire wasn't only her guard, the big blond warrior was a friend. Winds whipped at them as he took the wide steps into her brother's palace. Gefn breathed in the sea air, hearing the crashing waves against the rocky cliff below. Streaks of sunlight slipped through the swelling clouds as she swept past her brother's guards. They bowed their heads respectfully as she, Laire and her two massive black beasts passed, giving extra room to the irritated felines that reached waist high to the large warriors. The beasts were the ancient Guardians of Thule, gifted to Gefn by her powerful parents when she'd been but a babe. Gefn's sires had instructed all of the Gods to heed the powerful creatures' instincts in all things. It was said that they would help lead Thule through the end of times if it was possible.

At the moment agitation bled from the magical creatures. Their bobbed tails twitched as much as their pointed golden ears. She sucked in a breath, fighting her own tension as well as that coming from Laire and her animals. She knew her guard was concerned and she understood, but she was busy battling to control her body's wildly intense reaction to the mysterious winged male Laire had just caught her kissing.

"I am." She managed. Though she wasn't certain she spoke true. Her body ached with a need that could not be natural. Her nipples pushed relentlessly at her leather vest and she felt restless... *What happened to her in that garden?* She still felt the dark male's strong hands, the immense power whirling around them as she'd succumbed to a passion she'd never imagined possible. He'd rendered her senseless, and she still felt his primal growls vibrating against her tongue as he'd devoured her mouth.

She called cooler winds to ease her flushed skin, but it was useless. The icy gale only whipped at her hair and Laire's kilt. Her cheeks were still heated when they moved through the massive stone pillars and into her brother Hroarr's sanctuary.

She sent power to slip the long tendrils of hair off her face. The heavy mass was held back at the side with clasps, but the rest flowed free down her back in blonde waves. The winds usually soothed her, but not now. Not when she was on her way to her brothers to tell them that there'd been an otherworldly male in Thule. One who'd disappeared before she'd asked him a single question.

"You are sure?" She would have smiled at the big warrior if she were capable of assuring him, but she wasn't. She blew out a breath as they strode down wide halls lined with ancient tapestries. Her friend finally asked, "Who was the male?" She noticed Laire still hadn't sheathed his staff to rest with the twin blades at his back.

Spa and Velspar hissed at Laire, and her warrior stepped back with a frown.

"Spa, Velspar, cease," she bit out. The magical beasts had always liked Laire, but they'd made their anger known since Laire had interrupted her with the male. She rubbed a shaking hand over her side.

Feeling her beasts' agitation through their ancient bond wasn't helping her ragged emotions.

She mentally chastised them. *Laire's intention was to protect me. What did you expect when you tried to warn him away from the garden? He is my warrior. Of course he would venture in to be sure of my safety.* In truth, Laire was far more friend than guard, and it warmed her to know he had braved her powerful beasts' temper to check on her even though she was a Goddess with enough power to protect herself as well as her friend. She glanced back at the large male, he stood tall, but she could see the crease at his brow as he studied the cats through confused blue eyes. He was a good male, but the sight of him brought a familiar pang, knowing that one day she would be forced to watch him die. She had a few hundred more years with her mortal friend, if they were all lucky enough to survive the end.

Gefn shook those thoughts away before mentally snapping at her cats, *Why did you lead me to the male? Who was he? What is his importance to Thule?* She firmed her lips, realizing how ridiculous it was to demand answers when Spa and Velspar were incapable of responding with words. They were surely able to send their irritation through the emotional bond she shared with the infuriating animals. Velspar had the decency to move back to one side of her, allowing Laire to step beside her again without so much as a huff of displeasure.

Laire didn't hesitate to step back to her side. He was far braver than any other warrior she'd ever known. Most gave the cats a great deal of space, including Laire's ancestors.

She breathed out before admitting to the warrior, "I am unsure who he was. Or why Spa and Velspar guided me to him." She'd been in the middle of her sister's garden when the male had dropped from a portal, shocking her into stillness because in all of her and her siblings' travels they'd never encountered another race of beings able to move from world to world. Something about the magic had felt almost Thulian, but later he'd disappeared using some other kind of ability. One that had not felt familiar.

Spa chuffed.

What did that mean? She clenched her teeth, knowing the magical felines were powerful and to be heeded, but she wanted to know more. Certainly their instincts had led her and her siblings to locations of invaluable artifacts throughout the long centuries. They'd also ruthlessly fought at her side when her evil siblings had attacked her palace all those millennia ago. And after her priestesses had been brutally slain in front of her, the beasts' bond with her had become the only thing grounding her. She still felt the ache at the long ago loss of Togn, Skuld and Grior. A God had a bond with their þrír, their three, and having it severed had left a hole deep in her soul. It was a battle that still haunted her dreams, because the outcome was always the same, Gefn watching them die, powerless to stop it.

"He did not say anything?" Laire's words drew her attention away from memories of blood and the stench of death that would never be washed from her mind. Her emotions were all over the place. She felt raw and it wasn't normal. Something was happening to her. The only thing she knew for certain was that her beasts had led her to the male for a reason. He had to be important in either finding her missing sister or for some other purpose related to the good of Thule.

She felt a pang of renewed desire that flushed her cheeks, embarrassment traveling on its heels. She commanded a passing guard, "I need Hroarr to meet me in his study."

"Right away, Goddess." The male bowed before whisking away almost faster than her sight could detect. Now to collect her more reckless brother, Dagur. She mentally scoffed. Would she be considered the more reckless one now that she'd had an erotic encounter with a male of another world without so much as asking his name or at the very least checking him for weapons first?

The beasts turned toward the great hall and emitted a loud roar at the top of the steps leading down to the large room of people laughing and drinking. The area immediately silenced, and Gefn saw wide eyes immediately shift to her and then to the rarely vocal creatures.

Dagur's golden eyes snapped up as well before he issued a command to those in the room. "Out." His wavy brown hair was tied back, and he wore a leather kilt with nothing covering his chest. The occupants slipped away in mere seconds as her brother's brow furrowed. "What is it? Is it to do with Kara?"

She mentally cursed herself for barely giving her missing sister a thought. Kara's absence had been the reason Gefn had traveled to her cold sibling's palace in the first place. "And more," she admitted. There was a great deal she needed to share with her brothers about her trip to the other Goddess' palace.

"Hroarr's study," she commanded and turned with her beasts. A now silent Laire moved to walk at her back as her brother came to her side.

"What is it?" Dagur growled.

"I will tell you with Hroarr," she ground out.

She only wished she had her own answers. The first being why her skin felt too tight and why she mourned the loss of a male she hadn't even spoken to. One who'd enthralled her so completely. Why had her beasts liked him? She needed to know that they hadn't been caught up in some kind of magic with her. Spa made a spitting noise that sounded vaguely insulted.

Hroarr stalked toward them a moment later; flames in the hall flared brighter at his passing. The intense power of the ruling God of Thule whipped around a massive frame clad in dark leather from shoulder to boot, a match to his raven beard and long tied-back hair. Ever-present darkness shadowed his brilliant emerald eyes. She knew she was seeing his ancient power of backsight, or sjá. A harsh flash of the untold death and destruction he'd seen in the hundreds of worlds he traveled, ruthlessly seeking the key to saving their world.

"What is it?" Hroarr demanded the moment they were all inside his study. Laire stayed beyond the doors, with Hroarr's elite warriors, and she felt the impact of the heavy spelled wood wedging shut as she decided what to say. The scent of old parchment and burning candles in the space had always been relaxing. She had a feeling nothing would be able to ease her until she had answers to her own questions. Something was happening, and her beasts' behavior only put a fine point on how important it must be. Nothing in the old tomes and ancient artifacts of her brother's study could calm her now.

"Kara is gone." She informed both brothers of her findings at her missing sister's palace. The ring Kara had always worn was still oddly burning in Gefn's palm. A fact she hadn't even noticed as she'd traveled to her brother's palace.

Hroarr's deep green gaze darkened at her words, and she could feel his displeasure crackle in the hearth at the end of the room.

Gefn continued, "Kara's servants do not know where she went." She shook her head as she continued in frustration, partly at herself, partly at her sister. Gefn doubted Kara had intended to be cryptic or mysterious about her departure. "Kara left her ring in their care." The other Goddess was arrogant to a fault, which had always been her female sibling's most irritating quality. Yet, if Kara left the ring, it had to mean she'd felt reservations at her destination, just not enough to delay the trip. As a Goddess of Thule, her sister could open a portal anywhere inside or outside of their world. That meant she could be anywhere, but opening portals was their most draining gift. If she'd faced danger and been injured, she could be trapped somewhere, waiting for her strength to return. She might not be close to her sister, but she didn't like that idea. Gefn should have been thinking of that not lusting after her mysterious winged male.

"When did she leave?" Dagur gritted out as Gefn handed him the ring. Dagur was the most skilled in spells, and he'd hopefully be able to figure out where Kara was or if the ring had any significance to her location. If not, then why had Kara instructed her servant to give the ring to Gefn or her brothers if she hadn't returned within the hour?

"The blue stone is spelled. It would likely have a match to another stone of its kind. With the heated power coming from it, I would say it is a call to someone or someplace," he mused as he studied it. "Was it hot like this from the start?" Dagur demanded before Gefn had been able to answer.

"No, it started heating…" She stopped, attempting to remember the exact moment it triggered. It hadn't been hot when her sister's servant had given it to her.

It had started to heat the moment Spa and Velspar began leading Gefn to the gardens. To the male. She absently answered the other question as she wondered at the significance. There had to be a connection. Gefn's agitated beasts paced in front of them as she continued relaying information. "Kara's been gone over a week. The servant sent riders here, but they obviously have not made it yet."

"What else?" Hroarr commanded, his eyes trailing Spa's and Velspar's impatient movements.

There was indeed more. "The ring began heating as Spa and Velspar started guiding me to a powerful otherworldly male. One with dark ebony wings and a great deal of power. He dropped from a portal as I entered the gardens beside Kara's palace." She hadn't admitted that said male had kissed her to the point that she'd been rendered ignorant. She was sure she would have to, but she wasn't looking forward to it. Her cats would never have led her to danger, so she could point out that she wasn't a complete fool.

But why? She narrowed her eyes at her pacing beasts. They seemed to be just as anxious as she was.

Hroarr's intent gaze caught and held hers. "Where is this male? Who is he?"

She felt her face heat like an errant child instead of a powerful Goddess who'd lived thousands of years. "He is gone."

"Gone?" Dagur's tone was incredulous.

"Yes." She cleared her throat. "He disappeared."

Hroarr crossed massive arms over his chest and stared at her. "He opened another portal?"

"No, he... used a different kind of power to leave."

"We have never come across hints of another race of Gods that could travel between worlds. You are sure he opened a portal?" Dagur said, a spark of concern in his golden eyes.

She mentally cursed in several ancient dialects before telling them, "Yes, I am aware of what a portal looks like, Dagur." She gave him a pointed look before continuing, "And Spa and Velspar seemed to *approve* of him."

"Approve. How?" Hroarr's words brooked no arguments.

"They purred." Just saying the words seemed ridiculous.

"And," Hroarr demanded.

"My power whisked me into his arms."

"Whisked you?" Dagur's tone annoyed her.

She firmed her lips. "I did not end up there consciously."

Her brothers both looked at the cats before Dagur looked her over and continued, "He did not attempt to harm you? Did he explain his presence?"

Harm her. No. She shook her head, wishing to crawl in a hole. "We did not speak." A deep dark hole. "We kissed... before Laire interrupted." And then she remembered that the male had spoken. "Wait. He did speak." How had she forgotten the way his sexy words had seemed to enthrall her. "He used the ancient tongue. He... he asked if I had called him there." She frowned at the ring, wondering if her sister's keepsake from Agnarr, a long-dead brother, had somehow summoned the male. But how? She hadn't opened the portal that dropped him into her path. She looked at the beasts, who were now yowling impatiently for her to do something.

"Tell me everything." Hroarr commanded.

She itemized the details as if listing it without emotion would be less uncomfortable. "He dropped from a portal and asked if I had called him there. Spa and Velspar purred at him. After that my winds blew me into his arms." She paused to take a breath. "We kissed. Suddenly the cats hissed and Laire was there with his weapon raised. The male pushed me behind him. I instructed Laire not to attack and then a moment later the male disappeared." Spa and Velspar huffed at her words and she glared at the beasts who'd been her protectors and constant companions for thousands upon thousands of years.

Hroarr's expression didn't change as he stared at her cats. "They did not wish for you to be interrupted?"

She nodded, incredibly uncomfortable at the way her brother had said that, but she wouldn't deny it. "So it seems. I have no idea what it means." She needed to tell them everything because she had no doubt that this had something to do with Thule. An allegiance that the cats were hoping to forge?

"I feel... anxious to see him again." She added, "And as if new power is flowing inside me."

Hroarr's eyes flickered with interest at that. "What kind of power?"

"I do not know. Part of it feels like mine is strengthening, but there is something else in there as well." Their world needed more power. They all knew it, but it was unsettling to have an unknown force welling inside her.

"Are you well?" Dagur asked. He might have his faults, but her reckless brother looked truly concerned for her.

She sucked in a breath. "Whatever the power is, it feels pure." It felt incredible and unnerving all at once.

Gefn could almost see Hroarr thinking. Considering. He was their leader, the most powerful of their Gods. Her brother could be ruthless when needed, but he was above all else intelligent. He had never been threatened by her beasts. She imagined he saw them as tools, and Hroarr would use anything he required if it meant saving Thule.

It seemed Hroarr was not acting fast enough for Spa and Velspar because soon enough the cats yowled in annoyance, and she was shocked when they released the power to open a portal on their own. Her mouth fell open at the sight of the watery air in the middle of Hroarr's office. She heard the splintering of wood and glass crashing to stone with the force of energy released in the space. Spa and Velspar had never done such a thing. She hadn't known they held the ability.

Dagur staggered back, biting off ancient curse words, but Hroarr only stared down at her beasts for a moment longer, studying them... or making a point that he followed no one.

Their test of wills was not what Gefn's anxiety level needed. She felt her stomach twisting with need. The arousal seemed to be getting worse, to the point near painful. That meant she had no intention of waiting long for Hroarr to make the decision to heed the beasts.

This fact that they'd opened a portal was like a blow to the gut. How had they hidden this from her, and why hadn't they used the ability during her battle with her evil brother Tyr all those millennia ago. What else had they secreted from her? Twin sets of golden eyes met hers and she felt a well of sadness through her bond with them. She swallowed through the clenching of her stomach. If they'd withheld any power that could have saved her priestesses, she'd never be able to forgive them.

Hroarr turned to Dagur, and she forced her attention on her dark brother's words. "Find out where this leads and if it has significance to the ring or Kara."

Dagur nodded before turning to the watery air and spelling words she didn't quite hear. Magical winds surged from his fingers, moving over and through the ring as his tone grew nearly hypnotic.

Nearly as fast as the spelled air slipped through, it was back. Dagur breathed it in, his eyes glowing a brilliant gold. Scant moments passed before his muscled shoulders tensed followed by a string of curses as he slammed the ring down on Hroarr's desk. "It is the same world where I found the God. They may have come to retrieve him." Dagur had tracked and captured a God weeks ago, and it had been a bone of contention. He'd lost dozens of warriors when taking the arrogant male from the other world.

Dagur continued while shaking his head in obvious irritation. "The ring leads to that world, but I did not sense Kara. If she's there, they've somehow blocked her power signature."

Gefn breathed out, knowing they'd feel it if Kara were dead. Thule would feel the impact. So she was either in the other world, likely in a prison cell like the one they used to contain the otherworldly God they held, or she'd gone somewhere else. The latter wasn't likely.

Are we going to get Kara? Is this the purpose of your portal? To save her? she mentally sent to the beasts and had confirmation of her suspicions through a yowl that felt like assent. *Is she there?*

"Spa and Velspar think Kara is there, but it does not feel as if venturing to this world is necessarily about retrieving her. Not in their emotions."

"Then why?" Dagur growled.

"If they could talk, I would know that, would I not?" she bit out as the beasts paced, staring up at Hroarr.

"Does their purpose have to do with the good of Thule?" Hroarr demanded while looking at the beasts.

She felt a wave of emotion that seemed to confirm her brother's question as both animals yowled again. She nodded when her ruling brother's gaze came to her.

"I go through first," Hroarr declared as he sent out power, slamming the doors open and directing his elite warriors behind them. Laire stepped in line with Hroarr's warriors as she tried to still her anxiety and the desire to demand Laire stay in the palace, where she knew he'd be safe from the unknown. They'd already lost too many lives to this world. She would not lose Laire. One look at the blond warrior made her heart sink. She could not do that to him. It would look to the others as if she didn't have faith in him. She blew out a harsh breath, hating this while feeling drawn to it as well.

"Should Dagur stay?" she asked Hroarr.

Spa and Velspar snarled and pushed at Dagur.

Hroarr looked down and with a word, "No," he stepped through the watery air.

She built power inside her as she and her beasts strode through beside Dagur. She couldn't shake the feeling that her mysterious winged male was awaiting her on the other side. In a world that could lead to Thule's salvation, or possibly a battle for Gods.

Chapter 2

Mystical Lake, Earth Realm – Minutes later

Son of a bitch.

Pothos was ensnared in the beautiful lust-filled gaze of a Goddess of Thule.

His fated mate.

And potential instrument of his death.

Winds whipped through the dark forest flanking the turbulent banks of the moonlit lake. He sucked in the cool mountain air as he battled lust and the need to protect not only his family, but a female who could likely want him dead. Primal power raged over the water and trees while locking them in place. His muscles tensed against the magical hold unleashed by the beasts who'd come through with his female. His ears were still ringing from the roar of power the cats had unleashed upon stepping into his world.

The fact that several of his Guardian brethren as well as his fucking father were behind him only added to his agitation as he assessed the two male Gods that stood beside his Goddess just above the soft ripples of the once calm lake.

Kilt-wearing Thulian warriors had gone down on one knee above the waves and stayed there as massive power held them all immobile against the backdrop of the iridescent blue of the open portal turbulently flickering behind them. He barely heard the breeze rustling leaves in the otherwise silent forest beyond.

You will leave here the minute I free us of the beasts' hold, P's father ordered through their telepathic link. The God had been steadily losing his mind for the past several minutes. P understood that Hades was worried, but the last thing they needed was the furious Deity starting a fucking war. That was the reason P had positioned his body in between his damned family and the female who was fated to him. Hades was too damned powerful, and P could only hope the massive black lynx-looking beasts could maintain the magical hold until P could figure out a way to fix this shit.

Father, you need to calm the hell down, P mentally growled back. He knew his dad was convinced that the Thulian Gods would want P dead because of the secret of his birth. Apparently P had a Thulian priestess mother and she'd warned Hades to keep him away from Thulian Gods. All before handing P over as a damned baby. He understood that, but his father was conveniently forgetting that fated mates were exactly that. Fate decided, and in this case, it was relentless along with having an apparent sense of humor. P's flesh pulled tight with the need to claim his female no matter how dangerous she might be to him.

Pothos, you will do as I say. Hades had always been protective; the God's centuries in a stasis unit hadn't changed a thing about that.

I'm not leaving, he bit out.

His gaze slid back to his Goddess, watching as long tendrils of golden hair slipped from the clips holding the sides back. Those soft strands flirted with her bare shoulders and the heavy curve of her breasts pushing against her snug leather vest. She was the most beautiful creature ever fucking created, and he'd had her in his arms not fifteen minutes ago. A place he wanted her again as soon as possible.

Enemy or not, she'd sealed their fate the moment she'd put her soft hands on his chest. That single touch had turned him into a damned animal intent on nothing but having her. That thought should have jolted him, because all that should matter at the moment was protecting his brethren and father.

What do you need, P? Drake asked from his position behind him. The dragon leader of the Guardians was his closest friend. They were brothers more than cousins, and he knew the male was silent as he ordered all other Guardians to stay the hell in Tetartos, the Immortal Realm of their world.

He opened his telepathic message to include Brianne, Sacha and Bastian, who were all there with their mates and Drake. *Do not let my damned father do anything stupid. Remember that Goddess is my mate, and* nothing *is to happen to her.* He'd already given all the Guardians her telepathic image upon teleporting back from Thule, but he refused to take any chances.

The others gave their tense assent as Drake responded privately, *I won't let him do anything stupid. The weapons are still in the air, and they can't seem to move any more than we can.* The first thing Drake and his powerful mate, Era, had done was remove the golden staffs from the Thulian warriors.

His concentration was shot, so his only response was a grunt, while ignoring mental communications and rants from his furious father along with questions from other Guardians he didn't have the capacity to answer.

He clenched his jaw, hoping for some clarity. Everything was changing. His muscles pulled tight as power swelled from the depths of his body. He forced back a groan as he fought to hold the growing abilities while at the same time battling insatiable lust for the beauty in front of him.

He stifled a growl as his cock pulsed, demanding freedom. Through the darkness he could see her pouty as fuck lips and wondered if they were still swollen from his kisses. Mating frenzy seemed too light a term for what he was feeling. He'd seen his brothers brought down by it, but he hadn't truly understood how distracting it was. How fucking demanding the need would be.

Her heated gaze flickered over his bare chest and the nerves jumped as if she'd slid her hands over the sensitive flesh. There was no missing the lust and frustration flickering over her face before she trained her attention on the massive lynx. Her reaction to them was completely different. He saw anger and even pain on her face, and he assumed she felt betrayed at their actions in holding them all in place, not to mention the fact that one of her beasts had come to sit in front of P. He glanced down at the black animal who'd come to him. Its pointed golden ear nearly reached P's chest in its sitting position, not an easy feat when perched in front of a nearly seven-foot Demi-God. He wasn't sure what the hell was going on with the creatures, but they were too powerful to ignore. He glanced back to see his Goddess' eyes shutter for a split second before the emerald depths blanked of the pain.

The feathers on his outstretched wings lifted from both the turbulent weather and his agitation at seeing her upset. The massive black appendages had been the one barrier he could have created between those of both worlds before the cats stunned them in place. He gritted his teeth as he tried to flex and break the hold. He mentally growled at himself. He was a warrior and needed to fucking focus.

The Thulian God in the middle was the one to watch. The male hadn't spoken, but there was something dangerous about the silence and the way his gaze took in everything at once. The male's eyes had landed on him after taking note of their cat's position in front of P. Even Pothos could tell that it meant something for the powerful beast to sit in front of him. P studied the warrior God. His long black hair was tied back, and it was hard to see his expression through the short beard. There was a distinct air of power and savage ruthlessness that reminded him of a darker version of his dragon leader, Drake. The very air seemed to still at the dark Thulian God's command, "It is time we speak instead of fight." The words were spoken in the ancient language of the Creators.

"By all means, talk." Hades' autocratic command came from behind P's position.

He gritted his teeth. *Father, you need to calm the fuck down.* He wished the cats had done something to seal P's father's mouth when they'd locked down the God's powers. P added, *The Goddess is in this mating frenzy with me. That means if any of them kill me, she'll suffer the consequences.*

He wasn't entirely sure of that, but had seen lust in her eyes, and he needed to give his father some reason not to try to battle the Thulians when, or if, they were allowed any kind of movement. Who the hell knew how long the cats were going to keep them like this, and would they loose their hold on the Thulians before they freed him and his family? That was the question, and he didn't like being this damned powerless.

Explain this, his father demanded.

Sacha, his father's mate and the diplomat of the Guardians' calm voice filtered through the winds, using the ancient language of the Creators. "How about we start with introductions. I am Sacha. Who am I speaking with?"

The kilt wearing male spat out, "I am Dagur, and your male has disrespectfully addressed my brother Hroarr, the ruling God of Thule. I will have this insulting God's name."

Hades' response sounded like a sneer. "You are addressing Hades, God of Earth, and you will watch your tongue when speaking to my Goddess."

"Enough," Drake growled toward Hades.

Eyes shifted to the dragon. "And your name, male?" the one called Dagur demanded.

P could smell the smoke he knew was lifting from Drake's lips as he ground out, "Drake, leader of the Guardians of this world. And your Goddess, her name?"

"My sister's name is none of your concern, male."

He saw the Goddess' eyes harden in frustration, likely at her brother, but there were other emotions flickering in her beautiful features. Her attention was too focused between the cat at his feet and P. As if the rest of the world didn't exist or matter. It was exactly as he felt.

The dark Viking-looking God, Hroarr, didn't speak or even seem to care what his brother said. He watched, possibly as an intimidation ploy. P didn't have the concentration to deal with any of that.

Dagur's golden gaze shot daggers at the lynx in front of P. Some of the male's brown hair had torn freed from the tie, whipping in his face as the winds kicked up, flapping at the leather kilt he was sporting. The male growled, "Sister, do something about your beasts' hold."

Brianne spoke through the Guardian mental link. *It looks like we're about to get a view of what's under that kilt.* The wild redhead was standing behind P with her Demi-God mate, Vane. The tone held a hint of sarcasm, but his sister Guardian was bloodthirsty as shit; he didn't doubt for a minute she was looking for vulnerability.

I'm not sure if I should be furious and jealous or cringing at the direction of your damned attention, my lark, Vane mused, though there was definitely a hint of danger to the tone. The two were a unique hybrid pair. Vane was the lion shifter son of Athena, and Brianne was a powerful Guardian Geraki, an Immortal bird of prey. As individuals they'd been deadly. As a mated pair they were ten times as lethal.

Now P understood the sensation because he seemed to be gaining the power of his female. After one fucking touch, the elements themselves seemed to call to him, dragging the scent of his wet female into his lungs, forcing him to stifle a growl.

I'm more interested in what the male said, Sacha said with her usual calm. The logical diplomat of the Guardians was now his father's mate. Her words made P realize that he'd known exactly what the kilted God had said, and hadn't even processed the change in the God's language. He relayed the words through the Guardian link.

Hades snarled, *You can understand their language now?*

Anything to do with Thule in relation to P set his father off, and that was the last thing he needed when he was barely holding it together. The power pulsed under his skin as he answered, *When the Goddess and I were interrupted by her guard, their words started to unlock in my mind.* All Guardians and Gods could understand any language of their world. He wasn't sure if his connection to the Goddess was what gave him the key to hers, or maybe it had to do with his Thulian half. All he knew for certain was that he'd understood the words without thought.

After what seemed like a lifetime of posturing, Hroarr directed his hard green eyes at Pothos before commanding, "Your name?"

"Pothos." He said the word while gazing into the eyes of his Goddess. The apparent hitch in her breathing made his dick ache.

Hroarr's next demand shook the ground with power. "Why were you in Thule? *How* were you there?"

Even knowing he should be on guard and alert to changes in Hroarr, P's attention kept going back to his golden-haired Goddess. She was incredibly beautiful, and the wild need to have her was making it impossible to concentrate on anything but getting inside her. Being a Guardian and Demi-God warrior meant nothing in the face of the damned mating frenzy.

He swore he heard a sexy shudder in his female's breathing, one that matched the harsh thud of his own heartbeat. He wanted to hear her sigh as he thrust into her body.

He mentally bit off a curse.

"I was not there to start a war with your world," P stated cryptically in the old language because he honestly had no idea how he'd opened a portal to Thule, and in the end it didn't matter how he'd been led there.

P, are you okay right now? Sirena, the Guardian healer's telepathic tone held a world of concern, and he knew it was partly because she was one of the Guardians left behind in Tetartos. P had no doubt Drake was fielding frustrated questions from all of those itching to be here, to do something. They were warriors; being forced to sit still was not in their natures. But his sister Guardian and he had always been close, and he'd known she would be grilling him at any moment. Everything had happened too fucking fast. His unintended trip to Thule, meeting his Goddess, and the grueling way he'd teleported back from that world with only minutes to inform his Guardian brethren that he'd found his mate before the air charged to signal the portal was opening.

How much time had passed? Fifteen minutes? Twenty? It was as if time had slowed to a halt.

I'd say I'm pretty screwed, he pointed out, not bothering to lie to Sirena.

Hroarr interrupted his mental conversation. "Interesting. You say your world…" The dark Viking's voice was deep and too damn calm with the power it emitted. "Yet it seems as if you have a connection to Thule."

Hades growled, "*This* is my son's world."

Tension grew thicker as Hroarr eyed P's father.

Sirena's voice cut off those thoughts, but not the pain and power surging violently inside him, threatening to rip him to pieces if he didn't loosen his iron grip. *Do you feel a telepathic connection to your female?*

P cringed, thinking he would have already checked that if he were capable of thinking clearly, because all mated pairs shared a telepathic link. He swore he'd considered it initially, before his female had stepped into his world. Who knew if his bond with her would work the same as normal pairings? Theirs was far from normal. P's muscles twitched as he refocused. When he detected a bright mental connection to the female in front of him, he took in a deep breath and eyed her flushed face. *Yes*, he sent to Sirena before adding, *The connection is there.*

If anyone said anything else in the time he spoke with Sirena, he was deaf to it all. Only his female's face and the healer's voice were cutting through the ringing in his ears.

His mind conjured a million questions as more ability rose inside him, relentlessly. He breathed through it, wondering whether the strength he'd gained would allow him to break free of the beasts' magical hold. And if he were to gain freedom from the hold, would he be able to use this new powerful ability on the Thulians to protect his family? The problem was that the power was far from controlled. He wasn't sure he could single anyone out with how damned raw and wild it was getting with each passing minute. He could end up mesmerizing the entire fucking group if he unleashed it now. And that was only if it affected the Thulians in the same way it did his own damned brethren and father.

His father's soul ability had worked on the Thulian Goddess Kara, whom they'd imprisoned after her attempt to capture Hades about a week ago. The female was still unconscious after their battle and being put into the copper-infused cell that dampened her abilities.

Hroarr's next words broke through his thoughts. They held a challenge to what Hades said about this being P's world. "I can see that he is your son." He and his father looked a lot alike, aside from P's tattooed sleeves and the gauges in his ears, their dark hair, blue eyes and midnight wings were a family trait. Hroarr's attention shifted from him to where Hades stood behind him. "And yet my sister's beasts claim him."

"He has a way with animals." It was Bastian who'd calmly stated the words. The male was there with his mate, Tasha, just more members of his family that he wished were anywhere but here in this fucked-up situation.

"Why are you here?" Pothos bit out, drawing the male's attention back to him, which was exactly where P wanted it, not caring about his father's telepathic rants.

His eyes shot to his female without his meaning to. Heat and frustration rode in her emerald gaze, and lust hit him in the gut, slamming his cock against the denim of his jeans. He clenched his teeth and forced his eyes from her flushed cheeks. He needed to think. They still didn't know why the Thulian Goddess Kara had tried to take Hades or why they'd come to Earth and captured Apollo weeks before that. Just two more issues destined to complicate the shit out of an already volatile situation, because as a Guardian of the Realms, it was P's job to get the bastard Apollo back and contained again.

"It seems we are here for you."

Pothos felt his power violently pulse inside him, and he ruthlessly pulled it back as he clamped his teeth.

Fuck. It was too damned strong.

"I would level all of Thule before allowing you to take him." Hades' voice rocked with so much pent-up power that it shook the trees and rocked the water of the lake. "So take your beasts and leave."

Sirena's voice came through again. *Can you tell if she's going through any symptoms of the mating frenzy?*

Dagur growled, "That is a worthless threat, Hades. You have no idea who you speak to."

Hroarr roared, "Enough." And Dagur silently scowled.

He focused on his Goddess and Sirena's question. He didn't

actually need to see her to know the answer to whether she was in the frenzy with him. She'd been just as affected in Thule, and he'd seen the heat in her eyes, scented her sweet wet pussy in the winds. *Yes, she's feeling it.* He wanted to snarl; the most basic of his instincts demanded he take her away. That he claim her with his mouth and cock. The offending appendage chose that moment to throb painfully against the zipper of his jeans. Apparently, all the power holding them motionless wasn't able to do the same for his damned cock.

He clenched his jaw at another harsh surge of his ability. Her eyes dilated and a frown crinkled the skin between her brows. Had his Goddess felt that?

I'm going to need to test her blood with yours to see what the hell happens, Sirena bit out.

He mentally grunted in response. He knew the healer was worried about compatibility, but he wasn't sure it mattered. Once the frenzy hit, he was fucked. It didn't just go away, and Sirena knew that.

P wanted to rub his aching temple and his fingers twitched. Was he able to move his body? He didn't feel the hold on him anymore, but he still felt the cats' power in the air. His gaze watched for any movement from Hroarr or the others as P tried to find a way to deal rationally with Hades. *Father, you need to calm down. With a mating bond, if one of a pair dies, the other usually goes mad. They can't hurt me without hurting her.*

Hades scoffed furiously, *You do not know that that will pertain to her. I wasn't bound to the rules.* His father had connected souls with his mate, Sacha, another Guardian, without going through all the steps of bonding that usually happened.

Father, let me worry about her. I need you to deal with her brothers. P's concentration was shot and his father needed something else to focus on other than P's mating, but he was forced to add, *"Deal with them" does not mean try to fucking kill them*.

Another hard surge of power violently slammed into P's gut, and he just barely kept it from slipping his control. His muscles pulled tight enough to tear. The power was different, like a level five hurricane ready to unleash its furious wrath. He was completely losing his damned hold and he wasn't even sure what kind of power it was. It wasn't his old ability. No, this was something more. Something potentially dangerous to those he loved.

His shoulders and wings contracted as he searched wildly for some mental stability.

Fuck. More power than he'd ever wielded surged again. Just as fast as he locked it down, it was back that much stronger.

His vision hazed as he struggled.

As much as he'd tried to convince Hades everything would be fine, he wasn't so fucking sure. His cock throbbed again, and when his vision cleared, he caught his Goddess' sharp intake of breath. She was definitely feeling something. Was that pain in her eyes?

That look gutted him, but how the hell could he help her when he might be dangerous, even to her? He needed to get out of there.

He contacted Drake. *Fuck. I'm losing my hold. This power... I have to get out of here*. Without waiting for a response, he launched into millions of pieces, teleporting away. Thoughts of leaving his female nearly split him in half as his power surged with a force that whipped the air currents, turning them on end.

And then it did the unthinkable. That same power swept her away as well, pulling her into the air.

Into him.

Chapter 3

In Between Two Worlds

The second their very essence combined during the port, P'd been screwed. It was the most erotic thing he'd ever felt. His molecules merged with hers in a way that was too damned dirty and perfect. Inside the storm of their bodies he felt her panic and desire and couldn't do anything about it while they were soaring into the unknown. He felt her trying to fight it, which only seemed to bind them that much tighter, distracting him even more.

Focus had been the first casualty to carrying her away with him. His power surged, shooting them further out of control, thundering them through the ether. He hoped his subconscious had given it a destination, because rerouting to Tetartos seemed to be impossible now. Not when he felt her all over him like a second skin. He was inside her in a way that was baser, deeper than any physical touch could have been. His brothers had all said teleporting together while in the mating frenzy was a fucking erotic nightmare. They'd never said a damned thing about being unable to control where the hell they were going.

Calling this an erotic nightmare was an understatement of epic proportion.

He wanted more.

If it was possible to come in this state, he was about to.

Refocusing his thoughts to reroute to Tetartos Realm wasn't changing anything. They'd soared out of his world. It was like being sucked into the center of a storm; all they could do at this point was ride it out.

Sweet fuck.

The second they were finally whole, it was with her body wrapped around him and her tongue in his mouth. He groaned as his fingers gripped her ass, pulling her tighter to his body as he took command of the kiss and fucking devoured her. His wings flexed as those long-assed legs tightened around his waist, grinding her pussy against him as she made sexy mewling noises against his lips. He growled and lifted one hand to tunnel his fingers in the silky strands of her hair.

Her hands were running over his shoulders, his head, his jaw. Everywhere she touched made his muscles twitch as if there was an electrical charge firing every nerve. It was intense. Out of control.

An ounce of self-preservation existed enough that he sent out a mental scan of the area. Every synapse fired, demanding he keep his female safe above all else. His eyes narrowed for a moment, noting the change from night to day before sliding over high stone pillars. He heard tranquil water flowing into a pool, with a brilliant green forest beyond. There were lounges with soft white cushions, but he refused to loosen his hold long enough to set her down.

Birds and animals were silent, but out there. He didn't sense any people, and that was what he cared most about. Her safety.

The place was ancient, pure. Private. And so obviously not of his world that he knew he was back in Thule.

Mine thundered inside his mind over and over as he devoured her soft lips, riding her over his denim-clad cock. She felt so damned good. Perfect.

One moment she had her hands all over him, and the next she was in the wind, taking herself out of his reach. He growled low, a primal beast denied his mate. It took every ounce of his shredded control to stop from stalking her. His muscles fucking hurt from the tension in holding back. His father's voice in his head and the loss of her touch were the distraction he needed. It saved him from closing the space separating them. He still tasted her, smelled the sweet seduction of her wet pussy aching for him.

Fuck. He struggled for breath as his eyes refocused.

His family. He needed to be sure they were safe.

What's happening there? he simultaneously sent his father and Drake. *I have the Goddess with me; tell them she's safe. I didn't fucking take her on purpose.* He mentally cursed himself. He'd left them in order to protect those he'd cared about, but taking her with him was the opposite of protecting his damned family.

It was as if he were a babe with absolutely zero control of his abilities. The power inside him was like a living breathing thing, surging from every damned cell so that it completely flooded the space around them. Panic nearly drowned him before his mind computed it wasn't hurting her. Her breathing was uneven, her eyes lust hazed, and there was a tiny crease between her eyes, but she seemed otherwise fine. It was all fuzzy as he fought the lust and attempted to focus on anything but how hard his dick was fighting the bounds of his fly.

He sucked in air as he watched her pant while facing one another over the span of the sunlit temple. Her back was pressed against a large carved rock pillar. They stood on more stone with steps leading to some pools on one side. The entire platform was built on a high cliff surrounded by a forest of vivid green shot with the occasional brilliant red flower.

Is everything okay? he demanded, further stressed when neither his cousin nor father answered right away.

His female was taking in their surroundings while angrily glaring at him. "What have you done?" she demanded.

He breathed deeply, needing to make sure his father and the others were okay before he attempted to answer her question.

His ears were ringing by the time his father's voice came through. *We're still locked in place by these ridiculous creatures,* Hades spat out. *The Thulian Gods were demanding answers to what you've done with her, but the irritating animals haven't so much as twitched... Where are you?*

He felt a hint of relief that the cats hadn't freaked out; that fact should calm the Gods of Thule. He hoped. It made sense to him that the powerful beasts would have been agitated unless they knew the Goddess was safe with him. He shook his head, thinking how ridiculous that sounded in his head. As if the cats were all powerful. Maybe they were. Maybe his life had turned into Planet of the Lynx.

He glanced around again, taking a better look at where they were. Brightly colored blue and red birds perched as still as statues in the ivy-covered trees beyond the pavilion. When he glanced around the pillar at his female's back, he caught the view of an ethereal-looking waterfall. He narrowed his eyes at the familiarity of it. The beauty of glowing blue and silver orbs that made up the falls paled against the sight of his angry, lust-filled mate. He watched her closely and felt her trying to build power.

"Why did you take me?" she snapped and narrowed her eyes at him. His female was crouched as if they were about to battle and, fuck if her warrior stance didn't make his cock throb harder against his zipper. The damned thing was probably imprinted with the metal teeth by now.

"I have no intention of harming you," he assured her in the ancient language as calmly as possible though he could barely talk without growling. He felt like a damned animal. He wanted to fuck her until she was screaming his name. And nowhere in that scenario would there be any pain. Only soul-rending pleasure.

Son of a bitch, this was fucked. He wasn't sure if he should take her back to the lake. He couldn't be there though, not this out of control. His power had washed into the forest with the force and strength of a tsunami, and he wasn't sure he could contain it all.

Everything in him stilled when the implication of it finally sank beneath the lust.

His power was free and she wasn't affected. He'd been right to leave the lake if his power didn't work on Thulians. Even his father would have been rendered completely enthralled and at P's mercy with a fraction of the power he was unleashing now.

He took in every inch of her, paying special attention to her heavy breathing and swollen lips like a damned fiend.

Was she immune because she was his mate? That made the most sense, but he sure as hell wasn't going to test that theory. There was no way he was taking her back to her brothers if he couldn't get his power back under control. He tried to force it back and heard the soft gasp of his mate.

Her eyes flashed with fire that lit him up as she choked out a demand, "What are you doing?"

His cock ached at the glazed look in his female's eyes. She

moved as if by compulsion. A few steps until she locked in place, balling her fists, glaring at him.

He tried again and they both groaned.

For fuck's sake. His power was somehow linked to the raging arousal. For both of them. Each surge matched the throbbing of his damned cock. He ran a shaking hand over his head as he tried not to be embarrassed by the fact that they were both, in fact, ruled by his dick at the moment.

"What was that?" she breathed, and fury mixed with the arousal burning in his direction. "Have you put a spell on me?"

He eyed his female. The draw was a damned drug, and he could see her fighting it. Her tanned skin was flushed a gorgeous pink and her lips were swollen from his kisses. He smelled her juices and knew she was making more for him. He rubbed his lips and held back a damned growl at how much he wanted to taste it. Her eyes trailed his fingers and he was only seconds from losing his mind. He took a deep breath before telling his father what he was sure the God could already sense. What he sensed. *We're in Thule, and I can't leave until I get my power back under control. It's linked to her, and the mating frenzy is fucking with it. Do not start a war while I'm gone. I need time to figure out how to fix this. But tell me if anything changes there.*

This was a damned nightmare.

*****

Gefn felt completely out of control of her body, spelled to the point of animalistic need by the heathen in front of her. The dizzying effects of how he'd taken her away had worn off, but intense power seemed to fill her entire body. All that power and the arousal were affecting her mind. She was wild and needy, out of control, and somehow it was linked to the male in front of her. He'd stayed on his side of the space, but it was taking all her will not to go to him. They were alone. But where had he taken her? It felt familiar, but not. She'd tried to build power for a portal and cursed when it fizzled out. How could she feel so powerful and not be able to wield the one ability she needed most?

One minute she'd been in his world, feeling the crushing impact of betrayal. Spa and Velspar hadn't only been her protectors, they'd been her friends... her constant companions for thousands of years. She had a bond with them, had battled at their sides, so to be blindsided by the immense power she hadn't known they held was like a blade to the chest.

Her cats had effectively immobilized not only the powerful beings in the new world, but also her and her brothers. If they'd always had this hidden ability, why hadn't they used it to prevent her evil brother Tyr from slaughtering her priestesses?

She still mourned them. They were bonded to her at birth just like the cats. And she hadn't saved them, but knowing that Spa and Velspar could have infuriated her. She'd been trying to get some kind of answers from the cats before she'd been whisked away by the intoxicating male.

She was still angry with the beasts, and feeling their pleasure that she'd been abducted only angered her more. Was she some kind of pawn in a greater plan for Thule? When she felt her beasts trying to soothe her again, she pushed them away. She didn't need soothing. She needed answers, and she needed to get back to that lake.

"Return me to my brothers," she demanded, even though a traitorous part of her rebelled at the thought of leaving this soothing place, of ending whatever this was. She wanted to be in his arms far too much, but if she didn't get back to Hroarr, there was no telling what he would do to find her.

"I can't. Not with my power so out of control." His words were said through clenched teeth.

She scowled at him. "You were able to get us here. You should be able to return me the same way." She tried for another portal and again the power fizzled away. "You need to take me back." Hroarr would not wait long.

"I am not lying to you," he ground out, his chest rising and falling as harshly as hers. Lust? He continued more steadily, "Do you feel the power coming from me?"

"Yes," she rasped out as she tried not to moan at the comforting warm blanket of power he spoke of.

"It doesn't hurt you?" he growled.

She flushed, because it did the opposite of hurting her. "No."

He growled low. "Fuck. It feels good to you, doesn't it?"

She sucked in air, assuming the first word was a curse by the way he spoke it. "Yes." She wasn't about to admit how good it felt running along her skin.

He moved closer, and she was mesmerized by the animal grace of his movements, the way his muscled chest flexed with each step. The way his black wings fluttered in the building wind. He was more than beautiful, with the images on his arms and his piercing blue eyes drawing her in. His next words dried her mouth. "It makes you wet."

She licked her lips and watched his eyes focus there. She swore a shudder ran over his body as his eyes nearly burned with heat. She refused to answer him, but his voice lowered. "I can smell how good it makes you feel, and I can't wait to make it even better. Now, tell me your name."

She gasped a little as her entire body flushed and she grew impossibly wetter at his words. She spoke without thought. "Gefn."

"Gefn, I'm Pothos." He said her name as if it were a vow, just as he'd said it at the lake. As if the word were for her only. Air stuttered from her lungs.

He broke some of the spell after long moments. "Gefn, at this level my power could hurt everyone at the lake."

She narrowed her eyes. He seemed sincere, but it seemed too convenient an excuse. "If this is true, why would it not do the same to me?"

"Because it knows you're mine, *thea mou*."

"What do those words, *thea mou*, mean?" she demanded while narrowing her eyes at the male.

"It means *my Goddess*."

Her lips parted at the way he said the words, as an endearment instead of an acknowledgement of her power. And it was attached to blatant possessiveness from a male she didn't know. She heard purring and firmed her lips at her absent beasts.

"I am a Goddess. That means I belong to no male."

"In my world there is such a thing as fated mates, Gefn."

She just stared at him. "I am not an animal to mate."

His lips twitched before he continued, "No. We are not animals, but you and I are linked. We're bound to each other."

Her jaw dropped a fraction as she heard more infuriating purring. "Bound how?" Because the cats seemed to believe it and so did this male. She could see the truth in his eyes. Could feel it in his words and she should have paled; instead she felt her cheeks flush with even more desire.

"Our souls are trying to connect. What we're feeling now is what we call a mating frenzy."

"Frenzy?" Her ears were ringing as thunder crashed around them.

"This lust will get worse and worse until it becomes painful. We'll want each other constantly, possibly more than we desire each other now, and our powers will start to blend together."

She felt far away, like the words were said through a wind tunnel. Truth. This was the truth. She knew it.

Her nipples rasped the harsh confines of her vest as she took a deep breath, thinking more about the emphasis he'd used on *my*. The lust was truly affecting her mind. Her powers were slipping free just as wildly. Winds had kicked up and clouds were rolling in rapidly above them. Maybe he wasn't lying about struggling for control of his power, because she was as well.

He was still several steps from her, but she swore his scent was everywhere. It was on her skin, sliding through her lungs like an intoxicating fog. Her entire existence seemed to have been turned on end by... lust. By this male. It seemed that she was so affected by him that she had started making excuses to like him, to believe him. Her beasts had championed the male the moment Velspar had perched in front of him, so she knew it had to be true, but it seemed impossible. Immortals and Gods of their worlds had never joined or married, yet this seemed like an extreme version of just that.

An arranged one. With her beasts as the cosmic matchmakers.

Logic demanded she question it all, fight the male who'd stolen her from her brothers or at least attempt to escape on her own, but Spa and Velspar… This match was for the good of Thule. They would not have championed it otherwise. Reason infused her with doubt. He lived in the same world that her reckless brother Dagur had stolen a God from. And his world was holding her sister, if the cats were to be believed. Didn't that mean neither should trust the other? Wouldn't he see her as an enemy? Did he even know they held his God Apollo? Nothing had been said about it at the lake. She fought the lust, trying to figure out what to believe.

She gritted her teeth while taking in her foreign surroundings. "Where is this? And what do you call the power you used to take us here?"

He frowned at her. "This is Thule, Gefn. And we call that power teleporting or porting." The translations felt odd, but the more he spoke, the more it seemed she understood his odd speech.

She shook her head as she looked around. It was like Thule. "No, this is not Thule."

Her eyes slipped to the stone altar in the middle of the space. Frowning and distracted, she moved closer. Her eyes widened as she took in the runes etched in the stone. Spinning, she took in the soft-looking white lounges and fluffy white pillows. The open view was of a brilliantly colorful forest of greens, reds, pinks and yellow. Behind where she'd been standing was…

Her mouth dropped at the sight of the waterfall.

Spirits of the dead.

She rasped, “You brought me to Fólkvangr?”

*****

Pothos watched his female closely, curious as to how a Goddess of Thule could be unfamiliar with this Realm of her world. He’d known at once that it was like Heaven Realm on Earth. There was no mistaking the brilliant orbs or the tranquil feel. This was where the souls of Thule’s dead flowed.

Her beautiful emerald eyes had shot wide as she stared off to the falls.

He was attempting to give her time. She had no idea what they were going through, and no matter the agony to his cock, he would allow her questions for as long as they both could take it. He wasn’t sure how long that would be, because his fingers itched to touch her.

She shook her head and stared at him. “Your father was at the lake,” she confirmed, watching his eyes closely. “Who is your mother, Pothos?”

She’d figured out the secret of his birth. He guessed this would be the test of whether the Gods of Thule would really want him dead because of it. “Her name was Eir.”

Air rushed from her as she faltered away from the stone altar, seeming to speak more to herself than to him. “Your mother was a priestess of Thule?”

“You knew her?” he asked, more than curious about the mother he didn’t remember.

“She was my brother’s priestess. I did not know her well. Agnarr and I were not close.” She knew of his mother. That was an odd feeling.

He nodded, studying her closely as he fought his dick's reaction to her parted lips.

She closed her eyes.

"What are you thinking?" He wanted to know because she looked pained.

"I am thinking of all the reasons your mother would have felt the need to hide your existence."

"She told my father to keep me hidden from Thule. That the Gods of your world would want me dead."

Her eyes flashed with anger before she blew out a breath. "At the time she was right. Hroarr was gone a lot, and our evil siblings were killing priestesses and Gods alike for decades. It took a long time to finally build a cage for them." Her eyes flashed with regret. "I am very sorry, but your mother was one of those who died."

"I know." He'd gotten that much from his father.

The caring in her eyes gutted him.

She shook her head. "There was so much death then. Your mother likely saved you, Pothos."

He changed the subject because he suddenly felt uncomfortable. "You've never been here?"

"No." He could tell she was debating telling him more.

"Did your mother share this place with you?"

He shook his head. "If she did, I don't remember. Why haven't you been here?"

She studied him with lust in her eyes. "We cannot open a portal here. Only priestesses have access to this place."

"They couldn't take you here?"

She didn't seem to want to say more. Her lips had firmed, and he suddenly understood the implications of what she wasn't saying. She couldn't get out without him. Or his power. He swore he was feeling her emotions through their bond. He felt sorrow and anger when talking of his mother, and there was a pang of anxiety that he knew meant she was worrying he'd trap her in this Realm. It made him want to hold her, reassure her.

Fuck her.

He gritted his teeth as need slowly ate at him. Minutes seemed to pass like hours.

He sent a message to Drake and his father. *Is everything okay?*

It's the same. Drake's tone was not amused.

P sighed. *This information might help. We are in Fólkvangr; it's Thule's version of Heaven. Gefn has never been here because their Gods can't portal to or from this place. She said only priestesses can travel here, and they can't take passengers.*

He heard his father scoff. *Good, leave her there.*

Father, she is my mate, he growled. *And so far she knows who and what I am and doesn't want to kill me.*

So she says. His father was fucking stomping on his last nerve.

P snapped. *Fucking stop. I'm still on guard, but she says that Gods in Thule had been killing priestesses and Deities in Thule until they were imprisoned.*

Anything about Apollo? Drake asked.

Not yet. I haven't asked, he ground out. He was barely hanging on with all the need battering them both. *I have to go.*

When he saw her eyes flash with pain, he nearly lost his mind. "You're hurting?" he growled.

Chapter 4

Mystical Lake, Earth Realm

Hades was losing his mind with worry. Every muscle tensed as he fought the power holding them with a might that should have destroyed the damned cats easily. Sacha's soothing energies barely calmed anything. Those few minutes when he hadn't known where Pothos had gone were the longest of his existence. If that Goddess harmed a single hair on his son's head, every Thulian present would know the agony of his power.

As soon as their hold waned… and it would, because the beasts could not hope to restrain him forever, he would truly enjoy their screams as he ripped the souls from their bodies. One of the creatures had the audacity to stare at him and twitch its ears as if completely unfazed. He glared at the offending animal.

"Where is my sister?" Hroarr commanded with deadly calm. The only indication of the male's fury was the fire flashing in his eyes and the raw power flowing from him to the water beneath his feet. Waves rocked violently over the edges.

Hades narrowed his eyes at the display, wanting the battle that brewed in the other God's eyes.

Draken answered, "Your sister is unharmed."

Pothos isn't helpless, Hades. He's a powerful warrior and your son. Sacha's calming voice penetrated his wrath. *And what he just said makes sense. You told us that the reason Agnarr came to you for an alliance all those centuries ago was to gain your help in imprisoning the evil Gods of Thule. When Pothos' mother gave him to you with that warning, their world was likely just as different as ours was all those millennia ago.* She paused. *This Goddess is not evil, and you know as well as I do that even these arrogant male Gods don't hold that kind of tainted power.* She paused. *Just remember that if Pothos and the Goddess complete their mating, no Thulian will be able to harm him, not without harming her.*

If the mating rules are the same for her. We don't know that, Hades bit out.

Even your soul was affected by the mating rules, my love. The steps may have been different, but the results were the same, and P is half Thulian.

Hades vaguely heard the rumbling of Drake's and the Thulian's words over the agitation of the water as he listened to his female.

Though her logic made sense, the thought of his son in any potential danger brought back nightmarish memories of Ares and Artemis' attack on his palace when Pothos had been a child. His disgusting siblings had almost gotten to the boy, and Hades had never felt such rage as when he'd learned of their breach of his palace. The fear and fury had unleashed a power and darkness in him unlike any the world had ever seen. It hadn't mattered that the two had been the most powerful of his evil siblings, he'd made sure their blood soaked the palace grounds. He'd wanted to bathe in it, and he would have killed them, no matter the consequences to the world. If the two hadn't retreated, they would have suffered long and hard before he allowed them death.

Pothos had been his brightest light in the darkest of times, and his son was still his greatest creation. Hades would bring down all four Realms for him.

I know. And that's one of the reasons I love you so deeply, Sacha said softly.

Feeling her love through their bond finally eased some of his fury. *You know I'd do the same for you. Maybe worse,* he admitted.

In the background Hades heard the God's commanding tone; the fact that his confidence was absolute made the threat damned effective. "Return my sister or I will take this world apart piece by piece."

Hades watched Hroarr closely to see if the male's silent rage was having any effect on the beasts' hold, knowing Sacha was doing the same. He wasn't the only one with a son in potential danger. Bastian was standing to their left with his mate, Tasha, assessing the other Gods. His normal calm was replaced by the eyes of a male worried for his mate.

Hades made a vow to his female. *I will never allow them to harm him or anyone here. You will all be safe.* He was the most powerful of the Gods, and the Thulians would learn how dangerous he could be if any of those present he cared for were hurt. Brianne had been one of his most loyal warriors, and the wild redhead's mate, Vane, was his nephew, Athena's son. Drake and his mate, Era, were a force all their own. The dragon's female had a stillness about her now that spoke of her own readiness to fight if anyone threatened her male.

I choose to consider it a good sign that both sides are unable to move or fight, Sacha pointed out, but she was assessing the situation from the eyes of a warrior. *And I'm perfectly capable of doing just as much damage as you are if this tentative peace ends.* A fact that pleased him immensely. Not only was she a Guardian, she held immense power now as his mate. His female was as strong as any full-blooded Goddess.

Now he only needed to break the beasts' power over them so the soul rending could commence.

He heard a choked laugh through his bond with his female. He would have smiled if he weren't still worried. Not seeing his son's telepathic marker added to his frustration. If he could at least see him, it would be easier.

What is happening now? Hades demanded of Pothos. It didn't matter that he'd heard his son's report moments before.

P's worried tone came less than a second later. *Is everything okay there?* Just hearing his voice helped.

Yes, there is no change, Hades responded. *Now tell me what is happening with the Goddess.*

I just told you everything! Could you not scare the shit out of me for no reason? his son growled. *Contact me if there's a problem. I need to get my power under control before I can get anywhere near anyone else. And interrupting my concentration isn't helping me do that any faster.*

Pothos is far safer there, Sacha said before adding, *I know this is hard, but I had to learn to trust Bastian's skills in battle. The second we were both deemed Guardians by the Creators was one of the best and hardest of my life, because that meant we were a part of something so much bigger than ourselves. They are our sons, and we will always worry, but they are also powerful males and we can't fight for them. We can only be there when they need us.*

He understood what she was saying, but he was a God. He protected; he acted. A growl slipped from his lips as he watched the Thulian Gods, assessing them.

His female's calm voice rang out with a soothing yet powerful quality. "Your sister is safe with Pothos. Your beasts would not be so calm otherwise," she pointed out. Hades did not like that he couldn't move to see his female speak, and he made his displeasure known with a glare at the infuriating beasts.

Hroarr glowered at the cats before turning his ruthless gaze to Sacha. "And how do you know this?"

It was the wrong tone to use with his female. Hades gave the male his full deadly attention; his voice held enough power to send more water over the banks of the lake. "You will not speak to my Goddess without respect. She was explaining something you should have already figured out."

The air charged with power, and Hades' wings flexed only a fraction as he willed the beasts to free them for battle instead of holding them tighter. Hades decided he didn't like the male, and he relished the thought of ripping the God's arms off and beating him with them.

He felt Sacha's displeasure. *That's enough. We need things to go calmly. I'm to handle the diplomacy since you and Drake are incapable of doing it.*

Sacha had been one of the Guardians' diplomats for centuries, so of course the bad-tempered dragon and his worse-tempered mate would want Hades' female to handle it. That didn't mean Hades would allow anyone to talk to her without reverence. Ever.

Then you do your job, agapi mou, *but he will speak to you in the way you deserve, or I will cut out his tongue.*

She groaned mentally before speaking out loud. "I assure you this was not an act of aggression on our part. Pothos assures us she is well. And since you are unable to communicate with your sister, I will try to find a way to assure you of her safety. But this situation is delicate."

"How did you speak to your male?" Hroarr demanded.

"We can speak through our minds," Sacha explained in the most basic way.

"Then instruct him to bring her to me now."

Hades could almost feel his female's head shaking as she ignored the male's demand and asked a question of her own. "Do you have fated mates in Thule?"

"Gods are not beasts to *mate*," Hroarr bit out with authority.

Hades felt the tension and power building all around when Sacha spoke calmly. "Think of a very binding, permanent marriage or joining. One neither of them have control over. Your beasts seem to understand that part."

Hroarr watched them closely as the winds whipped around the lake. He seemed to be dissecting their words.

"Who is your son's mother?" The Thulian God's eyes flashed in Hades' direction.

Hades tensed. He sure as hell wasn't going to admit anything about Pothos' birth. Pothos said the Goddess knew. This big bastard didn't need that information. "It's none of your business."

"Isn't it?" Hroarr challenged. "I will accept this *if* my sister tells me she wishes to take the male as maðr. So instruct him to bring her back now." Husband was the closest translation to the word Hroarr had used. It was close to an old language Hades had heard spoken in their world.

"It's a little more difficult than that."

"No. It is not." The male's tone grated on Hades' patience.

It was Brianne who answered the bastard. "What Sacha is not saying is that your sister and Pothos are likely screwing as we speak, so unless you're into seeing your sister naked, I'd give them a minute." Hades wondered if some of the slang was making it through the ancient language of the Creators, but it seemed they were understanding.

The male did not speak, but the power he exuded uprooted the trees all around them. Wood snapped and Hades was on guard. He heard his Sacha bite out, *Diplomacy has really never been your forte, Brianne.*

Brianne returned, *What? It's mostly true and may gain us time.*

Unless he assumes his sister is being taken against her will, which I'd assume right about now.

Sacha soothed over the sound of snapping bark. "He would never violate or take her unwillingly. He would never harm her at all. With a bond such as theirs, it would be impossible for either to harm the other." His female kept going. Hades noted that one cat had moved to Brianne before sidling up to the Guardian's mate, Vane.

Hades tensed, but the beast appeared more curious than threatening. An eyebrow rose as he watched the beast eventually rub its massive black head along his blond nephew's hip.

The act drew Dagur's frown, but the male had been fairly silent since his brother started speaking.

Hroarr was still intent on Sacha as she explained how fated mates felt the compulsion to have sex until they went through steps that led to a soul bond. Hades heard Brianne cluck at the cat rubbing on her mate. "He is sexy, whiskers, but that kitty is all mine."

Vane scratched behind the tall golden ears as he spoke. "What can I say, I'm the pussy whisperer, aren't I, beautiful?" Vane said with gentleness and a hint of amused male cockiness. Was the beast drawn to Vane's lion half? Because Hades could barely twitch his damned wings and his nephew was using his hand. Was Vane free to move and use his power?

The other cat yowled as if to call the other animal back. Vane spoke again. "It looks like your sister is not pleased with this, sweetheart, but if you'd like to free the rest of me, that would be nice."

The arrogant Hroarr seemed to be assessing the information Sacha had given him. "You're so sure that a Goddess of Thule would be influenced by your needs and rituals?" He swore the asshole smirked under that fucking beard.

Brianne spoke through a telepathic link to Sacha and the others. *I'm hoping to hell Vane gets this animal to let us free. And I can't believe I'm actually a little jealous of this shit. It's a good thing I only get pure animal vibes from this beast, not shifter... FYI, living with Vane after this is going to be a nightmare. He'll never let me forget that his beautiful manliness tamed this powerful cat. Never!* Brianne groaned, but Hades knew she was just as intent on the volatile God in front of them.

Vane drew the God's attention. "See, we're already getting friendly. This precious girl knows we're devoted to our females. We don't force them into anything."

Brianne scoffed, "As if you could force me to do anything." They seemed to be trying to lighten the mood, but all Hades could see was a dangerous God ready to unleash his wrath.

Vane still spoke in the soft tone even to Brianne as the cat propped its ass on the male's foot. "Of course not, my lark."

The other cat did not appear amused in the least, and Hades would have shaken his head if he could. Neither beast had allowed any of the others freedom of movement.

Dagur snapped out something in the language they didn't understand. It sounded like a curse directed at the cat that was all over Vane. His irritation brought a smile to Hades' face.

"Why don't we discuss this like friends until Pothos and your sister get back? My name is Vane and this is my mate, Brianne." He paused for a second after an apparent glance at Dagur. "And look at her tits again, princess, and I'll cut your eyes out. Look at that, we're already acting like family. All the males want to beat the shit out of each other."

"Aww. Isn't he sweet when he's possessive? I'll try not to take it personally that he said it while stroking another pussy... So, gentlemen, while we're getting to know each other, you can explain why you decided to come here and steal one of our Gods. In fact, we can pass the time with you telling us where exactly you're keeping Apollo," Brianne said, and he agreed deflecting was a good idea, but it didn't seem to be working. Possibly because her sarcastic irreverence didn't seem to be translating well into the ancient language of the Creators.

Hroarr's furious gaze met his, and Hades knew something was coming.

Chapter 5

Fólkvangr, Falls of the Dead – Thule

"It goes against everything I am to see you in pain and not fix it, Gefn." Pothos growled as he moved into Gefn's space in the span of less than a heartbeat. He was nearly touching her, his tense wide shoulders and hard chest were so close to her face, her lips, that she could breathe him in.

"Are you in pain as well?" She narrowed her eyes, thinking he might have hidden it better than she had.

He clenched his teeth. "I feel yours. And that's worse than if I were in pain myself. All you need to do is tell me to touch you." He looked dangerous and wild, but his reaction to her discomfort somehow gave her reassurance he'd never attempt to harm her. His next words were gritted out through his clenched teeth. "I want nothing more than to replace the pain with pure pleasure. I'm struggling here, Gefn. I know you must feel like one choice has already been taken from you, that fate forced us together, so I'm trying to give you the chance to choose now, but I won't be able to hold it back for long. Tell me to touch you. Tell me to make you feel good, and after that I promise to explain everything."

Another sharp pang hit, and that time she anticipated it. Her features were set even though her entire body shuddered with the will she was exerting in order not to reach up and touch his chest, his hard jaw.

Another low growl issued from his firm lips and the sound vibrated against all her oversensitive nerve endings. She hid the pain from her features, but it seemed he still felt it. It was strange knowing he shared it with her. They were in this together. She felt it deep in her soul. Her beasts had already been trying to convince her of a fact she'd already known.

"It is not that bad." She swallowed. "I really must get back to your world to calm Hroarr before he does something to your family."

He narrowed his eyes. "You think the beasts will free him?"

She shook her head. "No." She ignored her cats' displeasure as she continued, "Though I am not sure they can hold him. He will demand to see me safe."

She snapped at Spa and Velspar through their bond, *I get that you want to whore me out, but the situation is a little stressful! If I am to be of two worlds, then I cannot allow Hroarr to rip them apart to find me, can I? He will not trust what any of them say.*

She swore she heard a huff from Spa. Point made. It wasn't as if she were pleased with them at the moment either.

To Pothos she said, "I need to get back there and talk to him, to calm him. You have no idea what you are dealing with." The ability to breathe was getting more and more difficult. How could desire be so debilitating? He smelled so incredibly good, like the woods at night, and she itched to taste the tense cords of his neck. Her eyes moved to the flexing muscle of his chest inches from her face. His majestic wings had flexed higher on his back, making him even larger and so incredibly magnificent.

She noted his eyes on her as if concentrating before he rubbed a hand over his head. "What are we dealing with? My family is trying to prevent war with yours over this. What will he do?"

"Whatever he has to in order to find me."

"If they tell him we are here?"

"He will not trust them."

"My power is too out of control to be around anyone. I'm guessing you're immune as my mate, but when I tried to contain it before, it only made the need that much stronger." He was watching her closely. So that was what had spiked the desire earlier. She'd felt the change in his power, felt the wild surge of need that came with it. It made sense that he hadn't tried again after telling her it was out of control.

Suddenly she felt the elements change around them and knew they were about to have visitors, and there were only so many options on who would be arriving in this sacred place. It was Hroarr's priestesses, his þrír, who appeared. Pothos was in front of her a second later, wings wide and flexed as he built so much power the air was sucked from her lungs. It was so strong, pure and intoxicating, and that protective streak of his aroused her even more, when it probably should have insulted her.

She forced herself to move, calling the winds to put her before Pothos. Hroarr's priestesses had already built power, and she didn't want them to attack in their shock at seeing them there.

"These are Hroarr's priestesses. They are not a threat to either of us," she said to Pothos even as she raised a brow at Reginleif, Geiravor and Mist before commanding, "Do not attack, ladies."

Clouds filled the sky, blocking out the sun as winds whipped through the forest, letting out an eerie song.

Three sets of wide jewel-colored eyes met hers, cooling some of the blinding desire. Mist was in front of the others. Her pale hair, the color of snow-capped glaciers, lifted around her wildly as her wide crystal gaze moved from Gefn to the male she stood in front of, protecting him, cradling him in her power.

The erotic sensation of his voice sliding into her mind made her stifle a moan. *Let me loose,* thea mou. *Don't make me break your hold.*

"What was that?" She nearly moaned.

Mind speak is one of my abilities. As my female, you should be able to do it as well. His voice was seductive torture and she did moan that time. He needed to stop. It was too much when she was already so incredibly needy.

Mist's voice and the fact that the priestesses were all still on guard drew her attention back to the situation. "What was what? Gefn, how are you here? Who is he?"

"He is my male... The son of a God from another world and Eir." She released her winds from around him and felt him move next to her as she took a deep breath to add, "He is my maðr." Her consort. Gasps rent the air, but she needed them to see this. She needed them to know, to go to Hroarr for her. "Pothos was championed by Spa and Velspar."

All three sisters' mouths dropped further if possible as they shook their heads. The renown beauties were clearly shocked as they spouted questions all at once. "This is... How? His power. All this power. It is wild and pure... But how did we not know of his birth?" Gefn had a hard time keeping track of who was saying what.

Reginleif was the one to shake her head, gaping. "His power is the same as ours. The same, but so much stronger. Out of control."

Geiravor was the first to step forward. She was the second

tallest with hair the color of the forest and eyes that sparkled a brilliant moss color. Her wide-set eyes were the shape of almonds, set in honey-colored skin, and her voice held awe when she spoke. "A nephew."

"Eir sent him away before she died." She felt Pothos' tension and she whispered through the winds for his ears only, "So many priestesses were killed before we contained my evil brother Tyr and the others. There has never been another birth to a priestess or God of our world. At least not that we are aware of. You are special, Pothos." To her and to the priestesses who'd never had young and never thought it possible for one of them to do so. She could see it in their eyes. They were being cautious, as cautious as Pothos was being with them. Tension and uncertainty filled the air.

Reginleif was shaking her head, and Gefn understood their shock. Her golden catlike eyes were stunningly wide against the backdrop of her dark skin. The trio's pale-colored dresses flirted in the winds as they moved. The silk slid over their curves as the currents carried them closer.

"How did you know to come here?" Gefn asked as all three shook off their apparent shock.

"We felt drawn." Reginleif stared at Pothos, speaking mostly to herself. "He thought to protect you when we arrived. He brought you here?"

"Yes." Gefn nodded as she took a breath.

"How did we not know he existed?" Reginleif demanded again, anger and sorrow in her tone, but they all knew it wasn't a true question. Eir had done what she'd had to do during a horrible and deadly time.

Mist spoke next. "The wings are from his father?"

"Yes," Gefn answered before doing a quick introduction. She had her way to get a message to Hroarr. It eased her mind right when her body seemed to reel out of control. Not caring that she had witnesses. He was close enough to touch, to set her lips on his shoulder. He'd said this would get worse and he'd been right. The pain was increasing.

The need was too intoxicating and she realized just how uncomfortable she was with them there. She was going to have to go on faith. Her cats had approved of him for a reason.

"Reginleif, I need you to go to Hroarr through the open portal in his study. He and Dagur are in Pothos' world. I need you to tell him that I am safe. And that I need time."

She felt the urgency to get them out. She was completely losing control of the desire.

Reginleif narrowed her eyes and nodded. "You are right, Goddess. This kind of power should have rendered you completely enthralled. Maybe worse. Even our combined power is but a fraction of what is flowing here. It would be dangerous in our world."

Mist turned to Pothos. "Do you need us to try to help you control it?"

"No," he ground out. "It's fate trying to connect me to your Goddess. It won't stop until we bond."

They frowned. "Bond."

"Our life forces are pushing to connect in the way of my people."

Reginleif narrowed her eyes. "This is safe?"

"She is mine. She will have my power. My protection," Pothos said with the authority of a God, but his eyes were burning into hers instead of on the other females. They needed the trio to leave now. If anyone could calm Hroarr and assure him of her safety, it was these three. But they seemed to need convincing.

Mist spoke. "I do not believe there is a choice at this point, Gefn. I am uncertain how you both came to be here, but I believe you will need his power to return home. Even we cannot bring anyone with us when we travel here."

They all stared at Reginleif as she spoke. "And this concentrated power should have harmed you. You are certain what you are doing is possible?"

"Spa and Velspar led me to this. And Pothos is half Thulian."

The trio nodded together. "We will go to Hroarr at once."

Her body ached for him. These moments felt like the longest of her life as both struggled to contain the building desire to touch, but this was important. "Tell Hroarr I am safe. That I choose Pothos. See that he returns to Thule and does not war with Pothos' family, and you may return on the morrow. Not. Before."

"Goddess, you may need us," Mist argued.

"No," Gefn said fiercely, "Spa and Velspar will know if I need you."

The trio breathed out and nodded, knowing what she said was true.

"Now go," she ordered.

Her skin flushed and a sharp pang hit hard enough that her vision blurred and air whooshed from her lips.

The females rushed to her.

P bit out a snarl as he lifted her into his arms. "Pain is a side effect of not finishing what we've started. Leave us; I will not allow her to hurt. She is mine to protect. To care for." It was a vow. His touch alone gave her enough relief that she felt her breathing ease and tried to get him to set her down even though it felt incredible in his arms. She was a Goddess, and appearing weak was not acceptable. His lips met hers, his tongue demanding entrance until she was sighing into his mouth. She felt his arms shaking as he pulled her tighter. She moaned, setting her hands to his stubbled jaw as she lifted up to meet the kiss with equal intensity.

He broke the kiss with a harsh hiss. "Better, *thea mou*?"

"Yes." She moaned with a relieved breath. She saw his hard gaze shoot to the trio of onlookers and commanded, "Go. She is safe with me."

And they were gone in a rush of power.

They were definitely Hroarr's priestesses. Protective, likely torn, but in the end they should have accepted Gefn's word and known to trust that Spa and Velspar would never have led Gefn into harm.

But what had finally assured them was her male.

Chapter 6

Fólkvangr, Falls of the Dead – Thule

Pothos had two things he had to do, and it was agonizing when all he wanted was to be buried in his female. He sent a message to both his father and Drake simultaneously, *You have three priestesses coming your way. They're going to assure Hroarr of her safety and help prevent problems there. She doesn't believe the cats can hold his power, so watch him carefully.*

Then he will know where you are. Take her to Tetartos, Hades snarled, and P shook his head as his father stated the obvious.

I plan to, he snapped back.

He was losing his mind with her soft lips on his neck. He had to get the messages out before teleporting to his island home. It would be secluded enough there for the raging power flooding through him.

Gefn wasn't in pain at the moment, but whenever she was, it gutted him. He'd truly underestimated the mating frenzy. Consuming wasn't a strong enough word. It was more. He felt the need to ease her, to care for her. He mentally growled at how intense and distracting it was.

Sirena butted in with something about blood and tests, but he ignored the healer's concern. It was far too fucking late for that.

"I'm taking you home," he said to the Goddess in his arms, knowing it was going to be hell porting with her and then fighting to take his time when he got her beneath him. Her lips were still on his neck as he teleported with her in his arms. The second they broke apart, he felt a barrier he hadn't remembered when they'd arrived there. He pushed through, but she wasn't with him. He tightened his power, his hold, and swore viciously as he felt her panic mix with his own.

There was a barrier out of this Realm, one she couldn't get through.

Fuck.

They reformed, this time with his dick in agony and a shocked look in her lust-glazed eyes. They both panted as she tried for words. "I cannot leave here?" She paused and narrowed her eyes. "Why did you even attempt to take me from this place now?"

*****

Gefn breathed deeply as Pothos rested his head on hers while moving. "Privacy. If anyone comes here when we are together… I might lash out to protect you. I feel like a fucking animal in need right now." The slang seemed to form in her mind as he spoke the words. He hadn't trusted that the priestesses or her brothers wouldn't come there.

She called the winds to slip from his hold, irritated that he'd thought she'd lied to him. She was sure her emotions were driving her, because she didn't feel rational. She felt raw and needy, and it was all new and uncomfortable.

When she was away from him, she steeled her back. "I told you that my brothers cannot get here. Obviously, if I cannot get out, they cannot get in." It was a thought that made her stomach turn, because she was the one who could truly be trapped if what he said about her gaining his power ended up being a lie. He was a few feet in front of her, shaking his head as if in pain. She glared at him as he spoke.

"You will have my power after we finish the bond. That means you'll be able to come and go at will."

His wings flexed as power and wind whipped around the area. More clouds filled the sky, completely blacking out the sun. Their need was primal and intense, and she wasn't sure if it was his or her power calling the storms.

She began again, "The priestesses will not return until tomorrow." Had he doubted her authority as a Goddess when the females hadn't left when she ordered them to? "They will not disobey unless Spa and Velspar think I need them, and right now the cats are more intent on whoring me out for the good of Thule." She bit out the words that felt sour on her lips.

He growled, his brilliant sapphire eyes flashing with fury. "Whoring?" he snapped. "Is that what you think you're doing with me?"

"I do not know you, yet my beasts led me to you for the sole purpose of spreading my thighs. And the compulsion to do so is far too intense and conveniently painful to deny. What would you call this?"

He balled his fists, and she felt the first drops of rain on her cheeks as he snarled, his anger should have scared her, but it only filled her with anticipation.

He stalked closer until he towered over her, his breath against her skin. "In my world a mating is a rare and beautiful gift. Only a lucky few are fated to someone whose soul calls to theirs. So whore?

No. You are *mine*. I've envied my brothers and sisters their matches, because Every. Single. One has found something incredible." He sucked in a deep breath as lightning crashed around them. "I intended to take you from here because I'm a warrior. Your brothers are not my mate; neither are the females that were here. *You* are, and I'm meant to protect and care for you. I'd rather not do so in an unknown place with the potential of visitors when all I can think of is being inside you. I'd much rather we be in a secure place the first time I'm deep in that wet pussy. A place I can control. If you wanted a male who trusts blindly and doesn't give a shit about safety, then fate has chosen wrong for you."

She was panting by the end of his furious display. The last word had barely spilled from his lips before she was in his arms, her mouth on his. He gripped her ass tight as he grunted against her lips. He slid her up and down along his shaft, ruthlessly pleasuring her against him until she was aching for more.

Her fingers dug into his shoulders before sliding up to his wet hair and down to his jaw as he devoured her. She relished the tangling of their tongues, becoming dizzy from the assault.

He controlled the kiss with a fierceness she needed. His words had turned her upside down. No male had spoken to her like he had, and he'd answered her hurt with a powerful protectiveness that pulled at her heart. He might indeed be a match for her.

Her nipples rasped against the leather of her vest as she wrapped her legs tighter around his hips. They were moving and she didn't care where he took her in this sacred place. Water slid over their cheeks, inside their joined lips as he angled her head for more. She trailed her fingers over wet feathers that moved under her touch. She moaned, needy for more. For skin against aching skin.

He broke the kiss and slid a hand into her hair. His fingers wrapped and tugged the strands until her neck arched to his questing lips. She panted when his teeth grazed over her rapid pulse beat. She couldn't stop touching him; she wanted his flesh to burn against hers. Her hands slid between them to her vest, and she yanked the fastenings with an urgency that left her breathless. When the tight material parted, she moaned and shrugged the firm fabric over her shoulders and onto the stone beneath his feet. The second her breasts connected with his hard chest, she cried out at the soft rasp of hair against her hard nipples.

"I want to lick every drop of rain from your sweet skin." His rumbling voice slid over her neck. He released her hair to kiss her again before nipping her lower lip.

She barely felt him take steps to an area far from where the priestesses had appeared. Thunder rent the air and she loved that wild sound; it was exactly how she felt, alive, charged... She heard the flowing water of a pool to the left and caught sight of ivy-laden stone statues. He stopped under a massive flowering tree and her skin tingled with anticipation.

She felt his power flood the space before he laid her out on the suddenly dry padding of a wide lounge. She lifted her bottom to help him remove her leggings, undergarments and boots. Within the blink of an eye she was bare to his gaze. He stood above her as his eyes took her in slowly. That perusal felt like a touch as he spoke. "Beautiful."

She moaned as a soft breeze teased her bare skin. His eyes flashed with need that matched her own.

His wings were unfurled and magnificent as wicked power whirled over her. No longer comforting, this was pointed, as if fingers were caressing her skin. She moaned and arched her back, sending her winds to divest him of his leggings. He shook his head when she lifted up on her forearms to watch as she sent the power to his fastenings.

He growled low. "Not yet."

"Why?" Her voice was breathy and her eyes were on the hard length she planned to reveal.

"Because the second I take them off, I'll be inside you, and I want this first time to be slow. As slow as I can." Her eyes shot to his at the seduction of his harsh tone. More lightning flashed in the dark skies as the spattering drops added more stimulation to her aching flesh. She was so wet and greedy for him the drops were a kind of torment.

She closed her eyes and moaned deep, barely hearing his next words. "I want to savor every inch, *thea mou*."

She gasped when she felt invisible hands on her breasts, pulling her aching nipples until she cried out. Her eyes slitted as she moaned, "What is that power?"

"Telekinesis of a sort." She'd need a better translation because she had no idea what he'd said, and his next words made her forget she cared. "Now spread your thighs. Make room for me, *thea mou*."

She swallowed through the erotic agony and did what he said. If she didn't relieve the pressure between her thighs, she was going to die of need.

When he climbed between her legs, she almost cried out at the pleasure of the coarse fabric against her wet skin. Her moan was swallowed by his demanding kiss.

He tunneled his fingers in her wet hair, angling her to best devour her mouth. Shivers ran the length of her body as she writhed beneath him, grinding her, what was his word... pussy. Yes, her pussy was against his hard shaft, but it wasn't enough friction. When her nipples connected to the muscle of his chest, she nearly lost the ability to breathe while matching the passion of his demanding tongue.

Those invisible hands of power gripped her hips, holding her down against the padding. She bucked and fought to get the friction back where she needed it, but the hold was true.

She protested against his lips, sliding her hands down to his backside. Digging her nails into the firm flesh, pulling him down to her, demanding contact where she needed it. His mouth broke from hers and he shook his head with a slight tense curve of his lips. Even pained, that sexy grin changed his entire face and made him even more beautiful. Her lips parted and he nipped at the swollen bottom one before saying, "I need the first time you come to be on my lips."

It took seconds for her mind to translate the words before she groaned, "Then put them there now."

He choked out a laugh and set his mouth to the sensitive spot behind her ear. Her head turned, allowing him to torment her more. Her entire body was covered in gooseflesh and shivers racked her relentlessly. She fought the invisible hold; the power was making her wild. Being held down only made her ache and fight for more when her skin was already on fire. By the time his mouth slid to her breasts, she was speaking incoherently. When he scored her tight nipples with his teeth, her entire back bowed. The pain in her womb was long gone, but the agony of not finding release was surely going to kill her.

"It won't, my greedy Goddess," he said with a tight smile against her skin. Either he'd read her mind or she'd said the words aloud, she wasn't sure. It didn't matter when his tongue flicked her nipple as he watched her before leaning in and sucking hard enough that she cried out as his hand plumped and tweaked the other tight tip.

"It will kill me," she snapped, feeling wild and out of control. The winds whipped around them as she sent power to cool her overheated skin. The rain turned to steam the second it touched her.

Too hot.

More water fell. The drops cascaded down her flushed cheeks and slipped over her lips. She licked them off, and when he growled against her skin, she opened her eyes. His were intent on her mouth.

She licked them again and watched his entire body tense. His outstretched wings rose above them as he lifted his torturous mouth from her breast. She breathed out. Finally he would finish this.

"Do you have any idea what I want to do to those lips?" he growled.

"Yes." She nodded, eagerly lifting her chest closer to his lips. "But you would need to free yourself first," she challenged, more than ready to torment him as much as he had her.

"Soon." He growled and shifted his body until he was kneeling on the ground at the end of the lounge before pulling her closer to his questing hands and lips. More water washed over her face, her hair... her exposed breasts.

She watched the drops slide over his short dark hair, down his neck, his wings, over his beautiful coarse jaw. She moaned. His eyes held hers as he leaned in. The second he set his lips to her mound, she cried out and bucked against the hold on her hips again. His hands slid under her backside to angle her up, spreading her wider with her knees at her sides, displaying all of her intimate places to his hungry gaze. Her breathing stilted as he lowered his head. Her back lifted the second his tongue slid over the wet flesh between her thighs.

A silent scream caught in her throat as her neck tilted back with an agonizing release. Her fingers grasped the short drenched strands of his hair, not finding enough to pull as he licked and sucked her slowly, groaning in pleasure.

His voice was harsh in her head, just one more erotic provocation that she couldn't process. *You taste so damned good,* thea mou. *Come again. Give me more.* His tongue lashed and circled before sucking her hard, drawing more pleasure than she'd ever known existed. He buried his face against her, his breath hot, his tongue slipping inside her body as water washed down her aching thighs.

She couldn't do it again, no matter what he demanded, no matter how much she wanted to. His ruthless kisses were destroying her, building the need all over again until she thought she'd die. When his tongue slid down to her backside, her body shuddered as her eyes shot to his in surprised pleasure.

His looked feverish, as feverish as she felt at his demands.

When he spoke, his voice was a harsh growl. "Do you give yourself to me?"

She moaned and nodded, thinking she already had. That apparently wasn't enough for him as he pushed two fingers inside her and lashed his tongue against her. *Say the words.*

She couldn't form more than the one. "Yes."

His fingers spread inside her as they pumped. "Good. That's it, widen enough to take me, *thea mou.*" Those ruthless fingers toyed with her for long minutes, stretching her until three fingers were invading her. He bit into her thigh as he watched her opening for him like a male starved. His tongue lashed at the sting created by his teeth. It was too much.

He growled, "I could feast on you for days, but right now I need my cock inside you so bad I can barely breathe."

"Yes." She echoed her last word.

"You want my cock?"

She could guess what that word meant before the translation became clear in her mind. "Yes. Now," she demanded.

His other hand rubbed the water from his hair as he lifted up, still watching her as he used power to slip from the dark leggings clinging to his body. The second he was bare for her, she was mesmerized by the beauty of her male. His cock jutted up against his stomach, enthralling her. She was intoxicated by everything he did to her; every glance and touch was like lightning charging her body. It had been a very long time, but never had anything been like this.

When he crawled over her, taking her mouth beneath his, she tasted herself. Her fingers wrapped around his neck, her nails digging into his skin. Wet flesh slid against more hot skin as her breasts meshed against him.

Finally. Her hips, no longer held immobile, tilted for him. He slid a hand between them and she breathed out when she felt the thick hot crown slowly push inside her. She moaned and her vision blurred with the primal pleasure of being filled. It was nothing like she'd ever known. It was as if they were one by the time he fully breached her, inch by slow exciting inch.

You feel so damned good wrapped around me. Your tight pussy was made for me, he growled in her mind, and she finally breathed when he pulled out only to push back in and hit a spot that made her cry out in pleasure. He rolled his hips and thrust inside her over and again, hitting a spot that made her keen and throb around him as she panted through it.

He wasn't finished. He slowed for moments and then powered inside her with a force that took her over. She mewled and begged for more. Her words were incoherent demands for him to take her harder. Faster. And he gave her what she wanted. Their bodies slapped together with brilliant force as water slid between them and down his wings. Harsh grunts and moans lit the skies thundering above them. Power barreled out like a hurricane, lifting water from the nearby pools. She felt the elements themselves spin and blend impossibly as they came together in a wild roar of passion. Her entire body lifted from the padding before they came crashing down. She watched, enthralled, as his neck arched while his thick arms tensed ruthlessly as he roared his climax to the sky. Hot seed pulsed deep inside her. They stayed like that, him on top of her, inside her as he kissed her forehead, her eyes.

Every muscle felt relaxed until she couldn't even hold onto his shoulders anymore. He'd given her some of his weight, enough that she felt perfectly snuggled instead of suffocated. His forehead met hers as their breathing evened out. She didn't remember his fingers in her hair, but they were when his thumbs stroked in soft circles along her jaw. She smiled as he leaned in to kiss her lips.

Gently. Reverently.

Beautiful.

That was her last thought before darkness took her.

Chapter 7

Mystical Lake, Earth Realm

Hades hadn't taken his eyes off Hroarr since the bastard issued the last demand for his sister's return. Pothos' telepathic warning from Thule indicated that they needed to be watchful of the God, but Hades had already known there was something wild and dangerous about the male.

I don't like this, Sacha said.

Don't worry, agapi mou. *I will take care of everything,* he answered with dark anticipation, finally able to breathe easier knowing that his son was leaving that damned world. It made focusing on Hroarr and the beasts his primary concern. The muscles along his bare chest pulled tight and his wings flexed against the magic of the beasts while imagining tearing those cats to pieces. The need to battle was strong and emotions were high with tension and worry. Fighting the other God would be a very satisfying release.

But first he would see that the others were freed and protected. For the moment he need only bide his time, because if Hroarr could somehow shake free of the beasts' power, then Hades had no doubt that he would be able to do the same.

Power was slowly changing around them. The wild winds had changed direction, shrieking furiously through the darkly shrouded forest.

Sacha's voice sounded over the angry tumult. "You'll soon have verification that your sister is safe."

Before her words were fully out, the currents shifted again, crackling with electricity as lightning sliced down from the black sky. Thunder rocked the ground beneath their feet while the powerful beasts hissed their displeasure. Both stalked to stand before Hroarr, confirmation that the bastard was responsible for the display.

Tension filled the thick, charged air before heavy gusts of now icy mist whipped over Hades' bare flesh and wings like shards of glass.

The male's voice rumbled over it all. "My sister's presence is the only acceptable *verification*."

A primal blast of power shook everything around them, even the watery portal pulsed and shimmered in its wake. And then Hroarr was free and stalking forward above the water's surface. The elements themselves seemed at the dangerous God's very command.

Sacha sent a wave of personal power through their bond, knowing his intention. Hades used her immense porting ability and snapped free, breaking into a million pieces before reforming a few feet ahead of his Goddess. He rolled his shoulders, reveling in the freedom to flex his outstretched wings.

Sacha was in his mind. *Do not initiate a war. Give the priestesses a chance to calm this.*

As if his mate had called the beings there, three beautiful females stepped gracefully through the watery air. Their silken dresses whipped in the gale as all three sets of intelligent eyes scanned the area before landing on the tense standoff. Flashes of lightning lit their delicate features showing somber expressions.

Hroarr didn't turn to them; instead he narrowed his eyes on Hades as he demanded of the females, "Why have you come here?"

Hades wanted nothing more than to grip the male's soul in his power and twist until the arrogant bastard screamed in agony at his feet, but instead he was forced to wait. To allow the priestesses to do what, encourage their God to attack? He mentally growled as his muscles tightened in anticipation of the females doing something devious instead of calming the situation as Pothos had hoped they would.

The palest of the three spoke with authority. "Hroarr, we were sent by Gefn. She is safe in Fólkvangr."

The cats produced a noise mixed between a hiss and yowl directed at Hroarr.

"Fólkvangr," the dark God confirmed, and Hades swore understanding flashed in Hroarr's eyes. Hades didn't like the knowledge flickering in the darkness of the male's eyes. Dagur's golden eyes narrowed and the sneer he'd been maintaining dropped. The Thulian Gods knew of Pothos' birth. Hades could feel it, and his muscles pulled tight, more than happy to war if Hroarr thought to harm his son.

Dagur's sneer confirmed his worries. "I would say your son's mother is of great consequence, *Hades*."

Drake growled into his mind, *Do not do anything stupid, Hades. P needs us to keep this shit calm.*

He felt the tension of the Guardians at his back as Sacha sent calming energy, but it was taking all his fucking will not to destroy them now and not take any chances that they would attempt to harm his son.

You need to calm, for Pothos. We need to see what they will do, Sacha added.

An ebony-skinned female continued, "Gefn requested we assure you that she is unharmed and she does not want you to war with this world."

The one with snow white hair said more in another language. Hades concentrated on the different cadence, it was very close to an old Nordic tongue, but the female hadn't spoken long enough for him to compare the two.

Hroarr didn't respond to them right away. The male stayed there studying Hades for tense moments before demanding of his females, "Return to Thule. I will be there shortly."

The females didn't hesitate before stepping back through the watery air.

To Hades the male bit out as lightning flashed around them, "You have another of my sisters. And her warriors."

"We have Kara," Hades admitted before growling, "Not all of her warriors survived her attack on my world."

"She better be unharmed," Dagur snarled.

Hroarr's eyes flashed and the ground rocked and he shifted his stance until his heavy muscles strained against the dark leather of his vest. "Release her and her guards."

"She came *here* and initiated war," Hades challenged, flexing his wings. "I see no reason to release her."

A pregnant pause filled the space as power surged from the God. The Thulian God ordered the beasts, "Return to Thule with Dagur and the others." Hroarr lifted his hand in the air, launching waves of violent power that cracked the invisible power holding the Thulian's people. The cats roared in displeasure.

Dagur's muscles pulled tight as he questioned his brother, "Brother?"

"*Now*, Dagur."

Hroarr's eyes sparked with brilliant power. It was a display meant to prove a point.

There was obvious tension between the two Gods, to the point that the one called Dagur opened his mouth to argue and closed it before clenching his jaw and turning to leave. Smart male. Dagur sent the warriors through first and followed. Hroarr stayed facing off with Hades for a second as tense anticipation charged the air until Hades thought the other God would finally give him his wish and they could finally battle this out.

Drake growled into his mind, *Hades, don't. Not unless he attacks first. Then by all means finish it.*

He swore the other God's eyes sparked with excitement for a second before he growled, "We will do this another time." It was a promise made with a hint of anticipation in the words. An anticipation that matched Hades'. "For now, I will give you your God for my Goddess and her guards. You *will* return her to me unharmed, or my kindness and generosity will end."

Chapter 8

Guardian Manor, Tetartos Realm

Sacha was at Hades' side in a room full of frustrated and demanding Guardians with their mates, and he wanted to growl in irritation at their questions and chatter. The room was too damned small. Already holding a huge wood table and various computer screens, it was now bulging with an excess of beings. There had to be dozens, including his nephew Erik and his female. Add in the entire damned pack of Lykos that belonged to Conn and that meant far too many people and more useless noise that didn't seem to please Drake any more than it did him.

They even had Uri's hellhound in there at the male's feet.

"Enough," Drake roared with smoke filtering from his lips.

Finally.

Sacha sighed with a hint of empathy in her calm tone. *They were all worried after being forced to stay here. There's no greater hell for a warrior than to stay out of the battle.* This was her family, his now as well.

A few seconds later she added, *I think you're most upset that you were denied the chance to battle Hroarr.*

Sacha was right about that, but he had a feeling that wouldn't be the only chance he'd have to fight the Thulian, but it wasn't only that he was considering. It was that Hades wanted to know what the priestesses had said to Hroarr in the other language. What exactly had he left to do? He'd just checked his link to his son and wasn't seeing Pothos in Tetartos. Or anywhere on Earth. An attempt at teleporting using his son's soul as a beacon got him nowhere. Hades clenched his teeth, knowing that Pothos was in Thule. Hades knew it and couldn't get there.

Sacha chastised, *Going to him would have made him furious, Hades. And I've already warned you—Do. Not. Contact Pothos right now.*

You know what they're doing right now, love, she issued in her most calming tone.

Yes, and he could be in danger. I don't know what those females told the God.

He felt her empathy before she even spoke. *Hades, Pothos said that his power is out of control right now, it could have effected them teleporting; we don't know. But have some faith in him, he is strong, powerful and one of the most logical and intelligent Guardians. It's time you trust that he can handle anything that comes. He would have told us if there was a problem.* She paused before adding, *He said that Gods couldn't portal into their soul Realm and that the priestesses couldn't take passengers there. Give him time, Hades.*

The females could have been lying, or they themselves could go back to harm him, he snarled.

Yes, my love. But telling him things I can guarantee you he's already thought of isn't going to help him. If something happened to prevent P and his female from coming here, then he's doing what he can. It's only been ten maybe fifteen minutes since you last spoke with him. Remember what he said last time you contacted him just to check on him... Your interrupting him could be a dangerous distraction when he needs his wits.

He mentally growled. She was correct, but he didn't have to like it. He hissed out a breath as his wings twitched. *He gets an hour,* he acquiesced, but didn't hide his displeasure. The reminder that his son was probably having sex with the Goddess and binding them closer was keeping him on edge. He'd rather his son never went near that damned Goddess. He hated that Pothos said they already had the start of a link. If she proved to be as dangerous as Hades thought, he'd find a way to free his son. Hades was sure he could sever any soul bond that formed.

No. You won't. Sacha's tone was forceful.

If she's dangerous, I will not think twice to free him.

"If" she proves without a doubt dangerous to P, I will help you destroy it myself.

He wasn't even focusing on the other conversations in the room, having already heard all the mental questions through Sacha's links to the others the entire time they were at the lake. Why they all felt the need to meet was beyond him.

The situation had a simple fix.

The next time they felt the air charge to signal the Thulians were opening a portal, he would go and meet the bastard and trade the Goddess for Apollo. If they didn't bring Apollo, then Hades was free to battle as he wished. It kept everyone a safe distance away, a point he'd already made to Drake.

Sirena's biting tone filled the room. "That arrogant God actually said that *he* was being kind and generous? They came *here*. They *took* Apollo. And *he's* being 'generous' to return him in exchange for not only his Goddess but the warriors she brought here?"

It was Brianne who addressed the healer's intense irritation. "Well, the good news is that we might at least get Apollo back in his box if this Hroarr is being straight with us about a trade." The redhead actually rubbed her hands together with obvious relish at the thought of getting her talons into Apollo.

Hades flexed his shoulders and growled, "Apollo is *mine*." He had plans for his brother; the bastard would finally suffer for all he'd done to Sacha all those millennia ago. Snorts and growling retorts spouted throughout the room, but he ignored them all.

Sacha sent soft emotion through their bond. *I won't say that Apollo doesn't deserve to suffer for all the experiments and suffering he caused in his time, but I'll be most happy to see him put back to sleep.* They'd spoken of this, but her calm hadn't stopped his desire for blood.

She rested her head briefly against his chest and he was pleased at her gesture. His female wasn't comfortable with displays of emotion, which made these moments all the more pleasing.

Sirena nearly growled her next words, "Kara is still unconscious. How's that going to go over?"

Hades smiled. The Thulian Goddess had come to their world at his summons, but instead of talking, she'd tried to forcibly take Hades with her. She learned the error of her ways. No one took him against his will, so he sneered, "She is alive and has all her limbs."

"And her warriors?" Sirena demanded.

Brianne was the one who answered with a smile, "Hroarr didn't wait for Hades to agree. The bastard seemed more interested in leaving. The arrogant male made his demands and then he was gone like the damned Flash."

He noticed Sacha was intent on the blonde pixy-like healer for long moments before asking, "Was something wrong here, Sirena?"

The healer frowned and ran her hands down the front of her skirt as she squared her shoulders. "Alyssa's baby blew another hole in a wall."

Hades raised an eyebrow, finding it amusing that the first of the Guardians' young was already causing problems and she was still in the womb.

Drake demanded, "Is everyone okay?"

Sirena sucked in some air and nodded. "Yes. Alyssa is a little worn out. Gregoire is freaking out and so are Alyssa's parents."

"When did this happen?" More smoke filtered from the dragon's lips.

"At almost the exact time you said the cats immobilized you."

"Why am I just now hearing this?" Drake snapped, and the others in the room looked guilty. Those that were at the manor had to have known.

"You had enough to worry about," Sirena dismissed. "Jax kept everyone back for me."

"You were with her?" the dragon demanded.

"Yes. Gregoire, her parents and I were all there." And he could tell the healer was leaving something out of the story and obviously he wasn't the only one.

Drake growled, "What happened?"

"The baby let off a blast of power that went through their bedroom wall, but it also kept us locked in the room."

"What the hell do you mean locked?" More smoke lifted from the dragon's lips as the others remained silent.

Sirena faced off with Drake, her violet eyes flashing. "Exactly what I said. It stopped after a while and we're all fine, but for a moment we couldn't move from her side. Alyssa's just really in need of a rest, so Gregoire's getting them settled in a new room."

"The baby is fine?"

Sirena hesitated and Hades felt air leave the room. "She is... but the pregnancy has progressed again."

Chapter 9

Fólkvangr, Falls of the Dead – Thule

Pothos retracted his wings, bracing the bulk of his weight on his forearms as he lay above his sleeping female. It felt too damned good cradled between her smooth thighs. His breathing had finally eased, but he couldn't seem to move from her. There was something about listening to her soft inhalations that both calmed and enthralled him.

She was a drug.

He stifled a groan when his cock twitched inside her warmth. Shaking his head, he gently slid from her body to settle at her side. There really wasn't enough space on the lounge, but he scrunched his bulk against her hip, letting his feet dangle off the end. He wasn't ready to leave her yet. This was the first time he'd actually been able to look his fill without lust and a thread of vigilance battling it out inside him. The frenzy had turned him into a damned wild animal.

A quick check on his Guardian links told him that his father and the others were in Tetartos Realm, and he exhaled in relief. He could take a few minutes to himself; this female was his. It'd all happened so damned fast and he knew they'd have hell to pay, but he deserved this incredibly rare moment of calm. That didn't stop him from mentally tracking his link to her. It seemed stronger. Brighter. He frowned as he saw two gold threads, bonds that connected where? To who?

The cats?

That seemed right; in fact, he swore he even heard purring. A deeper look gave him a location for the beasts. They weren't in Earth Realm anymore, which P took as a good sign. He quickly built a block to his thoughts, knowing his brothers had all been telepathically wide open when the mating frenzy started. There would be no blocking the telepathic conversations that came in, she'd eventually hear those communications, but his private thoughts could at least be locked away. That was if his bond with her progressed the same as other matings.

Everything felt so damned clear, crisp and contained. The power pumping through his veins was new and vaguely foreign, but it was there, just beneath the surface, waiting for him to wield it.

He'd need to figure it all out, but not now. Enjoying this quiet peace with his female was a first for him. A mating was special in their world, and he'd truly doubted he'd ever find such a gift.

And at any moment the tensions between their worlds would come crashing down on them. He mentally groaned. Their situation wouldn't have been simple even if her world hadn't taken one of their Gods and then attempted to abduct his father. There was nothing easy or ideal about any of it. By all accounts, they should be enemies. Maybe they were. As matings went, this was the most fucked of them all. There was no way any of this would be simple.

He glanced away. The clouds had already dissipated, allowing streaks of sunlight to break through the brilliant green canopy. Huge flowers of red, purple and blue brought a fairytale kind of beauty to the forest around them. Between the branches he could see the pale slivers of two moons in the now cloudless blue skies, more evidence that this wasn't where he belonged.

Or was he?

That was the million-dollar question. He'd barely learned of the fact that he was born of two worlds, but, nevertheless, his family was his true home. Though neither of them had asked for it, she was now a part of that family.

Yeah, fucked didn't quite cover it.

He inhaled the sweet smell of rain in the trees and on their skin. It mixed with the scent of sex and sweet female. He still tasted her on his lips and wanted more. More mindless pleasure. No thoughts of war and imprisoned Gods. Just them.

He was a Guardian, though, and was incapable of shutting off duty for long. Not when his family was involved, whether they were safe in Tetartos or not. He took a breath and sent a message to both his father and Drake. *What happened at the lake? Is everyone okay?*

Yes. We just briefed the others, Drake answered. *Are you okay?*

He was vaguely surprised that Hades hadn't interrupted him having sex, because he would almost guarantee his father had stalked his location when they'd left the lake. That meant P either hadn't heard the call, or he had Sacha to thank for keeping his father under control. His money was on Sacha.

I'm fine.

Where are you? his father demanded.

Hades wasn't going to be happy with the confirmation he was asking for. *We're still in Fólkvangr.* P trailed a thumb over her soft cheek, moving the wet strands of hair away from her skin as he listened to his father curse and demand to know what had happened. His palm cradled her face when she turned into his touch.

She mumbled something incoherent and then rubbed her skin beneath his hand before letting her head fall into his hold. He smiled at the trusting action. Maybe it wouldn't be so hard between them. They had some trust beneath it all, and Gefn *had* tried to stop her brother from warring with his family.

P answered calmly, *I couldn't teleport her out. There is something confining the Realm, which goes with what the priestesses said about not being able to bring anyone here.* It was odd that Thule's Realm of Souls had protection. Earth's Heaven and Hell versions didn't have anything confining them.

A flicker of sunlight reflected off something in her hair. The clasps he'd seen holding the heavy strands back. At closer inspection he saw that the one facing him was in the shape of a single wing. His lips curved at the irony of her choice, but he couldn't imagine they were comfortable for her. With a breath of power he unclipped them both before sending them to sit on the pile of her clothes.

But you can leave? His father's tone held a hint of exasperation mixed with relief.

Yes, he gritted out, knowing where his father was going. *I'm not leaving her here.*

Just the thought of doing that, abandoning her, made his jaw tense. He wouldn't leave her to feel stranded and trapped, especially not when he'd been responsible for taking her there in the first fucking place.

Add that to the fact that some deep-seated part of him hated the idea of being separated from her at all. He shook his head. The lust he understood, the protective instincts, but it probably wasn't normal or sane to have this much affection for a female he didn't know. Maybe it had to do with the fact that they'd both been thrown into this chaos together.

He moved to stretch his legs only to have her entire body turn into his. When her head snuggled into his chest, he stilled, his hand suspended in the air for a few beats before he let it rest on her hip. He leaned down and kissed her head before he could think about it. She felt good. *They* felt good.

Touch was something he'd rarely engaged in because his power to enthrall had always been barely leashed, keeping him at a distance from even those he cared about. It had always been smarter to stay in the shadows when small doses of power slipped free, always drawing others in.

His father sighed in obvious frustration. *Where is she now?*

With me. Sleeping.

His cock twitched, reminding him that the frenzy was still there. Need for her was already building again, because this was only a short reprieve. They were effectively screwed. *Pun intended*, he thought sardonically. At least until they finished the bond.

He added to his silent father, *When she wakes, we'll see if she has enough of my power to leave with me.* The words were meant to ease Hades, because P had a bad feeling that it wouldn't work, at least not until they were fully bonded. The spell confining this place was powerful.

It could very well be that she'd need his priestess mother's blood through a blood bond. That was one of the stages in a traditional mating ceremony. One of many steps he'd have to eventually explain, though he'd been hoping to skip that one. His father hadn't needed a blood bond to finish the soul connection that bound his father to Sacha for eternity. But that was Hades; he was literally the God of fucking soul abilities. P might be able to see a soul when he chose to look beneath the surface, but he'd never been able to concentrate power to manipulate a life force as a weapon, and he sure as hell hadn't ever been able to completely tear the essence from a body.

His female rubbed her forehead on his chest before tucking her hands under her face. He stared down at her before manipulating the air to softly dry her skin and hair like he should have done before. She made a small purr-like snore a second later, and his lips twitched.

His father was silent, and P could almost feel the male's mind churning with distrust of P's Goddess. *Have you gained any of her power?*

Yes, and it's strong. I also feel her connection to the cats. Now, tell me what happened at the lake?

He listened to the details of his father's account, frowning because nothing made sense about these Gods of Thule. His eyes caught on the pool beside them. There were animal heads carved into the ancient stone; he cataloged the shapes of dragons, wolves, bears, birds and cats all spilling water from their open maws.

He took in more details of his surroundings to make sure he hadn't missed anything. He didn't hear or sense anyone; not even animals or insects entered the pavilion itself. The closest he could tell, there were only those colorful, now chirping, birds outside the temple area.

He and his female were alone, unless he counted the souls in the falls and the statues of females with dresses made of ivy. He couldn't see the brilliant lights of the spirits from their location, but he could feel the magic of this place.

His father finally came to the end of his story… *and then the bastard left.*

At least a few things were positive, and P pointed some of that out. *At least Gefn warned us that Hroarr was powerful enough to break the beasts' hold.* She hadn't needed to, but he'd truly felt her desire to stop any problems between their worlds. The other interesting part of his father's detailed account was that Gefn's brother hadn't attacked or tried to harm Hades or the others when he'd had the upper hand. Third, the priestesses had done their part in getting Hroarr and the cats from Earth, though his father hadn't known what they'd said to Hroarr to motivate him to return to Thule. They were all positives in the way of finding some kind of tentative truce between the worlds.

When did they leave?

About half an hour ago.

No one has come here. And he had a feeling if Hroarr could access this place, he would have. P was a little surprised that he hadn't sent the priestesses back to check on Gefn. They had to be trusting his female's beasts to keep a mental watch on her through the bonds he'd seen. That was what she'd told them to do, not that P had expected them to obey. Not with how concerned they'd been when they left.

And if Hroarr is playing it straight, we'll have Apollo put back in a fucking box soon. He could hope.

Hades growled, *Not until I'm done with him*.

P understood his father's need for the God's blood. Apollo had done some horrible things in his time, and Sacha had been one of the victims of the bastard's experimentation to breed the perfect army all those millennia ago.

His female murmured something incoherent again, and he looked down at her closed eyes.

Once Gefn wakes up, I'll ask her more about her brothers and why they took Apollo in the first place.

His father paused. *Fine.*

Drake hadn't spoken much, no doubt waiting for Hades to finish his tirade, but P closed the link with his father, and they were on a private connection now. *Are you okay?*

I am, P assured the dragon.

Sirena wants blood tests from you both.

I think we're past that point. I'm not sure we'll have a choice but to go through the steps. He paused. *I'm half Thulian, so that has to mean something, and biologically Hades was compatible enough with my mother to have me. I also doubt that those cats would have encouraged this match if they thought it would hurt her.*

True, but they may not care if it hurts you, the dragon growled.

He nodded. *If I can get Gefn out of here, I'll get samples for Sirena to check.*

Good. Sirena worries. Hell, I worry with you in another fucking world, the dragon ground out.

I know. Is everything else okay? He now felt guilty for not adding Sirena on this call.

Alyssa's baby blew another wall out of the manor. Drake sounded tense as he relayed the details behind those staggering words. Something his father hadn't shared in his tale.

Fucking hell, but Alyssa and the babe are safe and healthy? And Gregoire?

He could feel the dragon's frustration and concern through the bond when he added, *Gregoire is out of his mind with worry for them both. Era and I were just there with them.*

P shook his head. Alyssa and the baby needed to be safe. Gregoire would lose his mind, they all would if something happened to the first Guardian child. That little girl was a gift to them all.

All we can do is watch. Sirena won't leave their side until the baby comes. We have months, which seems like fucking nothing, the dragon bit out. *For now we need information from your female before your pigheaded father attempts to exchange Kara for Apollo.*

You're really letting him go alone, P snapped, not believing that for a second, no matter that his father's reasoning made sense. Hades thought he was fucking invincible. Hell, maybe he was.

Fuck no, but I don't waste breath arguing with your father. I will take care of it.

P's lips curved. Having his father awakened after all the thousands of years the God had spent in stasis ended up being a full-time job. One P'd taken as personal penance for his part in the Creators sending all the Gods to sleep. It hadn't mattered that he'd rallied for his father's freedom, the Creators hadn't allowed any of the Gods to stay awake. That guilt had always followed P, and he knew the same went for Drake because the dragon's mother and father, Aphrodite and Ladon, were both still asleep.

He assured Drake, *I'll figure out why they took Apollo in the first place and see if this exchange is some kind of trick.*

Good. Watch your back.

P had known the second his Goddess had awakened. He'd felt her tense against him a while ago, but she hadn't spoken, and he wanted to know what she'd do or say. It didn't take long to know that she'd heard his mental conversation.

She was up in a flash. "Who was that in your head? He said Hroarr offered an exchange to get Kara back?"

He would trust her with as much as he could. If they didn't talk and figure this out, they were going to get nowhere. So far she'd proven she didn't want war. That was why he hadn't cut off Drake when he felt her wake up. "That was Drake, my cousin and the leader of the Guardians. He was at the lake with his mate. And, yes, your brother offered an exchange."

He didn't like not having her in his arms. She was gloriously nude and didn't seem to care about that as she faced him before starting to pace. Her thoughts were broadcasting to him and he tried not to feel guilty for creating a block to his own. This side effect of the mating frenzy was about to tell him all he needed to know to protect the ones he loved. The deception would let him know if he could truly trust her.

Too much was at fucking stake.

Chapter 10

Fólkvangr, Falls of the Dead – Thule

Gefn still had his scent on her skin and she mourned the loss of being wrapped in his strength. She'd been shocked that she'd slept with him. She'd been vulnerable to him, and her cats had made their approval known. Their trust in the male made her shake her head.

Waking up cuddled into the warmth of his hard body with the sound of voices in her head had jolted her. It had taken a moment to realize that it was the mind speak he'd told her of. After that she'd been completely caught up in what was said.

She gazed at Pothos and was instantly shaken from her thoughts. He hadn't moved, and the sight of his nude gorgeous body dried her lips. Licking them had drawn his eyes to her mouth and reminded her of his kisses. He looked so different, no less beautiful, but completely changed. She sucked in air and spoke more breathlessly than she'd intended. "Where are your wings?"

He stood with the grace of an animal, and with a rush of power the magnificent wings unfurled from his back. The sound of a harsh flap of wind against feathers was intense.

"Better?" His voice was a sexy rumble that called to her.

She wanted to explore every inch of his body, those magical wings, and even the intricate images on his arms.

"I was only surprised that they were gone." Air stuttered from her lips and she knew he heard it. She looked away from him. He distracted her too much, and she needed to focus. After a moment she added, "We need to see if I can leave here. I need to talk to my brothers."

"I don't think it's possible yet." She swore there was a hint of regret in his tone. She was about to ask more when he spoke. "Will your brother really exchange Kara for Apollo, or will he attempt to keep them both?"

"He will do the exchange." Hroarr would be more concerned about getting Kara back. And now that they'd found Pothos, the other God wasn't important. Spa and Velspar had been right to draw her to him, the male's presence in Thule was exactly what their world needed to survive.

Now she needed to figure out what that meant for Pothos' world? His family? Would they relocate to Thule? She wouldn't leave them to die, because no world could survive with only the power of two Gods, even if it also held the handful of impressive beings she'd seen at the lake. She was sure Hroarr would welcome more power in Thule. As long as they didn't cause strife.

Her heart beat rapidly as her emotions raged with all the complications in their situation.

She blamed Dagur for the mess, mentally cursing her reckless brother in ten different languages. They had been the ones in the wrong, and that left a sour taste in her mouth, especially when she thought of all they'd lost because of his actions. Dozens of their warriors had been senselessly destroyed, and with birthrates so low it was a blow to Thule.

A part of her wanted to hate Pothos and his people for those deaths, but his world hadn't invaded Thule. This was Dagur's fault.

If only Dagur had waited for Hroarr to get to the palace, none of this would have happened. They would never have blindly stolen a God. She understood Dagur's thoughts and reasons, but that didn't make it better. At the time he'd known that Pothos' world couldn't survive with only one God. But what of Pothos' father? Where had he come from? That begged the question as to whether there were more Gods somehow hidden from the spell Dagur had used to search the ether.

"Can your Gods hide themselves or leave your world?"

He hesitated. She knew he didn't trust her, but how were they to solve anything without talking? She changed questions, planning to return to that later. "Did my sister indicate what made her go to your world? Why did you keep her there?" She felt his eyes on her as she paced. She pushed the heavy waves of her hair off her face and felt her hands shaking. Desire. She wanted to be in his arms again.

When their gazes met, she felt the spark of heat all the way to her core. His eyes were on her lips before they dragged down her overheated body. How could she want him again so soon?

His eyes trailed over her body, and it seemed his mind was where hers was.

He finally took a breath and answered, "My father, Hades, sent out a magical call to an old ally in Thule. Your sister came to our world instead of this Agnarr." That statement stopped her need to pace. The stone in the ring her sister had left behind, that had called her to Earth. But if Hades had been an *ally* of her dead brother, had Kara always known, and why hadn't Gefn heard of it before now? It made sense that her brother had traveled to Pothos' world, because how else would his priestess, Eir, have met Hades? Venturing to other worlds was commonplace for the Gods of Thule, but forging an alliance with a God of another world was not. And not telling anyone about said alliance was outrageous. Or should have been, even considering Agnarr's arrogant and reclusive nature.

She needed to talk to Kara; obviously she had the answers they needed.

When Pothos continued, she watched him closely. "After your sister came through, she instigated a battle in her attempt to steal my father away to Thule. It ended with your sister locked in a cell."

Gefn hated the thought of her sister in a cage and firmed her lips. At least her frustrating sibling hadn't been killed.

Why hadn't Kara told them about the world if there were Gods still there? And why try to take a God with such obviously powerful beings at his side? Gefn had felt the power radiating from those who'd been at that lake. They were not full Gods, but a few were at least children of Gods, like Pothos. Had her sister truly been so arrogant?

She groaned, knowing Kara.

Pothos seemed lost in thought so she asked, "You were there?"

"I wasn't."

She thought of the warriors that had left with her sister and closed her eyes as her heart sank.

"What of her warriors?"

"Some are alive, imprisoned."

"Have they been harmed?" Gefn felt fury rise at the thought of them being tortured because of her sister.

"They haven't been tortured. They were questioned, but the language barrier was a problem. And your sister is unconscious, but otherwise whole." Winds whipped around her in wild gusts that howled through the trees as clouds built to match her roiling anger.

What had her sister been thinking? Gefn would gladly string up both her siblings for their combined idiocy. She didn't care what their motives were.

"I need to see my brothers. We need to at least try to leave this place." She had to see for herself that it wasn't possible. She inhaled the clean air mixed with sex. The scent of their coupling only reminded her of the erotic torment she'd suffered while... teleporting, as he'd called it.

The thought of being trapped here for eternity was reason enough to attempt it anyway.

He was suddenly there, towering over her. Instead of feeling threatened, she felt protected as he put his hand on her cheek. His touch was electric, sending shivers down her body.

He spoke gently. "I can try, but I doubt it will work. At least not yet." She had a feeling he was hiding something from her.

"What are you not telling me?" she demanded suspiciously.

Maybe it wasn't possible for her to leave. That made her heart rate speed. He'd said that she'd gain his power, and she was, she felt it in her veins. But she didn't know how to use it or decipher what was there inside her. Teleporting was the most important at the moment. He'd also said they would be mentally connected, but she wasn't sure how...

Suddenly each and every reaction and hesitation that had shone on his face passed through her memories. Every single one, including the guilt. She spun from his touch in the air current and felt like a part of her was ripped away when she faced him from several steps away.

Tension filled the air around them, making it almost too thick to breathe freely.

"Are you hearing my thoughts?" she demanded with narrowed eyes, because it felt true. He'd listened to her *private* thoughts and worries. Was listening to them still.

She could see the guilt in his eyes and in the way his jaw clenched and unclenched, but the world seemed to stop moving when he admitted his deception. "Yes."

Winds lifted her hair and the water surged up from the pool as she felt the full effect of her mortification. Her skin heated as she tried to remember each thought.

"You said we would have a mental connection. Why can I not hear your thoughts?" she demanded, raising her chin.

He hardened his jaw before speaking. "I have a shield for my thoughts."

She was furious and trying not to lose complete control of her temper. "When did you start hearing my personal thoughts, and why did you not tell me?" She held a hand up as he moved closer. It didn't matter that he had every reason not to trust her, he should have said something. The winds howled through the trees as she demanded the more important answer, "How do I build one of these shields? Explain. Now."

She wasn't sure if she were more furious, humiliated, or just hurt at having trusted him. He'd been blatantly listening to her lust over him among everything else... Her cats yowled in her head and attempted to calm her emotion, but it wasn't working, and she was still furious with them as well.

"I will do it for you," he said gently.

He moved closer and she snapped, "Do you need to touch me to do this?"

He growled, "No, I need to be in your mind."

"You were already there," she bit out. "So show me this shield."

"I didn't lie."

"Omission. I am aware of the difference."

She felt him slide into her mind and nearly moaned, which only embarrassed her more.

Her power was wild and spinning out of control, and she wanted to lash out, do damage. She understood him needing answers from her. She would have done the same thing in his position, so she wasn't sure exactly why she felt hurt that he'd shielded his own thoughts, protected his privacy. Perhaps because she was the one left wide open and vulnerable while he was left with his secrets.

She closed her eyes, trying to calm the wild emotion that didn't make sense. She only knew that lust was riding under it all, amplifying everything.

She'd allowed him inside her body. Not only that, she'd slept beside him, and her cats had encouraged her to trust him.

Lightning lit the dark skies and thunder crashed as she turned and stepped into the raging water of the mineral pool. She wanted his scent off her skin, the stickiness from between her thighs.

She needed space. She moaned when she felt something... a wall building in her mind. Water slid over her thighs, her breasts as she slipped through the warm liquid.

Even his mental touch was intoxicating, and she hated that he could spin her this far out of control without even touching her skin.

A shiver ran over her shoulders down to her breasts, and she knew it wasn't right.

The waters shifted and she knew he'd followed her in. The pleasure of his voice in her mind was nearly too much. *I'm sorry. Hurting you was the last thing I wanted to do. But I needed to know I could trust you. That you wouldn't set my family up to be harmed.*

She felt him coming closer as ripples lapped lovingly at her sensitive flesh. It was a kind of protection that should have soothed her tense muscles as she listened to him speak in her mind. *My mother adamantly instructed my father to never allow a God of Thule near me. She told him that you'd all want me dead, so he never even told me her real identity until a week ago. He didn't want me anywhere near that lake because he was worried. Now I worry about him. We may be fated,* thea mou, *but we've only known each other for hours. I'm here in your world, where your priestesses can pop in at any moment and put a blade through my neck. At the same time my family could be walking into danger with your brother."*

She turned to him and watched as he slowly stalked through the water toward her. His wings had gone away again, but he was just as magnificent and beautiful. His intent eyes were focused completely on hers as he moved with a grace that any animal could only hope to achieve. She'd already known his reasons had been valid, but she still felt hurt. It had to be all the lust driving her other emotions wild.

His gravelly tone filtered to her ears. "I hate that I hurt you.

You're the one female I'm bound to protect and care for through all eternity, but would you ever want a male who didn't protect those he loved?"

"I would not," she admitted before frowning. "Can you still hear my thoughts?" She swore she felt a wall inside her mind, but hadn't he just answered her mental question.

The intent look in his eyes was affecting her deeply. "Your thoughts are safe, but I can still feel the hurt."

"You can feel my emotions?" That was more like the bond with her cats.

He nodded. "You'll feel my emotions too."

That eased her. At least that felt fair.

Standing in front of her, he added, "From now on, think to me directly as if you're speaking aloud."

She sucked in a breath. "Now what must we do?"

"I need to tell my father and Drake that it's likely safe to trade the Goddess and her warriors for Apollo. You'll hear me because you share my telepathic links now."

She did hear him contacting them and felt how he was doing it. While he relayed the information, she slid her mind over the mental thread that led to him. She saw the web of those threads coming from her male while only seeing his brilliant white thread and two gold threads that must lead to the bonds with her beasts.

When she felt his wet hands slide up her arms and over her shoulders, her knees nearly buckled.

"How do I know you cannot hear my thoughts now?" she asked

to be prudent, when she'd been feeling anything but. Not when such a simple touch from him made her crazy with lust. "And what are all those threads?"

"I'm not sure how to test it... Come into my mind, and then you can see the shield and what happens when I lower it." He said the words as he did exactly that, and her entire body lit up as she felt his thoughts.

She gasped at the carnal words that filled her head. The things he wanted to do to her. She moaned in near agony as he pulled her into his arms. Soon his thoughts moved to safer things. His father and Drake. His cousin was more like a brother to him. He gave her an image of them both. "Do you see the shield?" he growled.

She could feel his tense muscles against her. "Yes."

"And when I close it?" Which he did, and then she heard and saw nothing from him, and it felt wrong to her. It had felt too good being in his mind; she wanted to see more. Needed to learn more about him personally, not just what they had to share to keep the peace between their worlds.

Gefn was panting with need as she went into her own mind and saw the same wall and practiced lowering and raising it before breathing out in relief that she'd accomplished something other than falling willingly into his arms.

When she opened her eyes, she was caught in the wild lust in his sapphire gaze. It set his strong jaw in a tense line as he looked down at her, and she knew that the frenzy was taking them over again.

And she didn't fight it.

Chapter 11

Fólkvangr, Falls of the Dead – Thule

Desire was ruling them both, and Gefn wanted his hands on her again, his mouth, the hard shaft that bobbed into her stomach.

All of him.

Her gaze trailed over the hard body before her as even the swaying of the water seemed to draw her closer to him, attempting to close the gap between their naked bodies. She sucked in a breath as everything charged around them, the forest, the water. Clouds were moving in again, but she was too caught in his addicting male scent and the sight of his body to notice anything else. She allowed her fingers and palms to slide over the taut muscles of this chest, enjoying the way the warm flesh twitched at her touch.

He growled, and before she knew it, she was lifted up until their naked bodies meshed together through the liquid in the pool. She eagerly welcomed his descending lips, opening hers to his demanding kiss. The tangling of their tongues made her ache for more. She moaned into his lips as her legs wrapped around his waist. She felt the first drops of rain as she clutched his shoulders and dug into his wingless back.

The kiss was wild by the time her fingers came to his jaw, reveling in the way it moved as he kissed her. She tilted her head, accepting the demands of his mouth and savoring his taste all the while he moved her body against the rigid shaft between them. He teased her with each grinding down sweep until she thought she might find release like that. Her ears were ringing in time to the sloshing water flowing over the stone edge of the pool. Evidence of the sheer power of his body tormenting hers.

It wasn't enough. *More.* She wasn't sure the mind speak would work, but the thought of breaking the kiss was not possible.

He groaned into her mouth as his deep voice filled her mind. *How much more,* thea mou? *Tell me.*

All of it, she sent and hoped it made it.

You want my cock inside you? He asked the question while controlling her hips until she was gasping for climax.

Yesss. The stuttered emphasis was enough to get him to move. He lifted her to hover over his hardness before slowly lowering her down.

He growled into her mind and she felt the vibrations all the way to her soul, not a spot inside or out of her body wasn't shuddering with pleasure.

I'm going to teleport and let you see if we can leave. His voice was harsh and getting raspier as he continued, *But, Gefn, wherever we end up, you'll stay as you are. Full of my cock.*

She was barely aware of what he was doing. His voice and those dirty words were too much for her mind. Yes, she'd wanted to find out if she could leave, but now? Before the thought was even fully formed, she was broken up into a million pieces. She couldn't gasp or do anything but feel; every single part of him was combining with her in the same erotic torment as before.

This power was different than being a part of the winds, but that was the closest comparison she could make. This was much faster and seemed so wild and out of control. She couldn't breathe. The same wall was there, and she felt it pulse, but she couldn't push past it no matter how she tried. She would have cried out in frustration and panic if she was able to, but she had no body, no lips.

The second they reformed, she did cry out in pleasure so deep it dissipated the panic, pushed it back to the innermost parts of her mind. The need was so intense that her head fell back as she mewled for more. The dizziness from traveling and the panic seemed to be no match against the blinding need.

He was inside her so deep that she thought she'd die if he didn't move faster. Water ran over the sides of the pool as she fought for some purchase. She used power and strength to gain leverage to meet his thrusts.

He grunted before biting out, "You feel so damned perfect."

Over and over he slammed her up and down his shaft as they moved through the water toward the steps. Mindlessly, she noted something moving from the corner of her eye. Instead of carrying her out of the pool, her back was pushed into soft padding. In the recesses of her mind she knew he had to have moved the cushion of the lounge into the pool, but she was more intent on his weight on top of her, his shaft pushing inside her as his hips worked harder. It was as if she were in another place, somewhere with no time, where all that existed was pleasure. Her body fused with his in the most primal of ways, his body inside hers, his breath on her skin, those gorgeous eyes blazing with heat.

She wanted that. Wanted him to lose control like she had.

"What would feel better?" she rasped as she lifted up and kissed the straining tendons of his neck.

He groaned and she felt how much he was holding back. *Tell me,* she said into his mind. Or she hoped she had.

Wrap your legs around my back. I want to feel you all over me, thea mou, he growled.

And my voice in your head... does it do the same things to you that it does to me?

Fuck. Yes. His response in her mind was making her lose her sanity as she continued to kiss his neck while wrapping her legs around his hips. She felt his entire body shudder as she slid her feet over the backs of his wet thighs. His thrusts grew harder until the sound of wet skin slapping against heated flesh was all she could hear.

She licked and then bit his neck, wringing a groan from his lips that affected her just as much. Her touch had done that to him. This big powerful male wanted her hands on him, her lips and tongue. That alone seemed to drive animalistic noises from his lips. His body rocked hers with a force that drove him against her mound, making her moan. Deep inside, he ruthlessly slid over a spot that stole the air from her lungs.

When his big hands moved from her to grip the stone lip of the pool, she knew he was lost. His eyes landed on hers with such intensity that it drew a gasp from her lips. She heard stone cracking as he powered into her, the edge of the pool no match for this male.

She dug her nails into his back as she writhed and fought to feel it all at once. Her eyes closed as her head lolled back and forth on the soft padding. She was spinning out of control into sheer perfect bliss.

"Look at me when you come," he commanded with a force that rumbled the ground beneath them. Her eyes slit open just as her body started to spasm in pure pleasure. She fought for purchase on his back, digging her fingers in as she crushed her breasts tighter against his chest. Every muscle tensed as she cried out her release while clutching his shaft with a force that made him roar with pleasure.

His head fell back and the elements bellowed for him, rocking and swirling around them in wild abandon. The winds lifted the furniture as the water rose from the pool. She could hear and smell the forest blooming and growing, but nothing was as magical as the way he felt. The way his staff throbbed inside her clenching body, demanding more of the warm seed already filling her up. It seemed to go on forever as he looked back down at her, chest rising and falling with harsh breaths that matched her own. He was incredible.

From the corner of her sight she could see the furniture settle back to the ground, the water from the pool that had lifted to shroud them washed back down.

He set his forehead to hers and she understood. There were no words for what had happened between them. She couldn't stop touching him; her arms wound around his neck, holding him close as their breathing evened out.

He lifted up a hair to gaze down at her before lowering to kiss her, a soft tasting that eased her jagged nerves.

How do you feel? His voice in her mind was soothing, and she wanted to relax in his arms and let sleep take her again, but there was too much they needed to discuss.

Her thighs moved over his hips in a caress she couldn't seem to stop. *I feel relaxed.* His flesh felt too good against hers.

Not sore or hurt? He looked at her then, his eyes assessing her.

She smiled. "I am perfect. I feel strong and warm." She felt safe and secure as well. So much so that she never wanted him to move. It wasn't logical, for the time that they'd known one another, but somehow she felt closer to him than she'd ever been to another.

He leaned in to take her lips in a fleeting kiss before agreeing. "You are perfect."

She ignored the tingles that slid over her skin at his words and instead asked, "Does this mean we have finished the bond you spoke of?"

There was so much power flowing around them, through them.

He didn't leave the cradle of her body. Instead he stayed there, hovering above her as he spoke. "No. Our souls aren't connected yet."

He seemed hesitant, so she asked, "You are certain of this?"

"Yes, *thea mou*."

She loved how those words sounded on his lips. She was his Goddess.

*****

Pothos couldn't force himself to leave her body. He wasn't even sure she was aware that her hands and thighs kept drifting over his skin, but it felt too damned good to end. He'd been scared for a minute that he'd hurt her. She was so damned tight and he'd lost control, destroying part of the pool in his grip.

Now she was gentling him. He'd never experienced anything like her touch; it lit up every nerve in his body and sent power flooding the forest beyond them.

Her next words pulled him from his thoughts. “When will it happen?” There was concern in her voice, and he wanted to wipe away her worry. She felt trapped, and guilt ate at him. He’d taken her to this place. He hadn’t done it on purpose, and she didn’t seem to blame him, but he blamed himself.

That didn’t mean he looked forward to completing their bond there, where he would be very vulnerable to threats. They both would be, and that wasn’t acceptable to his protective instincts. He rested his forehead on hers. She had a right to know the damned process. “There are several steps we have to go through before the connection is completed.”

Her next words were breathy. “What steps?”

He lifted his head and slipped from her body out of self-preservation. His cock had already started to twitch inside all that warmth, making him groan.

The soft intake of her breath and the way her eyes flashed with disappointment didn’t help. “I can’t talk when I’m inside you. I already want more.”

“You said that was how this would be.” A small frown creased her brow. “You said the lust would only get more intense. Painful until the bond was complete.”

“I did,” he agreed as he stood in front of her, washing the stone from his fingers. The pool now held a permanent mark of his loss of control. Sunlight filtered down from the canopy, flickering over her wet flesh flushed and spread from his possession. Her nipples were still tight little peaks and they begged for his lips. He forced his eyes away; the damned frenzy was killing him. He looked into the forest, to the thousands of flowers dotting the brilliant green around them.

He wasn't sure if it was the combined power they unleashed when they had sex that had caused them, because he'd been too completely lost in her to notice anything else.

The frenzy was out of control. Too damned relentless. It hadn't been this way for his brothers. They'd had hours between bouts of sex. Why did he want to bury his cock back in her wet little pussy all over again? Fucking hell, he hadn't wanted to leave her hot cunt in the first place. This couldn't be normal.

"Pothos?" she asked, and he looked at her again.

Shit, she'd asked him for confirmation that the frenzy would get worse until they completed the bond. "Yes, the mating frenzy gets more demanding until we finish it." What he didn't say was that it shouldn't be this demanding already. Hadn't his brothers gone hours before the need hit like a truck? He'd come inside her only minutes ago.

Her eyes landed on his cock, and desire flared in her emerald eyes. She shook her head. "I see that." And then she licked her lips.

Fuck. She was killing him. They needed to talk, but it was getting nearly impossible. He attempted to arrange his own damned thoughts, but at the moment nearly all of them involved having her again.

"What do we do to stop this?" He heard her frustration and looked back down at her. She stood inches from him and he could see her small hands fisted under the water. Her nipples were so damned tight, they begged for his mouth. He moved back a step.

He groaned and ran a wet hand over his head. "In a traditional mating ceremony it begins with vows. After making my vows, you would mark me as your male." Fuck if he didn't want that right now.

He telepathically sent her the image of the traditional mating mark, the tattoo of twin dragons interlocked by their tails in the dual shape of infinity. "The symbol represents the everlasting bond of a mated pair." His voice grew deeper as he continued, "That mark would signify that I am yours for all eternity."

Her mouth shot open. "I would need to do this to you?"

He smiled. "Yes. If we were in my world, our healer would funnel her power through your hands. Here you would tap into the healing ability I have."

"Healing ability?"

"I can do some, nothing like our healer, but enough for the mark to be permanently imbedded in my skin."

"And your females take marks as well?" He swallowed through the desire to mark her soft skin. It was a primal urge that he needed to curb. She'd firmed those pouty lips, and he could tell she was shocked by the traditions.

"It's tradition only for the male, but my brother Guardians' females have taken a mark as well. You choose whether you would like one or not."

Her eyes flashed with something. He felt her pleasure and wondered if it was the opportunity to have some say in all that was happening.

Her gaze went to study the designs on his heated flesh as she murmured thoughtfully, "Some in Thule mark themselves with spells or symbols of battle, but nothing for their female. They are not so detailed as this." Her palmed slid to his bicep and nerves twitched following her exploration. "Do these markings define you?"

Define him? He supposed they did. When her soft fingers trailed around the back of his arm, his cock twitched in response. It was a simple touch nowhere near his dick, but that didn't stop his reaction. He'd never felt anything as good as her small hands roving over his skin. Had he been so starved of contact through the centuries, or was it simply that his mate's touch was like air to a flame? All he knew was that he wanted more. His skin heated to near burning. He flexed the muscles at his back, feeling the flesh at his spine tingle.

He growled when he could finally speak. "The tattoos there represent my family."

She moved beside him, shaking her head. "But these are beasts?"

He gazed down at her, transfixed by her, wanting so much more. His tone was raspy to his own ears. "Many of my brothers have a beast half." He wouldn't get into a history lesson on how Immortals ended up with beast blood; it wasn't pertinent to explain that Apollo loved a good experiment and he used animal DNA to try to make the perfect Immortal army thousands of years ago.

Her eyes shot to his. "They are able to actually change form?"

"Yes. Some can." Not all could shift into their beast; some had just enough of the blood to give them an edge with added strength and enhanced senses. He distracted himself by using power to send the soaking lounge cushion through the air, using the winds to dry it before setting it back in its spot under the tree.

Her sexy-as-sin voice brought his gaze back. "There are dragons and wolves..." When she looked up at him, her pouty lips parted invitingly. A beat passed before she asked, "Is there a beast inside you?" That brought a groan to his lips. How could such a beautiful and powerful Goddess be commanding one moment and so damned seductively inquisitive, almost innocent, the next?

*****

Gefn wasn't entirely certain how she felt about P turning into a beast. His lips curved as he looked down at her; the small change transformed him from beautiful to sinful. There was no mistaking the lust glazing his brilliant blue eyes. Lust she felt in turn. Her body was out of control, but she needed to know more about the male himself. So much had been focused on their worlds, on preventing tensions between their worlds. If she were to be connected to him for eternity, she wanted to know more about him.

"I'm a beast for you, *thea mou*."

She sucked in a breath at the sexual undertones and the way his deep voice seemed to whisper over her skin, causing bumps to rise along her arms. He affected her body like nothing she'd ever known. She should move away to try to stave off the lust, but she couldn't. She needed to touch him like this. She reveled in the intense reaction he had to her simple touch, the way his muscles flexed and moved with the slide of her fingers. His skin had heated as she looked at the images on his arms. So incredibly detailed as if they could come to life beneath her touch.

She felt a little light-headed when he added, "I don't have an animal half."

He lifted a hand to gently trace his thumb over her cheek, and she turned into the warmth as her eyes closed for a moment, stifling a sigh, and it eased and enticed all at once. She swallowed and opened her eyes, catching the intensity in how he gazed at her.

She licked her lips and pointed out, "You have wings."

"I do. From my father."

His thumb slid from her cheek to the side of her lips before he pulled away.

She felt a wave of disappointment at the loss.

He groaned huskily. "Touching you makes me want your lips, *thea mou*. Ask your questions while it's still possible for me to answer."

She shivered with need and shook it off; he was right. She wanted to know more about him. "The other God did not have wings."

"My father was the only God born with wings."

She moved to look at the back of his arm. It was a swirl of colorful beasts mixed with the occasional symbol or face of those he cared about. She noticed a long wing on the back of one arm and moved behind him to see the other arm and stopped.

She gasped at what she saw. The unique lines of the markings ran down his spine, glowing just beneath the surface. She felt the raw beauty of them while a wave of emotion nearly choked her. She drew a hand to her lips, swallowing it back as he turned to face her with concern etching his beautiful face. "What is it?"

She took a breath. "You have magical runes on your back." Runes that held so much heartbreaking meaning that she wanted to go back in time and kill Tyr. Her evil sibling had been the reason Pothos' mother had placed the power in his skin.

He gazed down with a fierce look. "What does that mean?"

"They're protections," she answered. "If I am correct, these were placed beneath your skin by your mother."

He growled, "Show me."

"How?"

"Send the mental images in the same way you can talk in my mind."

She moved behind him again, feeling his agitation. She looked at the soft glow of the ancient symbols and tried to use the mind power, but she wasn't certain she was using it properly.

"Do you see them?" she asked when he tensed.

"Yes. I've never seen them before. What exactly do they mean?"

"Each of the sharp markings represent a powerful protection spell, but it is also a gift of power."

His muscles twitched and flexed as he watched her. Another growl slipped from his lips. "Why does it upset you? I can feel it, Gefn. What aren't you saying?"

Sorrow filled her. "She gave you her power."

She saw the understanding flicker in his beautiful eyes before it turned to anger. "You're saying she left me with my father and returned to Thule powerless?"

She swallowed through the lump in her throat before nodding. "I don't know that for certain."

"But you think so?" he growled. She felt his inner turmoil as if it were her own. She tried to send him soothing energies.

"A mother will do anything to protect her child," she whispered. "I'm only sorry she did not come to me or Hroarr before doing something so drastic. We would have done anything in our power to protect the child of a priestess."

She could feel his emotions spinning. He hadn't known his mother. Was it worse knowing that his mother had sacrificed everything to protect him? Gefn felt her own raw emotion tearing at her heart. The cats tried to soothe her.

Pothos shook his head, and she felt a surge of anger and so much more as he spat out, "My father would have protected her. She didn't need to make that sacrifice. Why would she?"

"I do not know." And she didn't. "Times were dark. Hroarr was gone a lot, searching for the key to locking our evil siblings away." Her voice turned hollow in her own ears as she shared her greatest shame. "I had just returned from Hroarr's palace when all three of my priestesses were slaughtered before my eyes, violently severing the bonds I shared with them." She breathed out. "Your mother was right to take you from Thule."

They stayed in silence for a long time with him looking out to the forest. She wanted to go to him, but she wasn't sure he'd want her comfort.

He growled, "Come to me, Gefn."

One step through the water and she was in his arms. She leaned her head on his chest. So many memories of that time haunted her dreams. His warmth eased the tension from her shoulders. "I'm sorry."

He held her tighter and kissed her head. She closed her eyes. "You didn't do anything wrong."

How could he know that? She had failed as a Goddess. Failed her own people, failed Pothos' mother without knowing it. If she and Hroarr had been able to contain Tyr earlier, they would have saved so many. Too many sightless eyes looked back at her when she closed her eyes.

He rubbed her back soothingly.

After they'd both calmed, he asked, "Why are the markings only showing now?" It was another question she couldn't answer with certainty.

"I do not know. It may have begun with your presence in Thule. Or it could be Fólkvangr." She looked around the sacred place. "This is where our priestesses renew their strength."

The desire that had been building before her discovery seemed to have only been waiting beneath the surface. She kissed his hard chest and was pleased at the way his muscle jolted under her lips.

He was dragging her up his body when they both felt the air change.

She cursed Reginleif and the others, knowing the trio had returned.

Chapter 12

Fólkvangr, Falls of the Dead – Thule

Gefn's voice whispered into P's mind seconds before the priestesses showed themselves, *Hroarr's females would never harm you. No one in Thule would dare. Nor could they.* He knew she referenced the runes heating his back; her voice had a sorrowful tinge that he hated. She paused. *Wait. It is me you worry for?* Her sex-kitten voice held a hint of confusion. She'd gotten very comfortable, very fast with their telepathic connection. Having her speaking in his head was destined to be a constant torture for him. Frenzy or not, it was like fucking phone sex on steroids.

Yes. P stifled a growl of frustration as his shoulders bunched with tension. Every instinct in him demanded he shield his mate, but these were her fucking people. Still, he'd set her down and turned in the pool so that he was between her and the newcomers. He should be happy they'd returned now and not ten minutes from now. His cock, the greedy fucker, wasn't pleased at being denied, but it wasn't only desire for her. It was the need to take away the torturous sadness he felt from her at the sight of the runes and the memories of her slaughtered priestesses. In all honesty he acknowledged that they both needed some easing. To him his mother's sacrifice felt like a senseless waste. Hades would have protected his mother if she'd stayed instead of dropping him off.

For Gefn it had been a harsher blow. She'd seen too much death; he felt it in her words as well as in their bond. As her mate he needed to give her enough pleasure to forget, even for a short time.

Are you always so protective? She moved to his side and he sucked in a breath as he looked down at her. There was a hint of a smile in her beautiful emerald eyes.

Of you, thea mou, he admitted honestly before nearly growling at how beautiful she looked with her lips curved like that, *always.*

He loved the way her breathing hitched and wished they were alone now, but the females were already at the pool. He'd tracked their movements without needing to look at them.

He finally turned to the visitors, crossing his arms over his chest. Their presence wasn't surprising. If Hroarr was half the brother his female thought him to be, he would demand to know she was safe. The fact that he hadn't come was telling, because Hroarr hadn't struck P as the type to send others to speak for him. He'd been the first through the portal to Earth. He hadn't sent warriors or his siblings; it had been the massive God and then the others. So that meant it was very likely that the females hadn't lied about not being able to take passengers.

"Why have you come early?" Gefn's demand was a mix of irritation and displeasure. He was caught by the fact that his Goddess could manage an air of power even with wet hair plastered to her naked flesh. He cursed the hip-level waters near the steps, but had no intention of retreating into the deeper end. His mind was too busy short-circuiting at the fact that his female's beautiful full tits were just above the water, displayed like some sort of sexy sea Goddess come to take over his fantasies. She stood tall and proud, completely unfazed by her nudity.

He was not. His cock didn't seem to care that they had company. He forced down the lust with an iron will, knowing his cock was barely concealed beneath the water and any more excitement would have it up and on display against his stomach. He gritted his teeth and kept his focus on the females before him.

It was Reginleif, the darker one, who answered, "Hroarr commanded us to see that you are safe."

The trio of females darted glances from the wet pavilion out to the forest beyond. He had no doubt they were seeing the changes since they'd last been there. In that time the forest had bloomed with thousands of flowers.

Gefn nodded regally before huffing out an irritated breath. "I assumed as much." She paused. "And as displeased as I am that you did not follow my instructions, it is good that you are here. I need you to relay information to my brothers." Her heavy sigh only served to draw his eyes back to her fucking tits like a high-powered magnet. He grinded his teeth, knowing the frenzy had started working overtime and it was a damned menace.

Her eyes shot to his for a split second. Long enough for him to catch the same mix of annoyance and blatant heat he was feeling.

She tilted her chin before directing her attention back to the females. "I am still unable to leave this sacred place." He felt a hint of his female's anxiety at that fact, and he sent her soothing energies without a thought. Her eyes shot to his and he watched her slender throat move as she swallowed. Concentration was a bitch and he hated how relentless it was. They had a lot to discuss and not enough time to do any of it. He still hadn't addressed some of the assumptions she'd made when he'd been hearing her thoughts. One was that Earth only had two Gods. Another was the fact that he was a Guardian of Earth and she seemed to need him in Thule. His main concern was getting the trio to leave. He felt his female send him soothing energies, and it felt like she'd stroked his cock under the waters.

The priestesses turned to him, and this time it was Mist who spoke. "You are sure she will gain your power to leave?"

"I'll get her out of this place no matter what." It was his fault she was stuck there, and he'd find a way to get her out.

Gefn did not respond, instead commanding the females. "I need you to warn Hroarr that Kara is unconscious," she said before quickly relaying all the information she'd learned from him about her sister's presence on Earth, including the alliance Agnarr had with his father. He was glad she hadn't shared the information about what his mother had done. That was too damned personal, which was something she seemed to understand.

Reginleif shook her head. "I cannot believe Kara would not have said something about this world."

His cock was completely unbothered by the tension or the female's words. The bastard was twitching beneath the water and was seconds from full wood thanks to the scent of his female and the way she was sending winds to caress his skin. He was forced to bite back a groan. *Gefn,* thea mou*, you need to stop,* he whispered into her mind. He was seconds from fucking her, audience or not. He forced his cock down with nearly all his focus. He wasn't his father, who was perfectly fine whipping his dick out for all to see.

She turned to him with a frown. "What is it?"

Your winds are tormenting me, thea mou. He had no idea air could do what she was doing, and the look on her face told him she wasn't consciously stroking him with it.

I didn't realize… she stuttered before she blushed a pretty pink.

He couldn't help the pained smile. *I love it. Just not when I can barely think as it is,* thea mou, he sent back, meaning every word. There was no denying how much he longed for her touch. For a male who'd avoided most contact with anyone, it was as if he'd been starved for so long all he wanted to do was gorge. Not on any touch, only hers.

"Were you speaking into her mind?" Reginleif questioned, and he had no doubt the female was information gathering for Hroarr.

"Yes," he ground out, finding it better to give them something to take back even though he wanted them gone. "And she was speaking in mine. Our abilities will continue to blend as we bond."

"When will this bonding be complete?" Reginleif spouted before frowning. "Will she get wings? Where *are* your wings?"

He chose the questions he was willing to answer. "My wings are hidden. And I don't think she'll get them, but I can't be sure. Our bonding is unique." That was an understatement. They were of two different worlds, but Sacha hadn't gotten wings after her mating to his father, so it was a fairly logical assumption that Gefn wouldn't get his.

The green-haired one was the quietest, watching, assessing him while Mist took a turn drilling him for answers. "You said before that your souls will be tied together. What does that mean?"

"It means that she and I will share a bond for eternity." He wasn't sure how much to divulge. He wanted less questions, not more. They kept stealing worried glances at his female, which would have been endearing if his cock wasn't ruling his mind.

"Will you have to stay together at all times?" Mist frowned.

He shook his head. "No. We'll feel the other and know the

other's location."

The three shared a look before Gefn spoke. "I feel his emotion. And he mine. Similar to the bond you have with Hroarr, only more detailed."

Reginleif asked, "What are the negatives of this bond?"

He answered through gritted teeth; the frenzy was already twisting in his gut. "If one of us dies, if the bond is severed, it usually leads to madness."

*****

"Madness?" The trio of females' mouths gaped. Gefn stilled, believing his words to be true. When her priestesses had died, it left a hole inside her, and their bond hadn't been anywhere close to what she already shared with Pothos.

They all took a long moment to absorb that information. The three females were aware of what Gefn suffered when she'd lost her three, but she needed them to understand, to explain this to Hroarr. "The bond between Pothos and me is already stronger than anything I have ever known, and it is still growing and changing."

They nodded while taking deep breaths.

Mist asked, "Do your Gods also have bonds with select Immortals as we have with Hroarr?"

"No. We have family connections." He paused, apparently thinking before adding, "But the strongest bond we have is the one with our mate."

He was creating his own place inside her, one that held immense pleasure, but also held the potential to destroy her. That fact didn't jolt her nearly as much as the fact that she could destroy him as well.

The fear that she'd fail him as she'd failed her females nearly paralyzed her. Her cats sent her soothing emotion at the same time Pothos did. She breathed through it and refused to let that fear rule her. It was a useless emotion since she knew deep inside there was no going back. The bond was already there.

A glance at him showed the tension in his massive muscled body. She could smell his addicting scent and was forced to bite off a curse when it sent a surge of lust coursing through her body. The frenzy was a nightmare.

Once the bond is finished, the lust will calm, will it not? she gritted out. Fate had already dealt the card.

Yes. I'll always want you, but it won't rule us like it is now.

The trio of priestesses had gone silent. It was time they left her to ask him more about what they needed to do. In private.

Gefn commanded the trio, "Tell Hroarr that I am well. And ensure he maintains peace with Pothos' family. He will not be pleased about Kara, but knowing ahead of time should help. We need answers from her. Now leave us and Do. Not. Return until the morrow."

Chapter 13

Guardian Manor, Tetartos Realm

Hades stepped down the dimly lit hallway beneath the manor. His nephew's deep bellow drifted to him from the last door of the tunnel. The blond dragon was standing by the cell they'd fashioned for the Goddess Kara, while addressing Sander. The dark-skinned Phoenix nodded his assent to whatever Draken had said while folding his thick tattooed arms over a sleeveless white tee shirt. The males of this time had the worst taste in clothing. His son included. Hades preferred silk dress pants to the harsh material of jeans or the confining material of the tee shirts.

His wings twitched at the thought of being contained and clothed over. He only did so when following his nephew's ridiculous rules in the human Realm. And only then to please his female, not the dragon. He played nice for Sacha and Sacha alone. At the moment he was agitated, but he'd promised his female that he would not interrupt his son. He agreed that Pothos needed to focus on any threats, and he begrudgingly admitted that his telepathic check-ins could cost his son an edge if the Thulians attacked. The only thing easing Hades' nerves was knowing that Pothos could leave the Realm if he needed to.

Smoke lifted from Draken's lips as he continued speaking to the other male. "Uri will bring Havoc here to transport her to Earth Realm for the exchange."

Hades moved to the side of the cell to glance through the hazy blue confinement spell to the sleeping Goddess beyond. The dark-haired female lay flat on a narrow bed in the copper-lined room. The Guardians had moved her once. Only because the copper had been draining her powers too fast to allow her to regain consciousness after the injuries she'd sustained in battle with him. Now she was back in the copper room.

When Draken's words sank in, he balked. "You must be joking."

Smoke filtered to the ceiling, a sign of his nephew's annoyance.

He glanced over at the dragon and demanded, "Have you attempted to teleport her normally?" Using a hellhound pup was the Guardians' secret way to get people out of the confinement spell around Tetartos Realm. Anyone could get in, but supposedly the only ones allowed to leave were Guardians and Gods. Hades had never had reason to test his ability to take anyone out of the Realm, but surely that was a more dignified avenue.

"Why are you here, Hades?" Draken snapped.

"I came to see if she was awake." And his Sacha had wanted to see Gregoire and his pregnant female. The growling Hippeus, half warhorse, had been trying Hades' patience, so Sacha had recommended he check on the prisoner.

"She's not. And I'd rather she stay that way," the dragon growled. Which was obviously why she was back in the power-draining copper room. Draken added a second later, "It will make for an easier exchange."

He had to agree that an unconscious Goddess would be much simpler for him to deal with, but it was sure to rile the Thulians. That thought actually brought a smile of anticipation to his lips. He only hoped Hroarr would initiate a battle this time. That would be just the thing to alleviate the tension of his son still being in the other world.

Waiting was not something he found appealing. The fact that they were on the Thulian's time frame at all aggravated him to no end. The bastard hadn't even waited for a response to his demands. The only real plus was getting his hands on Apollo. That was *if* Hroarr made good on his deal, and Hades didn't trust any Thulian.

Hades eyed the Goddess. She was in the same icy blue dress she'd worn the day she'd attacked him. "Why did you bring her to this Realm in the first place?"

"Hades, you're trying my patience. The last thing I was going to do was keep an otherworldly Goddess in the Human Realm."

Hades admitted Draken had a point. The protections here were much better in Tetartos, and there were billions of mortals to consider in the other Realm. His nephew was nothing if not overcautious.

"You already transported her warriors to Earth?" he questioned.

"No. Testing how we'd get them out of here didn't make any fucking sense," the damned Phoenix snipped sarcastically. The annoying male had been the Goddess' primary guard because it seemed he was immune to her energy power, and the babysitting duty hadn't improved the male's attitude.

Hades shot the irreverent male a glare. It was tempting to show him his place, but Hades had no doubt that would upset Sacha, so he abstained, barely. When he felt her amused gratitude through their connection, it made him smile.

"So the warriors were transported to Earth via a dog?" He raised his eyebrows. "You should have asked me for assistance."

More smoke rose to the ceiling when Draken spoke. "If I was unable to get one of them through the confinement spell around this Realm, then I doubt you'd have better luck." The dragon held up a hand when Hades went to speak. "I know you're a fucking God. Fine. By all means, go help Uri port the rest of the warriors. He's only able to have Havoc take one at a time."

Hades raised a brow at his nephew. "This is how you ask me for a favor?"

The Phoenix had the nerve to snort.

Draken growled, "That was not me asking for a favor. I don't need you to do what Uri is already doing. But if you have no intention of being useful, then get the hell out of my face."

Uri arrived before Hades could respond. The large black pup stayed at the dark-haired male's side, eying Draken through red eyes. Hades felt another smile tip his lips that the animal seemed to love everyone but the dragon.

Uri's silver eyes swirled in obvious agitation as he addressed Draken. "We may need Hades after all."

The pup bumped Hades' side and he looked down with a raised brow. Did the beast have no care that he could destroy it with a thought? He shook his head at the adoration in the animal's eyes, and with a sigh he patted its head. Sacha's amusement filtered to him, letting him know his kindness had been worth it.

"What is it?" Drake bit out.

"I just got reports of massive hell beast hordes in all the cities of Tetartos." The Aletheia Guardian's silver eyes flashed with irritation. The main Guardian telepathic link was not being used because no one was certain if or when Pothos' Goddess would intercept any conversations through them. That left individual links. Uri must have been too close to bother contacting the dragon that way.

He didn't have time to muse anymore when they all felt the ground jerk beneath their feet. He checked Sacha immediately, finding her unharmed, but surprised, as all three males tensed. "What the fuck was that?" the Phoenix bit out.

Drake spoke as Sacha informed him of the same thing. "It was Alyssa and the babe."

"Is she okay?" Uri demanded.

Draken nodded. "They're all fine, but we have more damage to the manor."

The dragon's eyes shot to Sander. "Stay guarding the Goddess and tell me if she wakes."

The Phoenix's eyes shot with flames. "I hate this fucking babysitting shit."

Drake was already walking away. "I don't care. Uri, you and Alex go to Limni. I'm going to check on Alyssa before I head out."

Hades heard his nephew telepathically contact Sacha through the link he and his mate shared. *I need you in Ouranos. We have hell beasts in all cities. And take your male.*

As if Hades would be anywhere else, but he smirked at the dragon's ingenuity in not requesting his help.

He would destroy the beasts for his female as he waited for the air to signal a portal. Then he would have his hands on Apollo. Or a battle with Hroarr. Either way he would have an outlet for his agitation, and that pleased him.

Chapter 14

Fólkvangr, Falls of the Dead – Thule

Sweet fuck.

They couldn't do this forever; it was to the point P couldn't even look at his female without his cock aching. And the priestesses had barely been gone a minute when he started feeling her pain through their bond.

He turned and lifted Gefn into his arms. His mouth descended on hers as their bodies slid through the water. Wild gusts of wind swept over them, and he growled in frustration. The pain he'd felt from her was replaced by pure pleasure, easing some of the tension in his muscles. Her hands gripped his shoulders, and he reveled in the feel of her flush against him.

They couldn't carry on like rabbits while so much was happening between their worlds.

When she mewled against his lips, he gave up thinking. A soft hand slipped between them, wrapping around his cock as he devoured her mouth. He lifted her ass higher, loosening her grip as he positioned her over his cock. Before he could sink into heaven, he was hit with a blast of compulsion, and suddenly he was breaking apart. *They* were breaking apart, teleporting until his female hit the barrier like a damned wall. He felt her panic as he moved halfway through it before locking them together and taking them back to the pool.

When they reformed, his gut twisted for a split second more until his need to get to Earth suddenly eased. He breathed out, his hold on her too tight, so he forced it to loosen a fraction.

"What was that?" He felt her concern in her breathy words, but he couldn't answer, he was busy checking his links to his family. They were all scattered around Earth. In various Realms, but otherwise accounted for as he demanded of Drake, *Is something wrong there?*

Alyssa's baby blew another hole in the manor, but they're all okay. I'm on my way to see her now. How did you know something was happening?

He gritted his teeth. *I felt it. I'm not sure how, but Gefn and I teleported until we hit the barrier to this Realm.* He breathed through the disorientation and lust coming from his female. He set his forehead to hers, holding her close. His hands were shaking. He wasn't sure if it was from feeling her anxiety at their near separation. He shook his head as he demanded, *Is that everything?*

There was a pause as P and his female stayed locked in their embrace. She rubbed circles on his back before tucking her head under his jaw. He knew she was shaken as she listened to the conversation.

Drake took a moment. *There are hell beast hordes in all the cities of Tetartos, but we have it covered. You teleported without willing it?*

Yes. He'd felt a similar compulsion once before. When he'd been in the garden with his female. It had hit him around the same time his father had pulled at his fucking soul from a damned world away. This time Hades wasn't doing anything. His father had been silent, a fact he was grateful for.

Do you still feel compelled to get here?

He took a breath. *No, but what the fuck?* And then he added with conviction, *I'm not leaving her here*. He couldn't.

There was another pause for the dragon. *I know what you're thinking, but I don't like it. You'll be vulnerable if you blood bond with her there.* Drake was right. It was tradition to have someone guard your back during a blood bonding for a reason. They'd be lost in each other's strongest memories, unconscious and vulnerable to anyone who came upon them, which was all information he hadn't had a chance to explain to her yet.

But there wasn't another damned choice but to do it at this point. They couldn't stay here forever, too much was at stake. He breathed out before explaining to Drake what he'd learned about the runes of protection from his mother. It would hopefully ease his cousin's mind about P's safety when it came to blood bonding where they were.

The dragon paused. *You're sure that's what they are?*

I am, he growled, knowing the dragon was concerned for him. Drake wouldn't trust a thing any Thulian said, but P had felt the truth in his female's words. He added, *The priestesses were here a few minutes ago. Gefn told them how Kara came to Earth and about my father's connection to Agnarr. I wouldn't be surprised if you see Hroarr very soon.* He paused, not liking any of it. The timing. The urgency. He shook his head and continued, *And the frenzy is a constant battle now.*

How constant?

Only a few minutes before it starts back up again. Neither of us can concentrate long enough to have a full conversation.

Fuck. I still don't like it, P.

I know. Just keep my father occupied for the next few hours.

Damn it, P, the dragon growled. *Tell me the minute it's done. And fucking be careful.*

I will, he assured him before cutting off the conversation.

Gefn lifted her head to look at him. "Why is he worried? What did he mean by vulnerable? And P?"

"P is the short version of my name. Pothos is a little dated in our world." He smiled a little before moving on. "I told you that the first step is the vows and markings. He's worried about the second step, which is blood bonding. That's likely the part that'll get you out of this Realm, but it's also a time when we'll be unconscious together."

"Why? What do you mean by *blood* bonding?" She narrowed her eyes at him.

"It means we share blood." Her nose wrinkled as he moved on to the more important part, the part he doubted she'd like any more than he did. "When that happens, we'll be thrown into each other's strongest memories. And we'll be completely unconscious for however long that takes. For my brothers it was hours."

She stopped breathing and he felt the wind chill around them. The pool cooled by degrees as he watched her. Sadly the cold didn't ease his cock as much as he would have thought or hoped.

"Why is this necessary? It is barbaric." He felt her hint of panic and anger mixing together. "My memories are mine." Her tone had iced as much as the air around them.

"I am not looking forward to you seeing mine either. There's a possibility that it won't work the same for us. We might not share memories. We're of two different worlds." It was true, but he had a gut feeling it was needed. He'd always trusted his instincts, and he wouldn't start doubting them now.

"There is no way to connect our souls without sharing blood first?" she demanded with her chin raised.

*****

Everything inside Gefn had gone icy at the thought of Pothos seeing her memories, her nightmares, her greatest failings. She would share that with no one.

"I don't have the power to connect our souls." His regret and frustration was as unmistakable as the truth in his words.

Her beasts' incessant purring and pleasure at the idea infuriated her. *Cease*, she commanded. It was obvious what they wanted of her. It was all too much, too fast. She swept out of Pothos' arms and knew somehow that it was only because he'd let her. She needed some space, but the second she was away from his warmth, the cold permeated her bones, and she felt as if she'd shatter into pieces of ice.

The air and water began warming around her.

His power calming hers.

She moaned at the way that warmth caressed her skin. The bond to Pothos was already closer and more encompassing than that of her animals or the one she'd had with her priestesses.

"You ask too much." She lifted a hand to the skies before biting out to the world at large, "*This* asks too much."

"I know." She watched him rub a hand over his short hair in frustration. "I'm not exactly sure what horrors you'll see from my life. I'm hoping like hell we won't see memories, but the odds are that we will." There was sincerity in his growled words. The bond with him was making it impossible to hide emotion from one another, and that was a comfort as much as an invasion. She used to crave the kind of intimacy she'd seen in the mortal families of her world. This was a thousand times more intense. And part of her loved it while the other distrusted it. Having this connection meant she had even more to lose when the end came.

He was there in front of her as the last thought was finished. "Don't," he said with a flash of intensity in his eyes. "No thoughts of losing what we'll have. I won't let that happen. And no dwelling on what we see in the memories. This cleans the slate of our pasts and begins our new life."

She sucked in a breath at his words. As if this would magically erase the nightmares. She huffed out the air. She could dream. Maybe they both could, because she could feel how much he'd rather not share his memories. She focused on the feel of his hands on her skin, knowing in her stomach that they were both stuck.

"Or we can continue as we have been until the choice is taken from us. You get to choose if we do this now, *thea mou*, or we wait."

"The blood sharing is what connects our souls? It will stop all of the need?"

His eyes flickered with heat before he growled, "Nothing could stop my desire for you, but the lust won't rule us after we complete the bond." He paused. "But the blood bond only paves the way to the soul bond."

She narrowed her eyes, not liking the sound of this. "What completes this?" she gritted out between clenched teeth. "And why are there so many steps?"

He shook his head with a tight smile. "There is one more step after that." He paused, and she held her breath, half dreading what he would say. "After we share memories, I'll make love to you in every way possible." She shivered in anticipation at his words, and her breath stuttered out at the ones that came next. "I'll claim every inch of your beautiful body until your soul accepts me as your male."

The desire wrought by his words drew her closer to him.

"What do you choose, Gefn?"

She swallowed, breathing him in as the wind slid over their skin. She ignored her beasts' encouragement, pushing them from her mind as she looked into his heated eyes.

"We will finish this now."

Chapter 15

City of Ouranos, Tetartos Realm

Hades reformed beside Sacha, near the blue-domed city of Ouranos. The winds howled in the snowcapped mountains above them. The sun was barely coming up in this part of the world. He noted Immortals wielding swords and fireballs against the hell beasts barreling up the hill toward the city. Of course Draken would send him to help a city defended by phoenix and dragon warriors. Battle cries and furious shrieks of hundreds of beasts rent the sulphur-filled air. He took in the sight of brilliantly iridescent dragons clashing with the oily black dragons of Hell. The pairs were matched in mass.

The mountain rocked with power and the thundering of hooves of Ophiotaurus, large bull-like creatures with snakes for tails.

"What would you like, *agapi mou*?" His love. Hades' muscles flexed along with his wings as he anticipated the battle with delight. He needed distraction until his son was safely back in Earth, where he belonged.

Sacha's dark eyes lit. "I've got the dragons." He was forced to watch her snug leather-covered ass disappear only to reform gracefully atop a moving black hell dragon.

He barely glanced at the three rabid hellhounds thundering toward him amid a cacophony of furious snarls. He absently tore the souls from their bodies, cutting off their growls as they crashed to the ground at his feet. He spared a look at two more hounds and unfurled his wings before sending power to slam them into a tree with a heavy crack of splintering wood. After dropping to the ground with pained howls, the evil creatures took one look at him and retreated toward the warriors. He shook his head.

His gaze reverted once more to the sight of his female. Her long hair was tied in a braid whipping in the wind as the beast writhed and roared beneath her, not pleased at having a passenger. He frowned when she and the creature disappeared.

He absently ripped more souls from thundering hell beasts with a flick of his hand as he searched for her.

That split second Sacha was out of his sight made his shoulders tense. He tracked her new position just as she reformed with the creature at the same time as she slammed her sword down into its skull. The blade pierced hard flesh and bone, silencing the furious roars and raging fire that was spewing from its gaping mouth. Sacha was already gone the second the wings went limp. He smiled as the beast plummeted toward the lake below in a haze of smoke. A massive blue serpent shot from the depths in a cascade of waves, crushing the dead dragon in its powerful jaws before taking it beneath the surface.

It was a rather convenient placing, and he wondered if Sacha had done the same before.

I have, she admitted, already on the next dragon as she added, *Leave the hounds for the phoenix warriors. I need you to take down the Ofioeidis that's rushing up the mountain. The massive serpent is too dangerous for the Immortal warriors.* His female did not sound pleased at the creature's presence, which was confirmed by her next words. *We try to kill all of them we can find in Hell before the bastard Tria can send them here. Their venom is deadly and the creatures are immune to phoenix and dragon fire.*

His eyes tracked the deadly serpent downing trees and brush as it slithered up the mountain. Two warriors crouched at the ready. The large males seemed small in the face of the giant serpent gliding in their direction. With a flick of his hand he teleported the warriors out of the way just as the serpent struck with violent speed and accuracy into the space one of the big males had just occupied.

He was in front of the beast with a thought. A big smile lit his face as the creature roared to a halt and hissed out flames he easily dissipated.

He heard the warriors' angry battle cries as they reformed out of harm's way. He downed more hooved creatures with a thought. He'd yet to even get his blade bloodied, but he planned to stay free of the acidic blood in case the Thulians arrived sooner rather than later.

His voice boomed in the direction of the ungrateful warriors he'd just saved. "This one is mine." And he flexed his wings wider, pleased when the serpent starting to coil, attempting to defend its throat. The phoenix warriors' furious noise silenced, but he felt their tension as they remained at his back. A moment passed before he heard them taking down a few snarling hounds.

The serpent lashed out with speed almost too fast to see. He ported out of its way with a laugh. He wanted a fight, not that this was much of a challenge, but it would have to do. It would calm his agitation.

He glanced over when he heard a few more creatures with thundering hooves snorting in his direction. With a thought he cleaved their life forces. The ground shook with the force of their muscled bodies crashing into the dirt and rock of the mountainside.

Hades toyed with the serpent while tracking his female and

killing any beast that came close. She'd wanted the dragons, and now they were all destroyed. He smiled when he felt her behind him.

"Are you done playing with it?" she asked calmly.

A pack of snarling beasts thought to catch them unawares, and he was pleased when his female used the power she'd gotten from him to rend the violent creatures' life forces with a wave of her delicate hand. A hand she'd obviously already cleaned of hell dragon blood.

She was everything beautiful, perfect and deadly in the world, and now she was his Goddess.

When the air charged, he lit with anticipation.

A portal was opening.

Hroarr was about to deliver Apollo to him. And if the Thulian didn't deliver, Hades would have a much more satisfying fight.

With little effort he destroyed the serpent with a thought. Its massive head collapsed, violently rocking the ground when the body unfurled in death.

Chapter 16

Fólkvangr, Falls of the Dead – Thule

P gazed into the eyes of his beautiful female, but magical protective runes or not, he wasn't looking forward to being unconscious and unable to defend her while in her memories. He didn't know the priestesses or what their agenda was in Thule. Or Hroarr's. His shoulders bunched in anticipation to get this part over with as quickly as possible.

He put his thumb on the tiny dent in her chin, angling her lips for his kiss. She was nervous about what would happen next, and it was best they get to it, but he wanted to ease her a little first. He used his other hand to lift her into his arms. Her legs wrapped around him sweetly as he moved through the water, his tongue slowly tangling with hers. She sighed into his mouth as her body relaxed into him. Her questing hands were all over his skin, and he knew he'd never get enough of it.

He groaned at how perfect she felt, at how eagerly she kissed him, no matter how much he controlled it.

He moved from the water, drying them with warm air currents before breaking their kiss and settling her on the white lounge. She looked so damned gorgeous that he wished he had time to drink in the sight of her laid out for him, but he didn't want her more anxious than she already was. She was trusting him in this. The cats had shared their approval, but this was a huge step she was taking entirely on faith. It didn't matter that she was intelligent enough to know they were running out of options, unless they wanted to stay in this place for eternity, feeding the never-ending frenzy.

He lay on his side next to her, and she turned to face him. "We can do the marking later, *thea mou*," he soothed, knowing she was too on edge for more ceremony that wasn't necessary to the bonding.

"We can skip to the blood part?" she asked without hesitation.

"Yes."

Air huffed from her lips as she asked, "How exactly will we share blood?"

With a smile, he answered, "A kiss will do it."

She narrowed her eyes at him. "A kiss... You are lying."

He laughed before adjusting his aching cock so that it wasn't jabbing into her stomach. "I'm not lying." He sighed when she looked unamused. "I'm guessing that will be easier for you than having to drink from a cut on my chest."

"You plan to cut our mouths? How?"

He brushed a golden wave over her shoulder. "The healing ability I have goes both ways. I can cause a cut as easily as I can mend one." He couldn't do much more than that and a permanent tattoo, but it was sufficient for what they needed.

Taking a deep breath, she demanded, "Then let us begin." Capturing her gaze, he took a moment to take in the sight of her before allowing the words to slip from his lips in the old language. "*Thea mou*, I vow to honor and care for you, with my body, soul and blood through all eternity." He felt the magic in the words and knew she felt the warmth of it settle into her as well.

Her eyes glazed with heat, and before he knew what she was thinking, she recited the same vow back to him. His heart thumped in his chest with every word she spoke. She didn't need to do it, but there was no mistaking the power binding them even closer than before.

*****

Gefn went into this partially with faith in her beasts, and even in Pothos, but also because her own instincts told her this was right. Not to mention logic dictated that they couldn't go on as they had been, but logic had nothing to do with the beauty of his vows. Once he'd said them, she'd felt compelled to return the words. To make her own promises to him.

She lifted a hand to his neck and drew his mouth to hers. With a sharp nip to his lip, she'd drawn blood along with his growl. The vibrations of it slid through her body as she trailed her tongue over the cut. His big palm gripped her hip, dragging her tight to him.

She moaned, barely feeling the sting of a cut on her tongue through the warmth of his power.

She had only a moment, and then she was taken into a dream world. Into his memories.

In some strange mystical way she felt taken back in time, as if the sun and moons had reversed themselves and now she was in a place where blue skies were filled with white puffy clouds and sparkling blue rivers cut through green forests. With the sight came knowledge. Pothos was a bright-eyed child of maybe five summers, laughing and flying, even half falling in the air when he wasn't sure of his wings. His small body was captured in the arms of his smiling father. Hades. Only in this time the God had long black hair and a brilliant smile filled with an overabundance of love and amusement. His features were so similar to Pothos' that it wasn't hard to imagine her male with a winged boy of his own. Her heart clenched at the thought. This was love. She felt it rolling from them both as father taught his son to use his wings.

In a dizzying shift, time moved a few years ahead. She wasn't sure how she knew that, but she did.

Now she looked at a Pothos of ten summers, standing in a sleeping room, looking out a balcony to a starry night. She tensed as she felt the boy's power unleash, his small wings lifting from the back of the child when a male and female appeared before him. Ares and Artemis... That information filtered in her head as she looked on. She could feel the twisted, tainted blood in their too pale bodies. The strength of their evil soulless power mixed with their sinister laughter. She tried to get to him, to yell for him to run even though she knew it was a dream. A memory. Just as they reached for him, a furious roar rocked the stone floor beneath his small feet. Out of nowhere Hades appeared, his massive bulk and unfurled wings an impenetrable wall between Pothos and the evil two. His twin blades sliced through the air as he unleashed some unseen power that made the two shriek in pain and fury. Pothos was lifted out of the way by a reassuring warrior, but watched as his father battled the evil duo. Witnessed as blood spattered onto the balcony. She felt the worry that choked the boy. Just as she felt the way his father sent him soothing energies even amidst a vicious battle. Her very soul ached at the beauty of their bond.

Time flickered ahead once again as she fought emotion and the desire to learn more.

This time he was older, maybe sixteen summers, with two youths of about the same age, both blond. A pixie-like female with violet eyes and a broody male that she recognized from the lake. The other boy had deep green eyes, and somehow, in her mind, she knew this was Drake. They were sitting beside a sunlit lake when green shimmery wings tore from Drake's back, and she felt Pothos' excitement at the idea of soaring with his cousin. With that surge of emotion came a rush of power that immobilized both his friends. He tried to call it back, shamed and embarrassed when they only stared sightlessly back at him. Her heart broke for the boy when they were finally freed. The girl, she felt in his mind that her name was Sirena, tried to reassure him, but he closed in on himself, disappointed and sick at his lack of control.

Another jump as her heart rushed to her stomach.

Pothos at around twenty summers, sitting with his father in a long room of warriors. A fight broke out at the end of a firelit hall. A female was involved and he worried for her. Brianne... The redhead from the lake. His power lashed out powerfully and for a moment no one could move. The warriors were completely at his mercy until they came to in a daze. A power-hungry male would have relished that kind of ability. Her male hid it, hated turning friends and powerful warriors into sightless shells, unable to control the blasts. His father slipped the hold and sent calming energies to his son, and finally the warriors came back to themselves, seemingly unaware of what had happened.

More years passed.

Females and males surrounded him. Mortals drawn to him with glazed eyes. They were captivated by the power that slipped from him without his intent. He tightened his hold on the ability before leaving the area to teleport to sit atop a mountain. Away from everyone so he could relax his hold.

A sequence of years tracked by.

Battles where he fought with beautiful yet deadly skill. His blade cut true as he fought at the backs of many a warrior. His hold on his power had grown more secure, but he still sought the solitude of the mountains to be free when the battles were over.

Time shifted again. She saw Pothos arguing with his father over the fate of the world, over the fact that the other Gods were destroying it with their madness. They needed to find the artifact to call the Creators back. She gasped at the knowledge that the Creators of his world had given them such a huge gift. She'd never come across such a thing. Her own sires had left and never returned to Thule. They'd said it was impossible. His father demanded that Pothos trust him to take care of it. Pothos was infuriated by his father's arrogance, knowing that three good Gods against nine who were unspeakably evil was asking the impossible no matter how strong Hades was.

Another flash of time.

He stoically stared out to an island in the distance. Impenetrable. There were imprisoned Immortals being experimented on behind the protections. Being bred like animals by his uncles Apollo and Hermes. They were amassing an army. A moment later a blond male broke through the waves with two young females. Dorian... The young Immortal females gasped for air as Dorian gently handed them off to Pothos, and Gefn noticed the females' intense reaction to her male's closeness. He teleported them to the sanctuary in his father's palace, and she felt the knowledge that his relationship with his father was strained, yet he was still confident that Hades would do what he could to protect those who came to him. And these females needed safety.

More years slid by.

She watched as he secretly searched for an artifact hidden by the evil Gods Ares and Artemis. Reporting to his cousins, Drake and Sirena. She wanted to shrink away from the dark palaces filled with the stench of death and despair. There were naked mortals bleeding in locked cages like animals, their blood flowing to the ground. The Gods had been feeding off the dark energies caused by their torment. Pothos' inability to free them ate at his gut. A dark-skinned male stood at his side with furious fire in his eyes. Sander... Another warrior with dark hair beside them. Jax. They had to keep their presence secret or risk never finding the golden box that would allow them to call the Creators back to their world.

Another year.

He arrived, crouched for battle against three malevolent males. The trio wouldn't die; each slice of his blade healed in an instant... Than, Deimos and Phobos. The Tria... Each massive male was pale as ice and had soulless eyes of pure evil. Their hands and bodies were coated in blood she knew wasn't their own. It was hard to even look at them. She could feel sinister tendrils of tainted power coming from them as their poisonous laughter filled the air.

And then she gasped at the sight of the twisted bodies on the floor of the palace. One female that looked nearly dead, her entire body was mangled, not far from the two half-dead young males. Alexandra, Alex... And her twin brothers Vane and Erik. She'd seen the older, Vane, at the lake. Pothos was sick and furious as he fought beside his aunts, his father.

They were all combining power to keep the males from teleporting away, and the evil trio were viciously fighting against their hold. Three Gods were there, Hades, Athena and Aphrodite, along with the two females' warrior consorts beside Pothos and Drake, and still the Tria were nearly breaking free. He felt, as well as heard, his father's commands. They were each to recite a spell, and the three Gods were preparing to sacrifice a portion of their life force to transport and hold the malevolent three beneath the surface of the Realm of Tainted Souls. She felt the power of the chanting words, and she knew the moment Pothos added his own portion to the spell, as did the consorts and Drake. She saw and felt Hades' displeasure at Pothos' sacrifice, but in a whirlwind of furious power and rage-filled shrieks, the three were gone. Locked away for eternity.

A short time passed.

He stood on a mountaintop beside his cousin Drake, the artifact to call the Creators in his hands as other Immortals stood behind them. A rush of power so immense and pure filled the world until they nearly dropped to their knees from the force. She saw the bright luminous lights in the sky. Their Creators had come back. They were in his mind, taking his knowledge as to why they were summoned back to Earth. She felt the wind turn icy with fury that their sons and daughters, the Gods, had caused so much pain and suffering.

Pothos spoke for his father and his aunts. Hades, Athena and Aphrodite had been trying to stop the evil wrought by their siblings, so they didn't need to be punished. She felt the sorrow of the Great Beings as a living breathing thing. It was soul deep. And then she heard their voices and it was like soft music. They denied him before giving him a choice to be a Guardian of his world. She heard their punishments. The Gods were all to be put to sleep. They could not be trusted with humanity any longer. Neither could any more powerful being.

With a force she was sure their entire world felt, the Immortals were freed from Apollo's island prison and exiled to Tetartos Realm. A confinement spell surrounded it, not allowing the Immortals to leave.

Pothos was nearly crushed with guilt at the knowledge that his father was to be included with the other Gods. He tried to champion the God again to no avail. The Great Beings had spoken to the world at large. When Hades was brought forth, Pothos tried to fight to get to him. Their relationship had been strained for years, but his father did not deserve a prison.

His father roared and fought the Creators' hold to get to his son before he was wrenched away into the spelled containment. The harsh wave of guilt and sorrow that he hadn't been allowed to explain or even say goodbye to his father gutted him. Twelve Immortals, including him, Drake and Sirena, were deemed Guardians that day. Power flooded in their veins as they were told to make vows. With their new power came a curse of ten times the pain they inflicted against any mortal returned upon them. Humanity was to be allowed to evolve, and they were charged with great purpose. To watch over the Realms, as one day the Gods of their world would be needed once again. And then the Great Beings were gone. A flash of light and no way to call them back.

Centuries passed.

She saw years of battles and the building of cities in the Immortal Realm. Then she watched as the Guardians formed their own family. There was laughing, arguments and fighting at one another's backs. It was a closer bond than if they were of the same blood. A bond that would never be severed, because she wouldn't allow anything to happen to those he loved. She would fight for their world as she would fight for her own. She saw their meetings to deal with the lack of mates and Immortal young, which was so much like Thule's struggles.

In all the meetings and patrols she saw that he always stayed somewhat at the edge. Not by choice so much as by necessity. His lack of belief in his ability to control his power always kept him in the shadows, part of the family, but never too physically close to those he loved. And then she watched as the Tria found the ability to send demon souls to possess humans; they also sent beasts to battle in the other Realms. The evil beings saw to it that the Guardians were constantly fighting some threat, never allowing them to have much time to themselves.

Less than a year ago.

Then suddenly his Guardian brother Uri found a mate. It was Pothos' cousin Alexandra. She'd been hiding in the mortal Realm with her brothers. After that initial mating, Guardians started pairing nearly one after another. And then the news of a Guardian baby to Gregoire and Alyssa. He could see the beauty of the bond, but since mated pairs became more powerful, it made them all edgy that the couplings were leading to some bigger purpose for their world. Gefn knew his assumption to be correct.

A few months later.

She watched Pothos using his power to calm an enraged Drake, who was denied his female, Era. Worry flooded him that his cousin would never be able to claim his female because of her torture by the same enemy who'd freed Apollo into the world.

She felt their knowledge of something wrong before a portal opened to their world. P had sensed something coming, and then all the Guardians had felt the way the air charged when a powerful doorway was opened from Thule. And then she witnessed the battle with Hroarr's warriors when Dagur had sent them to Earth to take Apollo. She wished she could close her eyes against the deaths that cut into her soul.

And then she saw the sleeping unit containing his father. Hades was lying peacefully inside. She felt Pothos' dread and anticipation at waking the God to help find Apollo through their sibling bond. His relief when his father hadn't blamed him for his captivity.

A few days later Pothos was rocked with the knowledge of his mother's identity. He'd been unsure of his place in the world, angry at his father's lies. Angered more that he'd been kept from the meeting where Kara started a battle with Hades.

And then she was in the garden with him, feeling all the emotion and need from him.

Feeling the connection and relief while they were in Fólkvangr at being able to be with her without fear of his power turning her into a being without thought. The rush he felt at her touch. The way she soothed him. He craved her.

She moaned.

She felt his certainty that his connection to her was the most precious thing he'd ever known. She gave him a sense of peace and freedom he'd never thought possible. Beyond lust and destiny, he wanted her. She felt powerful and needed, but also like they were halves of a whole.

Chapter 17

Fólkvangr, Falls of the Dead – Thule

Pothos slipped into Gefn's memories. Small blips at first, gaining detail as he moved through time.

He looked on as a small golden-haired Gefn, an angelic little cherub with a brilliant smile, toddled amidst little miniature tornados in a bright room of pink and gold. She rolled and grabbed at the two massive cats easily ten times her size. Her melodic giggles filled the room as a trio of beautiful females beamed down at her. Her priestesses. They were each unique in their beauty and coloring, just like Hroarr's þrír. He watched as one massive beast lay down to allow the babe to get on its back for a ride. Velspar, the one who'd sat in front of him at the lake. He wasn't sure where the knowledge came from, but it was there. He didn't see her powerful Creator parents. Had they already left her world, even though she was so small? Fuck if the sight of her chubby arms didn't give him thoughts of the tiny baby girls she might give him. His heart thudded against his chest at the idea of her swollen with his child. Their children would have parents. He would be as his father had been with him. He mentally smiled when he considered Hades as a grandfather. The God would be a nightmare with little baby granddaughters.

He was taken from those warm thoughts and thrown decades later. To image after image of death. Years of bloody battles with evil warring siblings. Her cats and priestesses at her side.

And then he was whipped into memories of all the mortal guards she'd befriended through the years. Some dying peacefully in their dreams while others lay in pools of blood on desolate battlefields. Their sightless eyes looked up at her when she slept at night, jolting her from rest. He was given the knowledge of every name, of every fucking life lost to her in a scrolling list of death.

Years passed.

Then he was with her as the ground shook violently, signaling the fact that her evil siblings had started systematically destroying Gods and priestesses to steal their power. Each one rocked Thule, forcing her and the other Gods to calm the tsunamis, hurricanes, and earthquakes that destroyed more lives.

Another flash of time.

He saw Gefn working with Hroarr and Dagur on a confinement chamber for their evil Gods. Then he watched as the Goddess P had never seen with his own eyes, Kara, stepped into the room. The female's icy gaze burned with tears as she handed over all the scrolls depicting the work of their most reclusive brother, Agnarr. He'd been devising his own prison plans before the male had been killed by Tyr.

Pothos realized his female knew a great deal more about a threat to their world than he and the Guardians knew about the one to Earth. He had a soul-deep feeling that the threats were one and the same. Some cosmic darkness set to descend.

Decades later.

The cats led her and her brothers to a world with special artifacts they needed to complete their God prisons. The desolate dark world had held magical bronze pieces that were the key to finishing the God prisons. The new discovery could allow them to siphon the power of a God into Thule itself. She left Hroarr and Dagur to work on the chambers, with hope after centuries with very little.

Another flash whirled him into a far deeper memory. So deep that he lived it through her eyes.

A furious roar rocked the polished stone of Gefn's ivy-laden palace.

Instinct had her hands gripping the twin blades sheathed at her back before she knew what was happening. With a rush of power, she called air to sweep her in the direction of her powerful beasts. She came soaring to a halt beside the felines. Their pointed golden ears had flattened against their massive heads, and both heavily muscled animals stalked forward, fur rising as if ready to launch across the entire room of healing pools. Gefn's gaze flew over the space, not seeing a thing out of place around the sacred waters, but it was silent.

Too silent under the charged air emanating from her mystical beasts. Both of their furious muzzles gaped wide, revealing razor-sharp teeth as they loosed another thunderous roar, sending waves from the depths of the pools.

Time stilled as her gaze flickered to the torchlit flesh of her three stunning priestesses stepping gracefully from the soothing liquid.

"What is it, Gefn?" Togn's golden eyes flashed as they met Gefn's. Grior and Skuld were beside her, with water slicking their nude bodies, all three shaded from light to dark. Power flickered over their palms as they readied to battle the invisible threat. The room was no longer filled with the usual mischievous laughter and playfulness of her family. Their tension radiated through the unique bond they'd shared with Gefn since her birth, and she knew they were feeling hers as well.

Gefn was denied the ability to answer as time stilled.

Everything happened in the same moment. Mortal servants scurried out the doors as her kilted guards streamed in, but Gefn's eyes were caught on the glimmer of sharp glowing blades appearing out of the air directly at the throats of her females. The spelled metal arced in deadly synchronicity as killing slashes cleaved through bone and flesh, sending precious Immortal lifeblood into the crystal pools. The act stole the air from Gefn's lungs as her females' bond was torn from her. The grotesque absence nearly forced her to her knees as she gazed helplessly at the only real family she'd ever had. Their jewel-colored eyes dimmed to sightlessness. Horror and agony choked her as their broken bodies spilled into the waters.

A wild cry of rage and pain split her lips as her fingers tightened on the hilts of her glowing blue blades.

Her cats' fury blasted inside the last and only bond she would ever have. It felt as if a piece of her had been pulled beneath the surface to drown in the bloody waters. As their Goddess, she should have protected them.

She couldn't even hear the water closing over their lifeless bodies through the pounding of desperate pain and anger thudding in her head.

The beasts roared in renewed fury as she fought through the searing agony tearing at her spirit.

"Greetings, sister." Tyr, the most evil of her siblings, stalked out of the air with two other Gods. His pale hair fell over sickly cloud-colored skin while half obscuring violent black eyes. The orbs were lit with the same triumph that curled all their lips.

Tyr would soon strike like the poisonous serpent he'd become. They should not have been able to slither through her wards and spells to gain access anywhere near this inner sanctum.

To those closest to her heart.

The three monsters before her had too much power. Tainted strength stolen from the Gods and Immortals they had killed over the past decades.

Her guards rushed to attack, but with the flick of her wrist she sent their bodies tumbling in the winds and out the doors. It was a fight her warriors would not have won, and she refused to see more innocent blood spilled. The second they were through the doorway, she slammed the heavy wood shut, locking her and the cats inside to battle.

Spa and Velspar snarled before rending another ground-shaking roar through the palace. The now crimson waters of the sacred pool spilled over the edges into the path of her brothers as they stalked forward.

She instantly built more power from within, but the blow to her heart, her soul… left her weaker than she should be. A weakness Tyr had obviously counted on.

"Now, I cannot wait to take your beasts' lives and feel their power in my veins." Tyr's sneered threat was filled with covetous hate. His soulless eyes were half directed on her cats. All the Gods had watched and feared the mystical creatures, and the Deities before her were about to feel the full fury of their power. The air in the room crackled with it.

"You will never have their power. Or mine." Her words were as icy as the steel of her blades.

As much as she detested her choices, opening a portal was her one wise course of action, but using that power took a toll, and she had only just used it returning home with her cats from her brother's palace. Had the monsters before her been watching and planning this during her absence? How long had they been hiding so easily in her sanctum?

Tyr's advance stilled for one brief moment as he seemed to take in all the energy in the room. She held her blades at her sides, anticipating an attack.

"So sure of your ability, sister? I'm surprised you have the strength to fight after your females were so easily slaughtered. The scent of their blood fills the air." He was taunting her, she was aware of his tactic, but that knowledge did little to ease the sick pang in her stomach.

She sucked in a breath, ignoring the metallic scent. Refusing to allow him to split her focus. She would not be so easily taken. She felt power rush through the bond she held with her beasts, strengthening her just as Tyr loosed corrupted flames through the steel of his sword. Spinning, she met them with a blast of icy wind through her own blades. With a breath she stole the air from his burst of flames while watching her icy shots strike his chest with a force of lightning unlike anything she'd ever wielded. His furious roar told her that he hadn't expected the sheer strength of power she'd unleashed.

Spa and Velspar leapt from the steps with deadly grace and accuracy, counteracting the two remaining Gods' fetid powers. Shrieks of fury filled the space, shaking the walls and painted ceiling above. Stone crashed around them, sending the violent bloody waters spewing into the air as dirt and rock erupted beneath the ground. The Gods attacking her beasts stood little chance against their might. It mattered little how much power her tainted siblings had stolen from those they had killed.

She couldn't watch the felines, she had to remain alert to Tyr, but that didn't mean she wasn't conscious of their every move as she dodged more fire and the crashing remnants of her once sacred room. The beasts were all that were left to her, and she refused to lose them too.

Retreat was the wisest course, but she could not force herself to leave her family to Tyr. To what he could do with the last shreds of light held within the shells of their bodies.

Sickness and fury fought inside her at the thought of him touching her priestesses' essence. Their bodies were becoming entombed in the rubble that was crashing into the water, but she could still see the bronzed skin of Togn beneath the bloody waves. The sight was a painful reminder of her failure in protecting those who were closest to her.

She exchanged more power and blows with Tyr and knew she wouldn't be able to do it all. Not retrieve the bodies and open a portal while fighting Tyr and keeping her beasts with her.

She felt the evil God's blasts strengthening with each surge of flames, and she fought harder. The dark glint in his eyes indicated how much he was enjoying this.

Her choices were few. If she managed to get to Hroarr's palace with Spa and Velspar, would he even still be there? She'd only just left. If he wasn't able to portal back right away, Tyr and the others would surely destroy her warriors with the same brutality they'd used against Togn, Grior and Skuld.

More death.

More suffering.

Would it never end?

"You should have chosen my side instead of Hroarr's, sister. If you agree to ally with me now, in this moment, I may be generous

enough to allow you to live." Gefn wanted nothing more than to cut the sneer off his lips.

Instead, she taunted, "You are but a pitiful image of your former self, Tyr, and even now you are weak. You could not hope to take me, much less Hroarr."

The moment the air charged, Gefn braced for another attack.

Instead, furious power blasted the heavy doors from the outside. Wood splintered and shot into the destroyed room as Hroarr's massive body stepped through. His enraged power flooded the space, and she felt portals opening in the room. The other Gods retreating.

Tyr wasn't so fortunate as to escape her brother's wrath. Hroarr had the evil God in his clutches within the blink of an eye, and relief filled her. Legions of Hroarr's battle-armored warriors came in at his back as Hroarr wrapped power around her evil brother, choking the male in his fury as flames started at Tyr's feet. His agonized shrieks rending the air was music to her ears.

Pothos was thrown into more memories while he was still furious and shaking at the last.

Gefn, Dagur, Kara and Hroarr used power to lock away their siblings into spherical cylinders of bronze metal etched with glowing runes. The spells held so much power he felt the way it filtered into the dirt and stone of the underground temple. With it came the knowledge that all four Gods infused a fraction of themselves into securing and powering the prisons. He also possessed the knowledge that there were four such prisons scattered to the four points of their world.

The next flash took him into her mind when she saw him for the first time. It was like a gut punch feeling her lust for him after seeing all the darkness of her life.

Then he was thrust into her memories of coming to his world, and the lust of before was replaced with the harsh agony of betrayal when she learned her cats had held the power to open a portal and then to paralyze powerful beings. It had come with the heartrending knowledge that they could have saved Togn, Skuld and Grior. Anger beat at his skull.

It was like mental whiplash when he was brought into her memories of their first time having sex. Fucking hell, he wouldn't survive any more memories of pain and then blinding pleasure. Of guilt and pain before being slammed with lust.

Her beasts' betrayal had hurt, yet she still trusted them when it came to Pothos. His female had been lonely. She had only her cats, Laire and her siblings. Two of which she wasn't all that close to. Laire, though. He was her friend. Another warrior she'd have to watch die. Fuck that. Pothos would find that male an Immortal mate if it killed him. That warrior would live for fucking ever.

He was finally jolted awake in time to breathe her in, his hands shaking from the roller coaster from hell. He gripped her too damned tight, but was having trouble letting go. He felt her soft hands on his chest, her lips on his heated flesh, making him groan.

"Are you okay?" he asked, mentally scanning their surroundings. They were alone.

He was unsure of what she would have seen in his memories. It couldn't have been good, but hers had definitely been bleak.

"Yes," she said, but he could feel that she was just as emotionally drained.

"I'm going to try to teleport us out of here," he said and felt her nod.

He used power, breaking them into pieces until they were combined in the erotic torture. He felt the barrier, but she didn't bounce off it this time. She pushed through with him, and he could feel her relief mix with his own.

And then they were streaming through air, heading home.

To his home. His bed.

Chapter 18

Mystical Lake, Earth Realm

Hades reformed on the banks of the lake after battling hell beasts in Ouranos. The sun had started to rise, giving a warm glow to the mist-covered water. His wings flexed and stretched wide as anticipation filled him; he'd either get to battle Hroarr or take Apollo. Either outcome pleased him.

Sacha appeared at his side the next moment, and he attempted unsuccessfully to teleport her to their island home. Agapi mou, *you were to shower while I took care of this.*

I don't remember agreeing to that, she pointed out evenly before sighing. *You can try to force me away all you want, but it won't move me.*

He growled in frustration that she was there; he was to have done this alone.

He felt her amusement, even as he was fully aware that as a warrior she was still alert to all threats.

Draken appeared at his other side a moment later, and Hades growled, "Did I not say I would handle this?"

"Yes," was Draken's calm and irritating answer. Hades noticed the dragon's frown matched his the second Era ported in at her male's side.

They both had infuriating females who refused to stay safely away.

You both mated the wrong females if that was what you wanted, Sacha drawled.

He shook his head at her before demanding of Draken, *Where are Kara and the warriors?*

Within porting distance, was all Draken said.

Are we expecting more Guardians? he drawled in irritation.

The dragon grunted as smoke filtered from the agitated male's lips. *No, and I wish they were bitching about it in your mind instead of mine.*

He didn't have time to question Drake more as he felt Hroarr's power before the arrogant male stepped through the watery air. His booted feet stepped above the waves of the turbulent lake. When their eyes met, the Thulian scanned the area and his gaze flashed with power. Dark clouds formed above them while the ground shook with the male's even words. "Where are Kara and her warriors?"

"Close," Drake said as the kilt-wearing God stepped through with a bound Apollo in tow. Hades' bastard sibling seemed incapable of using any power beneath a transparent golden net that fitted around him like a second skin, and he enjoyed seeing the male's weak struggles beneath the web. Even Apollo's pathetic threats were music to Hades' soul. The fact that those words seemed to fall on deaf ears infuriated his sibling all the more.

He couldn't wait to get his hands on him. A bloodthirsty smile that promised deadly retribution curved his lips as he spoke. "Hello, *brother*."

Apollo's shoulders tensed and the struggling stopped when he sighted Hades. The male paled a fraction, and he hoped that his sibling was imagining all of the ways he would suffer at Hades' hands. Apollo had enslaved his beautiful Sacha. It didn't matter that it was millennia ago; the male would suffer for every year she had been forced to serve a monster.

Hroarr's booming voice brought his attention back. "Bring me Kara and the warriors." The dark Thulian crossed his massive arms over his chest before adding, "Or I will find them myself and keep your brother for the inconvenience."

He scoffed, "You would not have agreed to a trade if you could collect her yourself."

"Would I not?" the male challenged.

"No."

"Not even as a token toward peace?" Hroarr's eyes narrowed, but his tone was that of a bored male. The power that whipped around them felt anything but peaceful.

"After initiating *two* acts of war?" Hades scoffed as he raised a brow. He allowed his own power to radiate against the Thulian's. With a thought he opened the skies and allowed them to pour water over the island while deflecting it from Sacha, Drake and Era as well as himself. The Thulians were unaffected. The only one to get wet in the display had been Apollo.

Hades actually smiled a little brighter at the sight of his soaking and furious sibling.

Hroarr stared at him for long moments before the dark God shared a look with Dagur.

The kilt-wearing male smirked before whispering something into the air. Magic filtered around them, and Hades tensed for a moment before realizing it wasn't anything dangerous. If he had to guess, he'd say the Thulian had sent out some sort of magical tracking spell for Kara.

How far away are Kara and the warriors? Hades demanded of Drake.

They're in the Earth compound at the west end of the US. An ocean and continent away, Drake growled. *I've allowed you leeway. Now get to your point.*

Hades mentally scoffed at the dragon. As if Drake were capable of *allowing* Hades to do anything.

"Are you certain you wish to deny me?" Hroarr challenged.

Hades' smile was all teeth. "Did I say I would not return your people, Hroarr?" He spoke the name as if they were old friends, and the male's eyes flashed as Hades pointed out, "Kara and her warriors are of no use to me."

Thunder crashed around them before the Thulian lifted a hand and the rains were cut off.

Lightning strikes glowed against the darkened skies above the forest as Hades continued, "You have come to this world twice and initiated battle. Thule owes recompense for its crimes."

Hades swore the male's eyes flashed with something akin to amusement. "What is it you feel Thule *owes* you? Before answering, remember that your son traveled to Thule and took liberties with a *Goddess*, and then he *stole* her after we arrived. I have been kind in my dealings. Do not mistake that for weakness. I will not allow your game for long."

Liberties? As if his son was not good enough for the Goddess? "Your sister was *fortunate* that fate chose Pothos for her. And as I see it, he was kind enough to return her to Thule."

Dagur snorted, but Hroarr only looked on.

Hades crossed his arms over his chest and flexed his wings. "You say that you want peace. What do you offer in return?"

The male's eyebrows rose and he said, "My sister agreeing to join with your son is a peace offering far above necessity in this case. Out of curiosity, what do you hope to gain?"

Apollo's voice boomed to the Thulians. "I have far more to offer than my brother. If you offer sanctuary in your world, you have no idea the power I can provide. In fact, I will retrieve your sister and her warriors for you as a gesture. You only need to contain my brother and the dragon while I do it."

Hroarr glanced at Apollo, and Hades didn't miss the disgust that flashed in both Thulian Gods' eyes.

Hades growled, "Brother, there is nowhere you will be safe from my wrath. Nowhere you can hide from me."

Apollo turned his attention to Hroarr and spouted desperately, "He did not honor your trade. I am far more trustworthy."

Hroarr glanced at Hades. "My lenience is at an end. I will hear your request, and then I will have my people."

Hades answered, "You are free to take them when you have given a blood oath that my son will never be harmed or caged by a God of Thule."

Hroarr narrowed his eyes and stared at Hades for a long time as tensions rose. "You have so little faith in your son's strength?"

Hades growled, "The problem lies in my lack of faith in Thulian Gods possessing honor." Winds whipped violently through the trees as the slight hit home.

"Guard your insults before I rethink any peace here."

He felt Drake's tension as they both moved ahead of their females.

Hades infused his next words with a blast of power to rock the waters beneath their feet. "Remember how that lack of faith came to be. I did not go to your world and steal a God. Nor did I travel to Thule and attack Kara. If my son is to share a bed with a Goddess of *your* world, then I will have your blood oath that he will not need to sleep with one eye open."

"So you lie when you say your son and Gefn will not be able to harm each other?" Dagur spit out.

Apollo started to speak again, and Dagur growled in obvious annoyance at the God before flicking a wrist and sending Hades' sibling to his knees in a heap. Hades wasn't sure what Dagur had done, but was happy not to hear the bastard. He was alive, and that was all Hades needed.

Smoke lifted from Drake's lips as he growled, "We did not lie. They will not be able to harm each other. Their souls will be connected."

And the dragon's voice filtered into Hades' head. *You're starting too much shit. I get that you need some kind of insurance for Pothos for your own sanity, but move it the fuck along.*

Hroarr growled, "So you want to make sure *I* do not harm him?"

Hades gave a nod. "Or *order* him harmed or caged in some way."

"You would trust my oath?"

"If you add blood and vow it." He'd had blood allegiances with Agnarr in regards to their battling at one another's sides and not attempting to kill each other. If he'd fought at Agnarr's side, the male couldn't turn on him and vice versa.

Dagur spit out, "You deserve nothing from us."

Hroarr lifted a hand in the male's direction and Dagur shut up.

Hroarr challenged Hades, "Then I will have your oath on Gefn's safety as well."

Drake's booming voice snapped, "Done. Now let's finish this."

Hroarr stalked forward at the same time as Hades. Power clashed wildly around them, and he could feel Sacha sending her own power to infuse his. She knew he needed this.

When they drew closer to one another, anticipation licked at Hades. The need to battle was under the surface and he could see the same in the other God's eyes. When Hroarr's lips curved, there was no mistaking that need to fight that always came when two such powerful beings faced one another. They both itched to prove they were the more powerful being. He and Draken had enjoyed friendly battle, but he cared for his nephew. This male was not of his blood. If he and Hroarr battled, there would be no holding back.

Hroarr mused, "I feel your desire to challenge me." The God's eyes sparked with a hint of excitement. "Nothing would entertain me more. Go against me and you will have your wish." There was a brutal ruthlessness under the male's surface, but Hades felt something else there, possibly a sense of honor.

Hades' wings flexed behind him. "It's very tempting. It would be enjoyable, and I have nothing else planned today."

Hroarr spoke calmly. "Indeed."

Hades nodded as Hroarr produced a dagger from nothing. The blade held a green cast, and the tension in the air made it thick and exciting. If the male charged him, it would be on, and Hades would relish the fight. Sacha sent him more power, he felt her readying for a fight, but Hroarr did not attack. The other God's lips twitched as he sliced his palm with ease, red ran from the cut for only a split second as the male raised a brow to Hades. "Would you like my blade?"

Hades used his mind to produce a cut in his own hand and showed it to the other God. Magic flowed through the air as they each whispered oaths. There were exceptions built in for defending themselves but nothing more. In this they would each suffer a thousand deaths if either attempted to kill or bind Gefn or Pothos.

When the power stopped flowing around them, Hades felt Vane and Brianne appear with the warriors and an unconscious Kara, but Hroarr's eyes never left Hades. A truce of a sort had been formed. He would wait to see how that played out.

Chapter 19

Pothos' Home, Tetartos Realm

Pothos reformed with his female in his arms. He growled before carrying Gefn to his bed. A mental sweep told him they were alone and that his protection spells were intact. The house was secluded atop a cliff that looked out to the sea below, far from any inhabited continents in the Immortal Realm. He heard the waves crashing against rock beyond the balcony as he moved to the massive four-poster bed covered in a dark comforter.

She moaned into his mouth, inciting more need.

Finally, he could have her without thought to interruptions, because he knew for a fact that his brothers would give him privacy, and Drake and Sacha would leash his father if needed.

He broke the kiss before sitting on the edge of the bed, with her straddling his lap. His cock throbbed between them, but it could wait. His hands roved over her hips to grip her ass, pulling her tight to grind her clit against him.

She grew more demanding, her kisses more frantic.

He loved it all.

He lifted her legs higher, tilting her off balance, and she gripped him. *I've got you,* thea mou. He smiled against her lips before breaking the kiss and nipping her pouty bottom one.

Her hands slipped to the back of his head, bringing his mouth back to hers.

You're a greedy Goddess. What am I going to do with you?

Give me what I need.

Tell me what my Goddess needs. He flipped her onto her back and ground his hips into the cradle of her sweet pussy.

More. She moaned into his mind.

More what? By the time we're done, there won't be an inch I haven't loved. So tell me where you want me to start, he coaxed.

*****

Gefn's mind went hazy at his words. She hadn't realized how on guard he'd been while in Fólkvangr. Pothos was a different male now, no less demanding of her body, but more relaxed in the passion that radiated through them.

Your cock. She moaned through their bond. She barely paid attention to the masculine space with dark furnishings and a balcony that led to deep seas. She heard the crashing waves, and it would have lulled her if not for the undeniable desire.

He groaned deep before capturing her lips. *How can you look adorable and so fucking sexy all at once*? She fell into the pleasure of his amused words and the wicked tongue tangling with hers. She would use more of his terms if they affected him so powerfully. When he broke the kiss, his blue eyes had darkened like deep stormy seas. That gaze landed on her lips with intensity. "These pouty lips are what dreams are made of." His chest heaved with a breath as he rubbed a thumb over her lower one before dipping it between them.

Her tongue darted out on impulse and was rewarded with the

pulsing of his cock between her thighs. She twirled her tongue around the digit, loving her effect on him while wanting more. Wanting him to feel as wild as she felt having his weight pressing her into the soft bedding. She was surrounded by his addicting nighttime scent, and she couldn't be the only one to lose her mind.

His gaze shifted from her lips to her eyes as he asked, "Where do you want my cock, Gefn? Your mouth? Maybe your wet pussy? Or what about your tiny ass?

The vibrations of his voice made her as dizzy as his dirty words. She had little experience, but she was centuries old and was well aware of all the naughty things Hroarr's priestesses had done with males and females alike through the years.

She lifted her head and kissed his jaw and then moved to his lips, tugging the bottom one with her teeth before lashing it with her tongue. *Why don't you tell me where you'd like to put your cock.*

"Fuck. You are a damned vixen."

She moved to the tense cords at his throat, feeling his control dissipating and loving every second of it. *Would you like to put your cock in my mouth*? she tempted. His fingers tunneled in her hair, pulling her head back so he could invade her mouth as he circled his cock against her most sensitive spot. She moaned, unable to stop taunting him. *Maybe you want to slide it inside my... pussy.*

Stop, you're killing me. If I lose control, I'll be rough, he warned.

She was a Goddess. She could take anything he wanted to do to her. And she'd love it. *Maybe you want to put your cock in my bottom instead.*

He ripped from her lips, panting and shaking. "Fucking hell! Bottom should not sound ten times as dirty as ass, but it does. And, yes, Gefn, I want my cock between your lips, inside your hot little pussy and tunneling into that beautiful little bottom. Choose where I go first, *thea mou*."

*****

Gefn lifted up suddenly with the strength of a Goddess, pushing P up to rest on his knees as she smiled wickedly. His lips curved, but his body was tense with the need his naughty girl had wrought.

"I've made my choice," she said, facing him while sitting on her spread knees before demanding, "Lie on your back."

He groaned, knowing what she planned. He would allow it, but with one change, gripping her by the hips, he flipped her around as he lay back. Her silky thighs were spread wide on his shoulders, positioning her sexy pussy in front of his face. He groaned when he saw just how slick she was.

Her small hands were buried in the bedding at his hips as his cock bobbed up against her chin, making her gasp. That noise made him smile as he kissed the sides of her thighs. "That's it, make more sweet cream for me to lick up."

Her breathing stuttered out, and she seemed paralyzed for only a moment before she ran her smooth cheek over his heated erection.

Her tongue laved his balls, making his hips jolt. "You're teasing, love."

"Then tell me how to do it."

She was truly destroying him. "You've never sucked a cock?"

"No. I've seen it done, but I was sure it started with licking." She breathed out.

Fuuuuck. He took a deep breath before instructing his innocent female, "Start by sucking the tip, *thea mou*."

His hands gripped her round ass and spread her for his pleasure. Fuck, she smelled so good. He licked the crease of her leg, and she groaned at his teasing before attempting to grind her sweet lips into his mouth. He smiled as he took a small taste.

The second she took his dick between her hot lips, he nearly shot off the bed. It was better than he could have imagined. Too good. He licked up her slit before sucking on her lower lips, intent on making her come before he did. His cock popped from her lips as she gasped.

"I don't think this is possible," she said with a groan.

He smiled. "It is. Open your sweet mouth and keep it that way. I'm going to do the work. Just be careful with your teeth." She did as he said, taking him all the way into the beautiful wet warmth of her mouth.

He thrust gently as he devoured her pussy. Her groans vibrated his dick as he used her sexy virgin mouth. A few flicks of his tongue on her clit and her hips turned frantic. He thrust up with each suck on that hard little nub before lapping up all the juices she made for him. *That's it, just let me use that pretty mouth while you feed me your greedy cunt. Grind it on my face, love.*

His words ignited her. Her throat worked around his cock, swallowing and sucking so fucking hard he saw stars. His thumbs pushed into her pussy to spread her for his tongue, and she bucked against him. When his tongue slid over her tight little ass, she shuddered in his arms, collapsing against the power he used to hold her in position.

Come on my tongue, thea mou, he demanded before pushing a

finger against the little puckered hole while still sucking her clit. He loved it when she started convulsing in climax, and he eagerly slid his tongue down to lap it all up.

Now suck me to the back of your throat and drink every drop I give you.

His hips jolted, but he clenched his teeth, controlling it so as not to hurt her.

When his balls pulled tight, he tensed and roared his release. She greedily sucked and swallowed the hot come she'd forced from his body. He bit the inside of her thigh as his body pulsed for her. A second passed when her lips moved from him, and she turned to collapse on her side. He rubbed the spot on the inside of her thigh while sending warm healing power to ease the bruise he knew he'd made.

"That feels incredible." She moaned. "What are you doing to me?"

"Healing the bruise from my teeth," he said as he rubbed circles along her skin.

He moved and lifted her into his lap, sending all the pillows on the massive bed to prop him up. She was flushed and so incredibly beautiful that he had to feel her in his arms. He needed to look at her as the desire resurfaced all over again.

He set his fingers to her cheek and the dent in her chin before moving down her slender throat. She turned her head, allowing him more access. "We're not done, love."

She nodded and softly said, "I know. It feels like it will never be enough."

Because they had only just begun. The bond wouldn't connect until he'd claimed every last fucking inch of her body. The next hour was a haze of writhing bodies as he relentlessly forced her to come all over his cock over and over until her pussy milked every last drop of come into the tight confines of her warm body.

They were panting, yet it still wasn't over.

*****

Gefn gasped for breath. She couldn't believe she'd climaxed so much, yet still ached for more. He positioned them so she lay with her head on his chest for long minutes until both of them calmed. After a while she felt the lust rising relentlessly. From the corner of her eye she saw something fly to the bed. A jar of something that looked like a kind of cream. She curiously watched him break the seal around the lid. "What is that?"

"It's what's going to allow me to fit my cock in your tiny ass. Have you ever taken a male there?"

She sucked in a breath. "No."

"But you've seen others do it?" he asked with a wicked smile, his brilliant eyes flashing with heat.

She nodded as his tone lowered. "Is my Goddess a dirty girl who likes to watch?"

She flushed. "I was curious. And, yes, watching the things others did aroused me."

He frowned. "But you weren't a virgin."

"No. But I found no real pleasure before. With males or females," she mused as he bit off a curse.

"You were with other females?" he choked out.

"Yes. I experimented with Reginleif, Mist and Geiravor long ago while enjoying the healing baths. Their hands and lips felt nice, but it wasn't fulfilling."

His whole body tensed, and she felt mixed emotions in their bond as he spoke. "I thought I'd enjoy the image of you naked with beautiful women touching you, but I don't, Gefn. I don't want to think of anyone's hands on you but mine." His tone was as fierce as the frown marring his beautiful face. That look aroused her, made her ache for more of her possessive male.

"If you like to watch, there are places I can take you, but I don't want anyone touching you. I don't even want anyone's eyes on your beautiful body." He softened the words with a fleeting kiss. "You are mine. Can you accept that?" His words sent shivers of pleasure running down her arms and chest.

"Yes. As long as the rules apply to you as well. No one touches you but me," she said with a pleased curve to her lips.

His features relaxed before a wide smile lit his beautiful face. His teeth were so white and straight beside his tan skin and the dark stubble on his face, and it was striking. He nodded. "Agreed. Now, tell me how you pleasured yourself. Did you ever fill up your pussy or ass with anything? Toys?"

He was gauging her experience, but the conversation was making her wet, and she knew it was having the same arousing effect on him.

She understood his reference to toys meant a shaft made for pleasuring oneself. "I've tried some shafts that were fashioned for pleasure but prefer my own fingers."

He ran a hand over his head. "Did you ever stretch your beautiful ass with these *shafts*?"

"I attempted it once. It was not pleasant. It wasn't like what I'd seen others experience. The hard material feels nothing like your cock."

"Fucking hell." His breathing was as sporadic as hers.

"I am curious what your cock will feel like," she admitted as she started to writhe her body against his.

He growled, "You're about to find out. This cream should make it so I can get my cock all the way inside you without causing you any pain. It'll feel good."

He lifted her so she was straddling his muscled stomach, her breasts in his face as she trapped his hard cock between them. He gripped one breast, flicking a nipple with his thumb before pulling her in to suck her tight nipple into the hot cavern of his mouth. She keened, knowing he was coating the fingers of the other hand in the cream. *Arch your hips; offer up your delectable ass to my fingers, love.* She gasped for breath as she did what he said, and when his fingers moved down her crevice, she shivered. He circled the area, and pleasure jolted her body. It did feel good. He growled against her nipple while pushing a finger into her bottom.

He added more cream until she was circling her hips with her bottom impaled by first one and then two fingers stretching her.

He nipped her nipple before sucking it harder while his cock throbbed between them. When he finally spun her around to balance on her hands and knees, she felt him losing control. His voice was a harsh rasp as he demanded, "Lift your ass up and put your face down on the bedding, *thea mou*."

He pushed her legs apart, and she felt spread and vulnerable in a way that only amplified the need.

"Good," he said as he fed more fingers into her tiny hole. Her juices slid between her thighs at how primal it all felt. She didn't think she'd ever get enough, and she couldn't help wiggling her hips, silently demanding him to take her there. She needed to feel his thick shaft inside her more than she needed air.

Anticipation was driving her mad by the time she felt his cock pushing into her. Her pussy clenched, feeling empty as pleasure rocked her body. The walls of her bottom were tingling with sheer pleasure, but she needed it harder. She lifted on her arms and slammed back against him, moaning deep as he cursed and groaned. "Fuck, it's so tight. Your ass is squeezing me to death."

She was blinded by need and couldn't help ramming back and forth, slamming her bottom into his hips until their bodies smacked together with a force that filled her full. With a moan she did it again and again, wildly searching for release as she keened for something more.

He stopped her, lifting her back so it was flush against his heaving chest, making it difficult to move on him. She fought the hold until he moved her hair and slid his lips over her neck as he slapped her mound. She gasped and jerked as she saw the mirror-lined wall in front of them. She could see how they were connected, and she was captivated by his tattooed arms wrapped around her as he pushed up from behind her. He plumped her breasts, and she could see his heated eyes on hers through the mirror. His fingers trailed down and curved into her empty channel and she cried out.

"That's it, my dirty Goddess. You love this. Your sweet pussy is clenching around my fingers, soaking them as your ass clamps around my cock. You're fucking incredible. Do you see how beautiful you are?" He growled.

She only knew that they were beautiful together as he rocked her harder and harder while thrusting his thick fingers into her depths. Her mouth fell open to a scream as she climaxed harder than she thought possible. He found his release at the same moment. His shout was muffled by his teeth digging into her shoulder. She felt him pulsing deep inside her, warmth flooding her body as power roared to life. A wave of it overflowed from them both, making her vision blur before blanking. It was peace and beauty. Pure blinding joy and happiness like she'd never known. It was so foreign she wasn't sure she fully grasped it. And then it snapped into place, relaxing her into darkness.

Chapter 20

Pothos' Home, Tetartos Realm

Pothos lay with his sleeping female in his arms, awed at how good, how right it felt with her soft breath warming his skin and slipping into his damned soul. Sleeping was the last thing he'd been capable of doing; he refused to miss a second of this. After their soul bond had snapped together, he felt fucking whole for the first time ever. It wasn't just the way it leashed his power, it was how she fit inside him.

After long minutes he forced himself to check in with Drake and his father to make sure everything was okay while informing them that they were out of Fólkvangr and had completed the bond. Hearing the details of the God exchange might have sent his head pounding if Gefn hadn't been bundled safely in his bed. It was attempting to convince his father that she wasn't still some big threat that had set his teeth on edge. He loved his father, but Hades' protectiveness tended towards suffocating, even with Sacha calming him and a caged Apollo to keep the God busy.

He breathed her in, putting those telepathic conversations out of his mind, grateful that after months of chaos he could take time away from duty. At least for a little while. With Apollo secured and the Thulians back in their world, it was a rare moment of calm between the storms, where all he needed to think about was his female. He wasn't deluding himself; they had a lot of things to discuss. The biggest was his role as a Guardian and her need for him to help Thule. They were heavy conversations he would find answers to, but for now both worlds were still spinning.

For the next few days he was officially off fucking duty to indulge in his female.

Drake understood his request for space, but his father had not been pleased. P honestly didn't care. Unless they needed him, he was free for the moment.

His female snuggled in tighter to his body and rubbed her cheek against his chest with another soft snore. It was taking all of his will not to laugh at the odd little snuffles that came from her beautiful lips. How those kittenish noises could come from a Goddess was beyond him, but he fucking loved it.

It felt so damned good to be home with her, but beyond that his power had never been so strong while so controlled. He'd never been so level. All because of his snoring little Goddess.

His dirty as fuck Goddess.

He smiled when the snoring finally stopped.

*****

Gefn awoke tucked into the blissful warmth of Pothos' arms, her head resting against his chest, her arms pressed into the hard muscle of his stomach. It felt so warm and incredibly peaceful, as if the cradle of his arms were a sanctuary she'd never known. She breathed him in and snuggled closer, because it wasn't enough. She didn't want the moment to end and reality to invade, at least not for a while. She closed her eyes when he kissed her hair and pulled her tighter into the strength and comfort of his hold while tucking the blankets around her. She sighed in bliss.

They lay there for long minutes, listening to the waves crashing against the rocks outside the balcony doors. “Did I sleep long?”

“Maybe half an hour.”

“That was the second time I was rendered unconscious,” she mused, shaking her head. “Yet you stay awake.”

She looked up to see him smiling down at her. “I was enjoying the view too much.”

She smiled, wishing they could stay in this bed forever, but there was a lot to discuss, and both had duties. Eventually it would all invade their peace. She sighed. “Did you know it would feel like this?” She’d never felt so… happy. Had her life truly been so lonely and bleak before this? It was like she’d known him her entire life.

“Yes and no. Nearly all the Guardians have found their mates, and I could see the purity of their soul bonds, but, no…” He seemed to be searching for the right words; she knew that without hearing his actual thoughts.

He gazed down into her eyes while sliding a strand of hair off her forehead. “I guess I never realized I had a hole in my soul until you filled it, *thea mou*.”

She moaned as her heart expanded in her chest. On a heartfelt whisper she agreed, “We fill each other’s holes.”

He threw his head back with a deep shout of laughter. She absolutely loved the sound, and when he gazed back down at her, his shoulders were still shaking. “Yes, and I’m happy to fill your holes anytime you wish it, my Goddess.”

She laughed, understanding why he’d been so amused. She nodded regally. “You have pleased your Goddess well. Your attentions will be required often."

More laughter rang into the room as he rolled her onto her back, tangling the sheets around them as he kissed her, both still laughing. There were no words for how good it felt to be weighed down by his big body, the soft bed cradling them beautifully. She could happily stay here for all eternity. She'd only shared sleep with her cats. They'd had a bed in her suites for millennia, though often Velspar slept next to her, even when she stayed at Hroarr's palace. With that thought came sadness and anxiety.

He gazed down at her. "Should we go and get them?"

The softness in his voice eased her. She wasn't sure how she felt. If only she understood why they'd allowed her þrír to die. If they could have stopped Tyr, why hadn't they? She rubbed her chest, feeling their regret, but also something else.

She whipped from beneath him with dizzying speed. "Something is wrong."

She started for the balcony, already pulling power to open a portal.

Pothos commanded, "Wait."

When she faced him, he was already moving through a doorway. "What is it?" she asked while whipping the doors wide.

"You're naked," he growled.

She looked down. She was indeed nude; her clothing was still in Fólkvangr. He stepped out of the room wearing dark leggings, boots and a black shirt that pulled over his chest.

"Lift your arms," he commanded, and when she did, he slipped another black shirt over her head. The material was soft and light against her skin. The arms fell to her elbows and the bottom came close to her knees. He was kneeling in front of her next. "Lift a leg."

"I can dress myself," she argued, but was already moving her legs, too rushed to care that he'd dressed her without her thinking twice. The soft black material slid up her legs, covering everything above her knees as he tucked at the top. She was already opening a portal outside his balcony.

Thank you, she whispered into his mind as they stepped through. The shimmering doorway had opened with an ease she'd never known before, but she didn't have time to think about it. They came through at the steps outside of Hroarr's palace. The guards stilled; she wasn't sure if it was her attire or the massive male at her side. His wings were hidden, but his clothing was that of another world. She infused her voice with power as they rushed the steps. "This is my maðr. You will show him the same respect you show me."

To a guard at the top of the steps she commanded, "Inform the others of his status and presence at my side."

"Yes, my Goddess." The mortal left in the blink of an eye to do her bidding.

My way will be faster. Pothos spoke into her mind and suddenly she was breaking apart. The erotic agony wasn't there this time. Only a closeness that comforted her as they reappeared in her rooms.

Mist, Hroarr's pale priestess, and Laire were standing at the side of the massive four-poster bed in white and gold. Her massive black beasts lay atop the blankets, unmoving. When her warrior moved for his weapons at the intrusion, she ordered, "No, Laire." Her heart was pounding in her chest, her stomach twisting into knots, but she spoke with as much authority as she could. "Laire, this is my maðr, Pothos. He is to be respected as you would me. Now tell me what is wrong with Spa and Velspar?" she demanded of Mist. The pale priestess had healing ability, all the þrír did, so why were they like this?

She felt them weakly sending her calm through their bond along with something that felt like goodbye. The emotion chilled her blood and tore into her heart. She dropped on the bed between them, her fingers frantically running through their silky fur while sending energy. It wasn't enough; it didn't seem to revive them at all.

Mist was at her side. The look on her face said it all as she gently whispered, "They collapsed the moment they came back through the portal. We have been trying to heal them, but they have only grown weaker."

"Why didn't you tell me this in Fólkvangr!" Gefn demanded.

"At first we thought it was only exhaustion, and we did not want you to worry when you could not leave that place." She paused. "Later, we were sure you would have felt them. They may have been shielding this from you."

Pothos was by her side, crouching before Velspar. Mist and Laire tensed, but she raised a hand. "He has healing ability."

"They could be depleted from all the power they used." Pothos attempted to reassure her as she felt his power sliding into Velspar. His massive hands were gentle on her beasts, and Gefn put a hand to her heart as she pushed her own ability into him while trying to think of a way to do more. Anything. She would do anything. Tears started choking her.

"Their organs aren't working like they should," he said softly. She felt his healing ability and a rush of his personal energies. It didn't seem to help them. Helpless tears slid over her cheeks.

She felt Pothos' words through the agony. *I want to take them to my world, but I don't know if moving them through a portal or teleporting with them is safe.* She felt the seriousness of his thoughts even if she didn't know the details.

"Tell me how to help them?" she choked out to him.

His eyes hardened as they tracked the tears sliding over her skin. She didn't care that Mist and Laire were there to see them. This couldn't be happening. Her beasts couldn't have led her to Pothos, to the peace and joy of their bond, only to die for it. Her fingers slid over their faces; their golden eyes were so incredibly dim.

She heard him contacting Sirena. The blonde she remembered seeing in his memories, a sister to him.

Sirena, I need your help... in Thule.

Are you okay? There was worry in the female's tone. She felt it as the concern of a sibling.

Gefn's beasts are... not well. I think the pressure in the portal or the act of teleporting their weak bodies will be too much. And I can't heal this.

They have to have a vet there, P. I can't leave Alyssa right now.

Era can stay with Alyssa. The beasts are connected to my mate. I need you, he said with a depth of feeling that made her heart ache.

The female only hesitated a moment. *Come get me. Era is on her way to Alyssa now.*

He stood up from the animals and breathed out with a hand warming her cheek. His brilliant eyes tried to reassure her as much as his words. "I'll be right back. Send them energy until I return."

Chapter 21

Guardian Manor, Tetartos Realm

Pothos' heart was beating out of his fucking chest when he reformed outside the Guardian manor walls, the forest behind him. He wasn't surprised to see an angry Drake standing next to Sirena. The healer was in a black pencil skirt and white top with red high heels, her usual retro look, with her shiny platinum hair in a ponytail. He was grateful to see her, but guilt tore at him for asking this of her. This was a harsh reminder of his new status between two worlds. Taking his sister to a place she couldn't leave, where only he could protect her, was the worst thing possible.

His female's worry tore at him. The fucking beasts were dying, and this was his only way to save them. He couldn't let her lose them. The link they shared with her was strong, and he had no idea what their deaths would do to Gefn.

"P, this pisses me off."

"Drake, leave," the healer demanded. The tiny blonde's violet eyes flashed. Her elven features were hard when she looked at Drake. She'd been a sister to them before they had become Guardians.

The dragon didn't move though P did hear him grunt when Sirena sent power to stop some organ from working. He was too anxious to get back to Thule to care what she'd done to make her point. His cousin snarled, "Sirena, you're too fucking stubborn."

Smoke was already filtering into the air as he turned back to P. "You better be able to get her back. And watch her damn ass every fucking second she's there."

Sirena glared up at Drake, violet eyes flashing with another wave of power. "Drake, I don't have to tell you how much you're pissing me off. I'm perfectly capable of taking care of myself. And making Pothos feel guilty is a shit move and you *know* it." She poked Drake in the chest with a sharp red fingernail before adding, "Now go watch over *your* mate and *my* patient."

P nodded at Drake as his gut twisted. *I'll guard her with my life and have her back soon.*

You'd better. Because I can't retrieve her from another fucking world, his cousin snapped.

Sirena grabbed P's arm. "Let's go."

P breathed out before warning her, "It's a longer ride." And then they were porting away.

The trip felt like it took a lifetime, but when they finally reformed in the massive bedroom, it was to the sight of Gefn in his tee shirt, wiping the tears from her beautiful cheeks. He was beside her as she took a shuddering breath, still caressing the fur of both black beasts.

His female brokenly whispered, "Thank you for coming, Sirena."

His sister wasted no time; she was beside the bed in a split second. "Let me see," Sirena said softly. Her Siren's voice sent a hint of calming to them all, something he needed because the sight of his female's tears was enough to bring him to his fucking knees.

He had enough thought to warn Laire and Mist, "No one goes

near my sister while she tries to heal them. You will both wait at the door." When his gaze landed on the two, they moved across the room, wearing matching worried looks.

The big blond warrior's muscles were tense as he vowed, "She is safe here." And P felt the male's sincerity.

P's heart nearly tore from his chest at his female's tear-filled words, "Can you help them?"

Sirena looked up with her hands running over Velspar, power flowing into the beast as she gently answered, "I will do everything I can."

The tension and worry in the ornate room was enough to choke him. And then the cat weakly purred, and he was hit with a blast of sharp relief that allowed him to finally take a damned breath.

"That's it, pretty girl." Sirena's powerful voice swept through the room like a soft blanket. "Let me see your sister and I'll be back." A few minutes later they heard the same weak noise from Spa, and his muscles relaxed a fraction more.

Back and forth Sirena did this until P felt power outside the door. He ported there with barely a thought, his wings outstretched as the heavy wood slammed open. His body was a shield between the wildly powerful Hroarr and his sister Guardian.

Hroarr growled low before demanding, "What is this power I feel?"

Mist and Laire turned to their God as Gefn slid to his side.

P's Goddess answered, "Hroarr, meet my maðr, Pothos. His sister Sirena has come to heal Spa and Velspar." The tears had dried when the cats started breathing easier, but he could still feel her upset.

The God narrowed his eyes at P. "I was informed he was here, but no one spoke of a female... How did she get inside my palace, sister?"

Before P could answer, the room chilled and his female sent power into her words. "She is of Pothos' family, my family now, and as such she can be anywhere she pleases while saving the life of the *Guardians* of Thule."

Hroarr narrowed his eyes. "My þrír were here attending to them. I was told they were exhausted."

The pale female in question shook her head. "They have been getting worse, not better. We have barely been keeping them alive, hoping Gefn would come home and somehow help them, Hroarr."

The room shook with the God's next words. "Where are Reginleif and Geiravor? They should be here helping." The God's ruthless power leached into the room, licking at the walls, and P saw the male's eyes narrow and his nostrils flare as he attempted to see what was going on with the cats. P blocked his view. Hroarr wouldn't even look at Sirena if P had any say in the matter. She was under his protection.

Mist tensed as she answered the God, drawing his attention by answering his question as to where her sisters had gone. "They went to get healing waters from Fólkvangr and to see if Gefn was finally able to return."

"Why was I not informed of this?" The male's voice rocked the ground as he faced the tiny blonde. She didn't cringe back as P had expected in the face of the God's wrath.

The sound of boot steps down the hall outside the room

interrupted the standoff. "What is it?" Hroarr demanded.

A warrior stepped forward. "A rider from the Norðri Clan, þjóðann minn." P mentally noted that the words *my ruler* would *never* pass through his lips when addressing Hroarr.

There was no mistaking the urgency in the warrior's stance when he added, "They need your presence."

The God bit off several curses before turning his attention to Pothos. "Do what you need to heal them and return your female home *immediately*." The God's emerald gaze shot to Gefn. "I will see you both upon my return." It was a promise and a mild threat, and then the God was gone. It was as if he'd teleported, but P knew it was sheer speed that left him barely a blur.

P didn't have time to think about the God's demands. He retracted his wings, happy that his tee magically returned in place. When he saw Sirena's face, he was instantly alert. "What is it?"

She swallowed and shook her head before schooling her features into calm. "I just need to get some energy."

P was at her side, sending her personal energies, which made her smile. "I'll be fine until I can get them from home," she assured him.

Velspar moved weakly to set her massive head on Sirena's lap. It took up the entire space and diverted his sister's attention. She smiled before gently petting the creature.

She did look tired. *When was the last time you refueled?* he demanded.

Don't start, she mentally gritted out. His sister was known for working beyond the point where she needed to replenish her strength.

He shook his head before asking, "Are they completely healed?" Spa was inching closer to his sister as well.

She smiled at the beasts before chiding them softly, "Do not overdo."

She looked up at Gefn and P seriously. "Their organs were so depleted of energy they were almost completely shut down. I repaired the damage and gave them a boost of my power, but they still need a great deal more strength." His sister eyed him seriously before sending telepathically, *Only so much energy seems to get to them when Gefn sends it. Maybe if you create a direct bond with them, the dual points will fuel them faster. I'm worried that their bodies are feeding on themselves. And I can only give so much after all I've used checking on Alyssa. If their organs start shutting down again, we'll be in the same situation.* She paused. *I need to go refuel now in case you need me again.*

He nodded. *I need to share blood with them now?* P asked. His female sent a blast of appreciation and... love to him. First her tears and now this. She was slaying him. Drinking beast blood sounded disgusting, but he would do anything to never see his female's tears again. And, fuck, if Uri could bond like this to a hellhound pup, P could bond with the two cats who'd paved the way for his and Gefn's mating.

Sirena responded, *You should have an hour, and sharing it through two cuts should be enough if you add some power to the exchange.* He wasn't sure how the others of this world would react to an otherworldly male bonding with their sacred beasts. He guessed Sirena shared the same concern or she would have spoken out loud.

"Thank you," Gefn said with feeling before she produced a blue spelled dagger from the air. With a sharp slice of the blade against the flesh of her palm, she vowed, "I owe you a debt. Anything in my power is yours, Sirena." P felt the magic of the powerful oath settle in the room, settle into his soul. And then his female leaned in and hugged his sister tightly.

Sirena smiled softly. "Welcome to the family, Gefn. When the beasts are feeling better, you need to meet the rest of us."

Gefn nodded. "I look forward to it."

"I'll be right back," he told her before porting his sister back to Tetartos.

When they reformed, he hugged her hard. "Thank you."

His sister hugged him back, laughing. "I can't breathe, P. And I don't think you've ever hugged me."

He gripped her shoulder to pull her back and smiled down at her. "Did I crush you?"

"Yes. Now get back to the cats and your female."

He breathed out. "I owe you." He shook his head. "You know I'm not great with words, but I'm lucky to have you."

She growled a little. "Go away. You're going to make me weepy. And I need to go get energy."

His smile widened. "All this time and I never knew that the way to get you to rest was to tell you how much I love and appreciate you. This kind of valuable information is going to make Drake forget he's furious with me."

Her melodic laughter filled the air, making him smile. Shaking her head, she warned, “Don’t make me hurt you. Now go.” And then she was gone, teleporting away.

He sent to Drake, *Sirena is home and on her way to get energy. I need to go back to Thule. I didn’t have a choice in asking for Sirena’s help. That doesn’t make it better.*

Drake growled. *I know. I don’t have to like it, but I get it. Watch your ass.*

Chapter 22

Hroarr's Palace, Thule

The second Pothos reformed after dropping off Sirena, he noted with a glance that Laire and Mist were already gone. Before him stood a beautifully determined Goddess somehow looking regal in his boxer briefs and tee shirt.

"I will do anything to save them, Pothos. I do not care what others of Thule think. Will you do as your sister said? Will you bond with them?"

He pulled her into his arms and felt her body shaking against his. "Did you doubt it, *thea mou*? Will the beasts be happy about this? They are Guardians of Thule." Weak purrs brought a smile to both of their lips.

He moved to Velspar, who was closest, as Gefn caressed and spoke gently to Spa. With a thought he split his palm before using the same power to cut beneath the fur in Velspar's shoulder. He sent a wave of ability to mix the blood, issuing ancient words to cement the bond. Instantly, he felt the magic settle inside his mind. Gefn set one hand to P's shoulder as emotion flowed from her. He moved on to Spa and repeated the process before mentally checking the threads; they were a brilliant gold.

The intense rush of love and gratitude coming through the bond he shared with his female almost brought him to his knees.

Later, P lay in a massive bed full of furry bodies and soft female, listening to the surprisingly relaxing purring of the healed beasts. After he and Gefn spent hours sharing their energy with them, their eyes had finally brightened. The odd part was that he should feel at least a little depleted, but he didn't. He felt strong. At some point he'd sent power to open the balcony doors to allow the sea breeze inside, enjoying the soothing air currents.

He curiously asked, "How do you normally refuel your strength?"

She glanced up at him with a frown. "What do you mean?"

The look on her face made him curious. "In my world Immortals have caverns where they go to refuel their power while surrounded by the Earth itself. What strengthens your power?"

She nodded in understanding before answering, "Energy is everywhere here. A God of Thule need only breathe in the air to gain strength. Spa and Velspar are the same. The þrír are a little different in that they need the sacred energy of Fólkvangr to replenish their spirits."

It was interesting to learn of her world, the world of his mother. He wondered if trips to Fólkvangr were in his future. He couldn't imagine needing anything more than he was getting already.

He was curious. "What of your mortals? Like Laire?"

"They need physical sustenance. Cooked meals. Water... Laire enjoys mjöd." A word that he translated to mean a kind of beer. Her tone had softened at the mention of her friend. He would need to get a sample of the warrior's blood to Sirena and see if he was compatible for an Immortal mating.

"How old is Laire?" he asked, wondering how long he had to

find the male a mate.

"He just celebrated one hundred fifty-six."

Pothos' mouth gaped open; the male looked no more than thirty. Tops. "Years? How long do your mortals live?" Had he heard that the mortals were longer lived here? It seemed familiar, but he might have felt it in her memories and not truly realized what he'd been seeing.

She smiled up at him. "When we imprisoned Tyr and the other terrible Gods, their magic infused Thule and our mortals became stronger and longer lived. Their spans changed from around two hundred years to roughly half a millennium. How long do your mortals live?"

"One hundred is considered a long life for them."

"Such a short span of time," she said with a hint of sadness. "I can't imagine getting close only to lose them in the blink of an eye for those who live as long as we do." She sighed before adding, "There was a trade-off to our people's longer lives. We have incredibly few births. It is something we are constantly researching." This conversation was leading to things he'd secretly been dreading. He needed to learn more about Thule if he were to be a part of saving it. He was a Guardian, and that meant he had loyalty to Earth and his family there, but as a Guardian his life was also dedicated to preventing powerful beings from subjugating the weak. With what he'd seen of Hroarr's palace, the warriors and even the furnishings, their culture was antiquated. He knew Gefn's heart, but what of the others? There were villages and warriors in her memories, but little of what she did daily.

She looked up at him, frowning. "Something worries you?"

"Yes. You have my memories, *thea mou*. You know what I am," he said softly and then sighed. "I need to know about the world you want me to protect. I need to know that this place doesn't go against everything I am. Everything I believe is right."

*****

Gefn actually felt a shiver of desire from his words. Her male was not only a warrior, he was incredibly honorable and just, qualities she loved. Her memories couldn't have shown him everything about Thule, just as his hadn't shown her all there was to learn of Earth. "It would be easier to show you than to explain how things are done here, but I assure you that our people live freely. The mortals have ways of governing themselves until major strife happens."

That seemed to ease him some. Spa stood and moved to Pothos, proceeding to rub her massive face against his cheek, head and then down to his chest before dropping into his lap. Well, part of her landed on him, a paw landed on Gefn. They laughed and scratched the cat's stretched body as Velspar purred from her spot lower on the bed.

Now that her beasts were safe, she understood why they'd never used the kind of power they had at the lake. Thule had been in too much turmoil when her priestesses were killed. At the time she and her brothers had only just found the answer to finishing the prisons for the evil Gods. And Thule's elements had gone into wild turmoil when they'd finally caged Tyr and the others. Thule had needed the cats' power.

It seemed that the great beasts felt leading her to Pothos was worth their sacrifice. She knew he was the answer to Thule's salvation, to hers.

She smiled as she mused, "Spa definitely feels better. She has never done such a thing with anyone but me. You've won her, *elskede*." Her beloved.

Pothos had a way of gazing at her as if she were the only being in the world, and it made her breathing hitch a little.

He tunneled his fingers into her hair, and she leaned up for a sweet kiss. It wasn't meant to be arousing, but gooseflesh rose on her skin. Her reaction to him was a beautiful thing.

Velspar purred a little louder, making Gefn laugh. She was so incredibly relieved that they were well again. She'd thought for sure she was going to lose them.

She turned and laid her head back against Pothos' hard chest. His warmth slid inside her as she rubbed her fingers over Velspar's soft neck.

She and Pothos had a lot to figure out, and as much as she didn't want to do anything but bask in the comfort of his touch, they should start. "All of your Gods are still in Earth, in sleeping chambers?" She'd been shocked at seeing that in his memories. Obviously the sleeping units had been protected from Dagur's seeking spell.

"Yes."

She shook her head. "We have been looking for a God for centuries, but Dagur should not have sent Hroarr's warriors to take yours." She looked up at him with regret. "There is no true defense for his actions, but he thought you only had Apollo and a world with only one God was doomed to fall. When he detected the God in your world, he sent out summons to Hroarr, Kara and I, only we did not arrive right away. Apparently he kept checking and Apollo disappeared for a time. When he finally detected the Deity again, he acted without thought. Things would have been done much differently had Hroarr or I have been there." She would love to throttle her brother for all he'd done. For all of the lost warriors, for all the pointless deaths.

Her male trailed his fingers in her hair, and her eyes grew hooded at the pleasure of his simple touch. His voice was set low when he spoke again. "Since Dagur didn't detect the other Gods through their sleeping units, maybe his ability doesn't work through protection spells."

"I don't know," she admitted.

"How much do you know about why the Gods are needed in their worlds?"

"Our sires left instructions that all the Gods would be needed when darkness came. They said the power of Thule would be our only hope of surviving it."

"So this Tyr decided to take all the power he could to be the last God standing." She heard and felt his disgust. It matched her own.

"Yes, but the power was perverted and in some ways diluted. He couldn't consume it all. What was in him wasn't pure or complete. Nor in the others who tried the same thing, and with the deaths of so many, it left Thule imbalanced. We did what we could, but Hroarr has been certain that we need at least one more God to power our world. Maybe more since we'd be dealing with a foreign God."

Pothos tensed. "If your brother even thinks about sticking me in one of those fucking boxes, it will not end well for him."

She couldn't help but laugh. "He would never dare attempt such a thing. You are mine and he will respect that." At his grunt she continued, "I assure you he cannot do such a thing without my help. It takes the power of four Gods, one for each of the elements, to trap such a powerful being in one of the confinement chambers."

"If your Gods' powers are so important to this world, what happened while Kara was on Earth?"

She shook her head. "There are constant disruptions in our world. We may have felt her weakness in parts of Thule, it would have gotten worse in the months to come. We are free to come and go all we want, but prolonged absence or death would definitely have caused massive elemental reactions. She was still linked to Thule at some level."

*****

Pothos was curious about what she knew of this darkness. "It seems like you know a lot more of what's coming than we do. That's if our Creators were warning us of the same things yours did. Ours were very cryptic."

She nodded. "As were ours. And yes, they were warning you of the same plague to come, because it comes for all worlds at some point. It feeds and then it's gone. If not for Hroarr's power, we would not have nearly as much knowledge as we do."

"How does he know about it?"

"He has the power of sjá."

Sight? P wondered exactly what that meant. "How does that work?"

"Hroarr has the power of backsight. His ability allows him to see all that has befallen a world, from birth through to destruction. He traveled to hundreds of worlds, seeking knowledge of what the darkness does to a world." Her tone held a hint of sadness. "And then he used that information to form a plan to prevent us from making the same mistakes they did. He's given us the ability to fight it."

He looked down at her, shocked. "Your brother has seen what's coming?"

"Yes."

"Does he know when?" He felt his female's shoulders tense a fraction more.

"Dagur has been able to track it through the ether. For our world it's a matter of decades before we battle it."

"Can Dagur teach me how to do this?"

"I'm not sure. It's not even a skill I possess to any degree, but he *will* do it for you." Her tone was that of determination. "It's the least he can do."

"You said fight. Has Hroarr ever found a world that has survived it?"

"No." She breathed out. "But some have gotten closer than others."

"How?"

She shook her head. "Power. The biggest part of Hroarr's plan involves using the power of the prisons." She breathed out.

"How?"

She seemed a little hesitant but spoke. "We've set them up to be a sort of weapon."

"What kind of weapon?"

"It will set off a burst of energy into the skies to allow us to fight it all the way back to the ether. It is a chance though, because if we destroy Tyr and the others in the process, it could permanently disrupt Thule's balance."

"You could always leave before it comes."

She sighed. "Our power is linked to Thule. We have no idea what would happen to us or our people on another world in the long term."

He was absorbing all of this information. "We can't destroy it?"

"Hroarr thinks it's too powerful to destroy. Too immense."

Too powerful for Thule, but P wondered if Earth could destroy it. They had more Gods to put in those prisons. If they could build them. "Could you teach us to build prisons like yours for Earth?" Could they put their evil Gods away and use them to kill this thing?

"We would need Dagur and Hroarr, and you'd need four of your own Gods to do it. Or we could attempt to move your people to Thule, but it holds the same risks we were concerned about if we left."

"How did you think a foreign God would power Thule, then?"

"Dagur thinks it's a matter of bringing and trapping the God's elements with them in the chamber." She sounded skeptical. "It was a chance, but one we were willing to take before finding you."

There was a lot to figure out, but knowledge was indeed power. He agreed with Hroarr about that and planned to talk to the other God about all of it.

She turned her head to look up at him. "I would like to see your world."

“I’d like to show it to you.” He paused. “But it looks like I need to have that talk with your brothers. And I need to share this information with Drake.” It wasn’t at all how he wanted to spend their day together, but it was what needed to be done. As a Guardian he had a duty to Earth, to his family, that he could never ignore.

She sighed and he knew she felt the same way. Spa and Velspar jumped up, both stretching their legs the second they hit the ground. He guessed that meant they would have an entourage.

Chapter 23

Hroarr's Palace, Thule

After Gefn quickly changed into her own clothes, they were out the door and into the wide torchlit halls of the palace. Pothos had already relayed the information about the darkness to Drake, and it was incredibly odd to always hear his conversations, but she liked knowing.

Pothos slid his fingers into hers and eased the tension she hadn't realized she was feeling. Velspar sidled closer to her and she smiled. Spa had taken Pothos' side. Her beasts were showing their loyalty to them both, and it clenched her heart a little.

The first warrior they came upon bowed to them, but kept his features bland when she asked, "Where is Dagur?"

"He just arrived with Kara's þrír. He's gone to her suites." That explained why her brother hadn't come to see what was happening with the cats. She would ask Dagur about Kara when she saw him. Gefn wondered if her sister was still unconscious.

"Has everyone been informed that this is Pothos, my maðr?"

"Yes, we have, Goddess. I offer my congratulations."

"Thank you. Now please find Dagur and have him meet us in Hroarr's study." When the warrior left to do her bidding, she noticed Reginleif coming down the opposite hall.

The sheer relief on the dark beauty's face was intense as she whispered her thanks to the fates. "They are completely recovered?"

Gefn smiled. "Yes."

The female bowed regally, her pale silk dress flowing over her skin as she vowed, "We owe you a debt, Pothos. And Mist said that we owe your sister as well." And then she turned to Gefn. "We also need to prepare ágæti." A celebration. For her joining with Pothos.

Gefn smiled. "Maybe in time. Right now we have more important issues than preparing for a party."

"Gefn, the people need this. You are the only God to have ever taken a maðr. And they need to understand that Pothos is a powerful being here to help save Thule." The female went on and on.

She looked up at Pothos as he gazed down at her. There were very serious emotions coming through when he spoke in her mind. *Would you like a joining witnessed by your people? We still have a lot to figure out about how I will be a Guardian of Earth and do what you need me to do here, but I want you to have all that you deserve and wish for.*

Her heart expanded at his words.

Reginleif kept going, "We also need to do this right away to set the tone that he is to be accepted completely."

Gefn shook her head; it was all too fast. "We will discuss this later. Right now I need to speak with Dagur."

"Do not worry, Gefn. We will take care of everything." And then the female was gone.

She pinched the bridge of her nose.

Pothos took her hand in his and squeezed. "She's excited. And I believe she means well."

"She does," she agreed. That didn't mean she felt like dealing with any of it when they hadn't had any time together.

She smiled even though she felt the tension from the warriors in the hallway. Maybe Reginleif was right.

She explained, *They lost many of their friends in your Earth. It's not your fault, it is Dagur's, but I imagine word has spread that you are from that world.* She was already wanting to escape back to his home. Back to his bed, where there were no people around, just the two of them—where she could sleep off the emotional exhaustion from the last hours.

I know, thea mou. *It's understandable. They will eventually adjust. Or they won't.* He seemed unfazed by that fact. She'd known that Pothos was very aware of the tension in the palace as he remained alert to their surroundings. He was also curious and taking it all in. She vowed that as soon as they spoke to Dagur, they'd get out of there at least for a short while.

When they made it to the study, she smelled new paint and noticed some of her brother's artifacts were now missing. Evidence that the portal her beasts had opened in this room damaged Hroarr's sanctuary, and she had no doubt he was displeased by that fact.

"What are these?" Pothos asked as he studied the shelves.

"Artifacts from Hroarr's travels to other worlds."

He was noting some of the ancient daggers. "Only the most special items are stored here. Hroarr has an entire other room lined with swords and different specialty weapons."

She felt when Dagur came to the door. When it swung wide, the male took one look at Pothos and growled, "He should not be in here, sister."

"Dagur, this is my maðr, Pothos. And do not order me. He goes where I go."

Pothos faced the male with his arms crossed over his big chest. Her male was not worried in the slightest; in fact, she felt that he'd expected this.

"You took her from our side," Dagur bit out.

"I did," Pothos admitted. "We were linked. And now she is mine."

Gefn loved when he called her that.

"She is a Goddess of Thule and my sister. Remember that before you overstep. You will treat her with care."

"I will."

She closed her eyes. "Enough! I'm tired. Pothos was forced to bring his healer here to save Spa and Velspar. Where were you when the Guardians of Thule were on their deathbed?"

"The beasts were only exhausted. I was tracking down Kara's þrír so that they could help wake her. They'd traveled to her palace before attempting to get here. Remember that your sister is unwell because of his people!" He stabbed a finger at Pothos.

"After she went there and thought to take one of their Gods. You and Kara are too much alike at times. You mean well, but you are reckless."

"You side with him now?" Dagur demanded incredulously.

"He did not attack our world. Do not let your guilt be the cause to place blame where it does not belong, brother," she said icily.

Pothos watched in silence.

She and Dagur stared at one another for a long moment before he frowned. "He brought one of his people here! Spa and Velspar were in the care of Hroarr's þrír. They were being cared for."

"They almost died, Dagur." Her brother needed to know that Pothos' world was not the enemy. "And my male's healer saved their lives. His world, Earth, has done nothing but good for us. We were in the wrong. And now I expect *you* to make part of that right."

Her brother's shoulders tensed, and she knew he wanted to argue more, but was glad he decided against it. "What do you want, sister?"

"I want you to send a spell through the ether to see when the darkness will reach Pothos' world."

He shook his head and sighed. "They only have two Gods in that world, Gefn. Though his other warriors are powerful... we cannot help them like you wish."

She was getting a headache. "His other Gods are confined into spelled sleeping chambers."

Dagur's mouth dropped. "Have you told Hroarr any of this?"

"No. He was called away, and I'm leaving, so you will tell him. I need rest and some time for my maðr and me to get to know one another and our worlds."

"Hroarr will not be pleased you have not shared this information."

"I just have. When will we have an answer on the darkness and Earth?"

He crossed his arms over his chest before seeming to consider it. "A few days at the least."

"I will check in then."

He sputtered, "Days!"

"Yes, I am a newly joined female, and Pothos and I need time together."

"Here?"

"Both here and in his world. I will be back."

She grabbed her mate's hand, more than ready to leave. "Is it possible to take Spa and Velspar with us?" she asked Pothos. She would not leave them so soon after nearly losing them.

"You cannot think to take them with you," Dagur protested.

"I can. They always go with me. Nothing about that has changed." Her brother was just blustering, and it was annoying her.

Her male smiled down at her with a wink. "Anything my Goddess wishes."

And then they were teleporting away.

Chapter 24

Gefn's Palace, Thule

"This is my home," Gefn said as they stepped through a portal high in the snowcapped mountains of Thule. Pothos was taken in by the beauty around them; his female lived in a castle above the clouds. The charcoal stone face was built into the rock of the mountain, several stories high with a wide balcony. It was beautiful and tranquil there instead of cold.

He could feel her excitement in sharing this with him. She was proud of the massive structure and she should be.

"It's incredible," he said, gazing down at her with a smile. They'd spent the night at his home, where it was quiet, and then debated on where to start exploring. He'd won. She'd seen his home, and it was his turn to see her sanctuary, but before taking him to her home, she'd spent an entire day showing him different parts of Thule. He'd seen some of the villages and bigger towns of her world, travelling through each of the Gods' territories, and they'd spoken with many kilt-wearing locals. He was definitely an outsider, so they'd been cautious and very watchful of him. Gefn and the cats' obvious approval of him seemed to help alleviate some of the tension. Word of their joining hadn't reached many of the places because they didn't have cars or planes. He had seen ancient-looking ships and curious beasts; there were even massive steeds with eight legs. And damn, those bastards had been fast.

All in all, it was a successful day. The people of Thule seemed respectful and even adoring of Gefn. He didn't see poverty or homelessness in any of the places they went. It was much like Tetartos in that respect.

As they ascended the steps to her home, a servant swept the door wide. She wore a plain dress of green with light-colored curls piled on her head. Her green eyes sparkled in obvious delight at seeing her mistress. She moved to him curiously, but without any hesitance in smiling. The female appeared to be in her thirties, with round curves and pink cheeks that eased him at once. Her musical voice was cheerful. "Welcome home, my Goddess."

Gefn smiled as they slipped through the heavy wood door that led to a massive staircase. "Thank you, Eerika. This is my maðr, Pothos."

He felt the female's shock. "Oh my! Congratulations, my Goddess. Are we to prepare a celebration?" There was so much excitement in her features he felt a little bad when Gefn shook her head.

"We have a lot to see to before any celebrations. For now, I want to show him our home."

"Yes, of course. Laire did not come with you?"

He could feel his female's guilt at leaving the male behind. "Since this is a short trip home, I left Laire to relax at Hroarr's palace."

"I understand," she said with a smile before scurrying off. He saw more servants. An older male who appeared in his forties and two women who looked closer to sixty. Gefn introduced them all as if they were family members. If he had to guess, he'd say some were truly related to Laire.

Thule was definitely old world. The stairway banister, carved by hand or magic, was intricately beautiful. The top of the stairs led to a long hallway that passed a library and a study before arriving at a hidden staircase that wound up to a massive bedroom suite with windowed doors to a balcony that looked down at the clouds. Her bed was twice the size of the oversized one he owned, and Spa and Velspar were already making themselves at home on the white blankets.

"What did you think of Thule?"

She'd taken him to a tavern down the mountain from her home, and he still remembered her eyes lighting up when he'd sampled the bitter brews. She was excited to share her world with him. And it was a good world, with people who seemed to govern themselves. The Gods were charged with ensuring the world itself was safe, that the wild elements were calmed and didn't cause destruction where there were lives at stake. There was magic all around them. The people used it for power, for taking care of the crops... for everything.

"I like it," he said honestly. She'd shared that crime was dealt with by magical mortals called the Forseti, who were born to the task of seeking justice. He needed to learn a hell of a lot more, but one day of portal jumping all over the place had eased some of his tension with regards to the Gods in Thule.

She moved to the glass doors and opened them. The look on her face when she breathed in the air was almost orgasmic.

"I love being up in the skies." Something he could see by the way her eyes sparkled as she looked out at the clouds.

He pulled her into his arms and smiled down as he moved them outside, where the winds whipped lovingly at them. "How high would you like to be?"

His wings unfurled with a wild burst of power, and her delighted laughter filled the air. He'd never get enough of that sound. He held her close to his chest as he launched them into the sky. Her legs wrapped around his waist automatically, and he wasn't sure he'd ever known such bliss. Her head moved to rest on his chest as they flew above the clouds.

She whispered into his mind, *I'll never get enough of this. Of you.*

He felt his heart clench and kissed her head. *I'll never get enough either,* thea mou.

*****

Hades stood at the side of the war room, listening to information he'd already heard from his son's check-ins. Once again the room was too damned crowded with his nephews, Guardians, mates, wolves, and he wasn't pleased that Pothos wasn't there to share this information himself instead of exploring Thule with that Goddess. Who knew if her information could even be trusted? It sounded to him as if Hroarr was only guessing on how to save their world.

Any information is good, my love. I know you're anxious that he's not here, but he's learning what he can while getting to know the female he's bound to. Keep in mind Sirena likes her, and Sirena doesn't even like you most of the time.

He mentally grunted.

He heard Brianne point out, "The Thulians owe us after Sirena saved their cats."

Drake growled over the chatter of everyone weighing in at once. "We'll know more soon, but there are other issues to address. The

Tria are obviously up to something. We've been dealing with escalating attacks, and they're sending those damned serpents and hell dragons to strike cities in Tetartos. I'm sending more of you to patrol Hell to try to eradicate the worst of the bastards before they're loosed here."

Hades flexed his wings, readying to battle. Maybe he'd pay Apollo another visit. He'd generously allowed the Phoenix's female a turn with the bastard because she wanted to know how the God had located her and her twin in Paris. Now, after the female's enthusiastic interrogation, his brother was unconscious. If only she'd asked Hades, she would have had her answer before they'd found his damned brother, but the Guardians and their females were forever forgetting he was a God. It would have been a matter of trial and error. Immortals would be drawn to live in a location where the power of the Earth flowed heavier above ground. Simple. There were maybe a dozen such places in the human Realm, and not all were cities like Paris.

You never told me that there were such spots in the mortal Realm, Sacha pointed out.

You didn't ask.

Since he was denied his time with Apollo, he would deal with Draken's hell beast issue until the bastard was awake again. As much as Sacha wanted to lock the male away, Hades just wasn't ready for Apollo's suffering to end. Not yet.

I know, love. But not too long. He's toxic, and I don't like him anywhere near you.

He tucked his female into his side and breathed in her sexy scent. *I may forgo his torture tonight to give you enough pleasure that you pass out with my tongue still inside you,* agapi mou.

He smiled when he felt her shiver with desire. He decided to make quick work of the hell beasts so he could get home with his female within the next hour.

Chapter 25

Pothos' Home, Tetartos Realm

Morning sunlight filtered in from the curtains as P held his female close. They'd had a few days of making love and exploring worlds, and now he lay awake with her tucked into his arms. Today was the day they would meet with Dagur and see what he'd discovered about how long they had before Earth was under threat. And he was anxious, instinctively knowing that he wasn't going to like the answer. He had so much in this world to protect. And now in her world as well.

He'd found that the more he'd learned of Thule, the more he liked it.

Vane's laughing voice in his mind jolted him away from his thoughts. *P, I think you're missing something, man.*

What the hell are you talking about?

He could hear more laughter and then Brianne's disgruntled, *Come get your damned cat, P.*

Fucking hell. He felt the link to the cats and saw Velspar was not in the spare room like she was supposed to be. Spa sauntered into their bedroom at that exact moment and made a humpf noise.

He felt his mate's frustration as he demanded Velspar return. He had no doubt his mate was doing the same thing at the moment.

How the hell did she get there? And Do. Not fucking hurt her, Brianne, he growled at his bloodthirsty sister.

Then come get her furry ass. Your animal teleported directly beside Vane a minute ago. And now she won't stop snuggling up to him. I guess you missed the part where the beast started crushing on my mate at the lake?

He closed his eyes and growled, *Make sure nothing happens to her. We're on our way.*

The animal had to have acquired his ability to teleport with their blood bond, and that brought up the fact that he hadn't had any trouble getting them through the confinement spell in Tetartos, either. He'd half assumed that was because of how powerful they were, but now he wondered if his blood was giving them too much access. If Velspar teleported directly to Vane, it wasn't a stretch to assume the intelligent creature had found P's telepathic links and located Vane among them. Fucking hell.

The damned cat certainly didn't seem to be listening to them and teleporting away, either. She'd found what she wanted, and she was ignoring their calls to return. He'd have found this all fucking amusing if he weren't feeling Gefn's worry that something would happen to the apparently lovesick beast.

They both dressed as quickly as they could. His female had donned some of those sexy leather pants that hugged her ass. An ass he didn't have time to pay attention to when they were forced to collect an errant beast.

He and Gefn teleported to the manor's courtyard, and a moment later Spa appeared right next to him. He was so fucked. The beasts had his ability to teleport and could travel anywhere they damned well pleased. Drake was really going to love this. Not.

"Velspar!" Gefn commanded when they saw what was happening. The massive beast had her massive front paws on Vane's shoulders and was rubbing her head along Vane's as the big Demi-God laughed and scratched her fur.

Brianne pointed at the display while perching one hand on her hip. "P, what do you have to say for yourself? Aren't you supposed to be controlling these things? Uri can control his hellhound, and Havoc is just a pup." Just as his sister Guardian's snide words were fully formed, he heard barking as the pup she referenced came barreling from the manor doors as if they'd called him.

P groaned, "I don't see fucking Uri right now, Brianne?" He and Gefn needed to figure out some way to keep them from getting into trouble in Earth. Now.

Vane pushed Velspar back to the ground before scratching behind one pointed ear as they all watched Havoc's approach.

"Havoc, no," he commanded, seeing Uri and Alex coming from the opposite side of the manor.

Spa hissed, and just as P was about to put a stop to all of it, Gefn snapped, "Enough," and caught all three animals in violent whirlwinds, moving both cats to her side and the pup next to Brianne. He heard rumbled yowling from the indignant cats while the pup woofed.

After a moment she released the wild power, and all of the beasts wobbled a bit, dizzy after being spun in circles.

"What the hell just happened?" Uri said as he moved toward the pup. Brianne and Vane burst into laughter.

"Well, that was worth it." Brianne snorted.

He smiled, pulling his female into his side as he introduced his frustrated mate to Uri, Alex, Vane and Brianne, as well as Havoc, who seemed a little wobbly, but otherwise unfazed.

She smiled and nodded to each of them, but when Velspar started to move in Vane's direction, he felt Gefn tense and swore the beast was about to go for another spin. "Do not even think it, Velspar," she warned with power in her voice. He tried not to laugh as the cat let out a huff and sat staring at Vane. All the while Spa was issuing furious spitting noises from her perch. They definitely had their hands full, but his female had controlled the situation well.

Gefn finally shook her head when the animals were all under control. She addressed Vane and Brianne, "I apologize for Velspar. I have no idea what's gotten into her."

Brianne groaned when Vane spoke. "All the kitties love me. I think she wants to see my lion half." And then he got serious. "It was fine here, but it could have been dangerous for her if we'd been patrolling."

"What happened?" Uri asked, and they explained what the cat had done. The dark-haired Guardian lifted an eyebrow beneath the dark sunglasses that protected his silver eyes from the sunlight.

Alex's lips twitched as she scratched behind Havoc's ear. "Drake's going to love that."

P snorted at that. The dragon was going to be furious.

P could tell Uri was using his bond with the hell beast to keep Havoc in place, but the pup was making soft whining noises in Spa's direction. His big red eyes hadn't left the temperamental feline. The two creatures were roughly the same height, but the hound was built a little narrower, similar to a very large Doberman. He was young, he just wanted to play, and Spa obviously found this beneath her.

The indignant cat actually turned her body so she wouldn't be facing the pup.

"I'll make sure she doesn't do it again." Gefn growled in both cats' direction. In his mind, P was already thinking they were screwed. His female's beasts were too damned intelligent and played by their own rules. He half wished Vane would have just shifted into his lion form and played with Velspar, but with his luck, the cat would have only become more infatuated.

Gefn started to relax into his side as she asked after Sirena.

After a moment of conversation and questions, Brianne informed them, "Everyone else is patrolling or they'd be here to meet Gefn and the cats. Drake and your dad have kept us updated, but it's nice to actually see your damned face."

"How has it been here?"

Uri answered, "The Tria are being a pain in the ass. We've had hordes of beasts every day and then packs of possessed on Earth. You picked a good time for a vacation."

"Call me in if you need me," he told them, shaking his head. "We need to see Gefn's brothers now to see if there's more news on a time frame for the threat." He knew his father had been keeping them all updated, but he suddenly felt guilty for not having seen them sooner.

How do you feel about coming back here after our meeting? he sent to his female.

I'd like that. He felt the warmth in her response and was glad she felt comfortable with his family.

"We'll be back after we see her brothers. Hopefully by then

everyone will be done and can meet Gefn."

After a quick goodbye they were teleporting away, and he hoped to hell they weren't about to receive bad news.

Chapter 26

Hroarr's Palace, Thule

Gefn was shaking her head as they stepped through the portal she'd created to her brother's palace.

With a great deal of exasperation, she said into P's mind, *I can't believe Velspar.* Her beast had lost her sanity; maybe the near-death experience had the animal behaving oddly.

She felt her mate's amusement, but there was absolutely no remorse in the emotional link from the animal, and she saw his lips twitching at that fact. When they passed her brother's guards, Gefn asked one of the males, "Are my brothers here?"

"Yes, Goddess."

"And Laire, my guard?"

"Yes, Goddess."

"Please find him and send him to the receiving room."

The guard bowed and was off. She felt guilty for leaving Laire behind. When she'd sent him from her room when the cats were sick, she'd told him to take time off to rest while she and her maðr saw to the beasts. Her friend hadn't been happy then, and now it had been days later. She only hoped he'd been enjoying time with Hroarr's females.

He was at the door a few minutes after they arrived, and she noticed the stony look on his handsome face. "My Goddess."

Pothos covertly stepped from the room to allow her time to speak with her friend, and she appreciated it.

"Laire, I'm sorry to have left without word." She and Pothos had discussed this. She wasn't about to leave her friend behind; his position as her guard was always going to be his. It was considered an honor to be chosen to directly serve a God or Goddess in their world, and she would never dream of stripping him of the title unless he did not want it anymore. "Things have been hectic."

"Yes, my Goddess," he said while standing at formal attention. "Does this mean I will be dismissed from service?"

His words felt like a knife wound. "I deserve that... But you would only be released from your position if you wished it. I do not," she admitted while watching him take in a relieved breath. "I do need some more time alone with my male to figure everything out, but you will be my guard as long as you desire. I have only come to ask if you would like to take your time off here or if you would rather we take you home when we leave. At some point you will need to travel with me to and from Pothos' world as well."

Velspar and Spa both went to him and nudged his side.

"They missed you as well," she said with a smile.

He gave her a small smile. "I have worried for your safety."

She nodded. "I should have come sooner. Things are strained between the two worlds, and I needed time to show my male that Thule is a wonderful place. His world is so much larger. The things you will see there are incredible, and I do believe you will come to like Pothos and his family very much. But for now, I need more time with only my maðr."

He breathed out. "I understand. How long am I off duty?"

She shook her head. "I am not sure. Days or possibly even weeks. I believe Hroarr's þrír would be grateful for your presence when traveling his territories, but only until I return for you." She smiled, knowing the three would love nothing more than to have Laire with them.

His eyes lit a little before he shook his head. "If things are strained between the worlds, I should be at your side."

She smiled. "I will be fine. Pothos will protect me, but he has duties in his world, and I have duties here. It's something we need time to figure out."

"Reginleif wishes to have a celebration."

She groaned and smiled a little. "Then your duty is to stop that. Or at least postpone it; there is too much for me to do at the moment."

He grinned. "I will see to it."

"Good. You know we are friends, Laire. And I did not treat you as such when I left you. I give you my deepest apologies."

He shook his head, seeming at a loss for words.

"Now, will you stay here, or would you rather go home?"

"I will stay here and make myself useful attending the priestesses during travel if they wish it."

She smiled. "Indeed they will. Now I must see my brothers."

"Hroarr is in his study, and Dagur is in the great hall," he said.

She found Pothos leaning against the wall outside the room. He nodded and smiled at her before addressing her guard, "Laire." Spa had already come out to stand by him at some point.

Her warrior nodded. "My Goddess' maðr."

"You can either call me Pothos or P as my Guardian brothers do."

Laire frowned. "P?"

"Pothos is a very old name in my world and one I've never cared for all that much." Pothos' voice whispered into her mind, *Unless my Goddess is using it.* She smiled at that.

After a few steps she instructed a warrior to have Dagur meet them in Hroarr's study. A meeting she was anxious to commence with.

She sent Laire off to save her from Reginleif's celebration planning right as they neared Hroarr's inner sanctum.

The guard at the door was a sign that Hroarr was indeed inside his study. She nodded and the male swept the door wide for them.

The God in question was sitting at the massive wood desk. He leaned back when they entered. "I see you have found time to finally return, sister." She could tell he was irritated. When he narrowed his eyes, it was as if he were looking at her for the first time. "Your powers have grown." His knowing eyes slid to Pothos to assess him just as closely.

"They have," she admitted.

When the cats moved to stand at either side of her and Pothos, he noted that as well. "Dagur said that your beasts were fully recovered. Good."

"Yes. Again, that was thanks to Pothos' healer," she pointed out.

"Indeed. I will see this healer."

"No," Pothos said. He was protective of his sister Guardians. "You're welcome to send your thanks through me."

Hroarr raised an eyebrow, and Gefn interrupted before they started one of those infuriating male matches to see who could best the other. She was in no mood. "Hroarr, is Kara awake?"

That darkened his mood. "She is. And she confirmed what you said about Agnarr having an alliance with Hades. But millennia ago when they went to Earth to gain Hades' help, he was gone, all the Gods were, and it seemed as if they'd all been destroyed."

P nodded. "When the Creators came back to our world, they destroyed all of our Gods' palaces before putting them to sleep."

"Why would Kara not share any of this with us?" Gefn asked, shaking her head.

"She went there herself and saw the destruction. When Agnarr's ring heated with a call from that world, she became infuriated, convinced that Hades had somehow hidden instead of helping save Agnarr during his time of need. When Hades told her that another God had been stolen by warriors with a dragon staff, she decided to take Hades for the good of Thule. I believe it was her way of retaliation. She was too angry to think." Her brother's eyes went to Pothos. "It seems your father's powers are quite painful and damaging."

Pothos nodded. "They are. I assume she is fully recovered now?"

"Yes," Hroarr bit out.

The doors swept wide, revealing Dagur, and Gefn didn't waste any time in asking, "What were you able to find?"

He growled, "Something skewed the spell. But do not worry, sister, I recast it and will have your information in another couple of days at most. You would know this if you checked in."

"You said three days," she pointed out.

Gefn turned to Hroarr. "I'm sure you were worried, but I am capable of caring for myself, and Pothos and his family would never harm me." She raised a hand. "I have seen his memories as he has seen mine. His people are honorable and just. They would never harm me to begin with, but now that Pothos and I are soul bonded, any harm they did to me would come to bear on him."

She noticed that Spa and Velspar both moved to Pothos and rubbed their heads against his hips.

Hroarr lifted his hand and bellowed, "Enough. If I intended him harm, it would already be done. What I demand to know is how Pothos intends to be of use in Thule."

Before P could answer, Gefn shot back, "He is a Guardian of his world! He protects four Realms there, and he is *tied* to Earth. I've felt his call. That is why I need Dagur's answer on when the darkness will come for them. Whether you like it or not, *both* he and I are tied to two worlds now with our soul bond. We will be fighting for Thule and for Earth." She'd been considering this for some time, and she wanted them to understand how serious this was for both worlds. If the attack came to Earth first and she and Pothos were both to fall, Thule would likely fall as well.

Her brothers were silent.

She said, "We will be back in two days for the results. If you need me, you can open a portal to his world and we will know."

She teleported Pothos and the cats away, wanting her brothers to think on what she'd said instead of their male posturing and blustering. Her powers were strong enough that she'd actually used Pothos' powers without thought. If only she had the ability to cast her own spell into the ether, she'd have answers already.

The waiting was making her edgy.

Chapter 27

Guardian Manor, Tetartos Realm

Hades and Sacha reformed in the moonlit courtyard of the manor. Pothos had informed them all that they had no new information on the darkness, but he wanted to introduce his female to everyone that evening. Hades flexed his wings, still displeased with the fact that his son was mated to a Thulian and that Pothos hadn't come to him. That he was forced to meet his son's mate at a party.

Sacha's voice slid through his mind. *You haven't exactly made this easy, love. You snipe about her every time you speak to him. The mating is complete, and by all accounts he is happy. Make an effort to accept her.*

The second he laid eyes on his son, he saw it. The soul bond between Pothos and the beautiful Goddess nearly choked him with its sense of finality.

The Goddess wore a leather vest in tan with a matching long skirt. She was a stunning creature, he had to give her that, and he noted that she was talking comfortably to Brianne, of all people, while her cats milled around freely. The menaces should not have been allowed loose like that; they were too dangerous. It seemed the Goddess and her animals had won everyone over but him. He shook his head when he saw one of her annoying beasts bat an adoring Havoc into a tree. Apparently it hadn't been hard enough to hurt or deter the pup because he was stupidly loping back by the beast's side a moment later.

See, love, all is well, Sacha said, and he mentally huffed. *You need to give her a chance for the sake of your and Pothos' relationship.* His female's tone was stern this time.

When the Goddess put her hand in his son's, P looked down at the female with love shining in his eyes; that same love was reflected back at him from hers. Hades' heart felt torn as he was forced to admit his son was happy. Happy to live in Thule. A part of him was dying at the idea of finally being awakened and able to spend time with his son only to have him taken away.

He can portal and teleport to and from that world. And we can speak to him telepathically. You are not losing him, love. I promise. Sacha sent him warm loving emotion, and he hugged her close.

The Goddess and Pothos turned smiles in their direction when he and Sacha approached. The female actually looked happy to see him as Pothos formally introduced, "Father, this is my mate, Gefn."

The female beamed at him before bowing a fraction respectfully. "You have raised an incredible male with his father's sense of honor."

Hades arched a brow. Damn, he might just like this female after all. Sacha snorted in their bond, *Well, she sure has you figured out.*

They spent the next hour speaking of Thule and all she'd seen of Earth in the past several days. Their conversation relaxed into something that eased him.

Drake broke it by urgently snarling, "We have possessed all over the cities in the mortal Realm. Conn is sending you all locations."

"How many cities?" Pothos asked.

"Twelve," the dragon growled. "Sirena is busy with Alyssa, Gregoire and the baby. That means the rest of you are up. Someone take the wolves and Erik as well.

"I'm back on duty, then," Pothos said when he looked at his female.

Hades didn't like all the attacks. He felt like it was linked to the end. To the darkness coming for their world.

I agree, Sacha said before telling Drake they would take Paris.

*****

P gazed down at Gefn, and she could see that he planned to leave her behind even before he spoke. "Take the cats to my house; they can't be in the mortal Realm."

She shook her head. "No, I will go with you. The other females are going with their males; why would I not do the same?"

"You've only been to a few human cities, and where I'm going is nothing like what you've seen. I'm going into an ugly, dirty part of the Realm, and I don't want you anywhere near it," Pothos argued when Gefn insisted on going with him. He continued a second later, "You're unfamiliar with all of this, Gefn. Guardians are not allowed to harm humans, even possessed ones. We can only contain them." She remembered that from his memories of when the Creators cursed the Guardians with ten times the pain they inflicted on a human.

"I can contain them easily," she said with confidence.

She wasn't going to let this go, and she allowed him to feel that as she sent the cats to their room in Pothos' home. They disappeared easily. Maybe too easily, so she tracked them to ensure they reached their destination.

Pothos looked at her and she could tell he did not want her to go. "Remember the humans don't know about Gods and Immortals. Which means tornados coming from an alley would draw attention." He took another look at her and sighed. "You're only going to follow, aren't you?"

She crossed her arms over her chest and replied archly, "I wouldn't recommend you attempt to leave me."

He groaned. "You should probably change into something comfortable. I need to grab cuffs anyway, so we'll go home first."

When they reformed, she quickly donned some leggings and boots while he went to the cabinet where he stored weapons. Spa and Velspar poked their heads into the room as Pothos attached metal restraints at a back loop of his pants before lowering his shirt to cover them to a degree. Gefn shook her head before commanding, "We'll be back. Do. Not. Follow." They weren't exactly happy, but they seemed resigned, which was good.

When they ported again, it was into a dark alley. The stench of human waste forced a hand to her face as she groaned. "And you were worried about Thule? About how our mortals lived under a God's rule?" She'd been shocked at how some of the humans of his world were allowed to live.

"I know," he agreed on a groan. "We were told not to interfere with humanity's evolution and we haven't."

"I do not believe you did them any favors," she said as a large rodent scurried by her foot. She glared at him the second it was gone.

"I warned you," he pointed out with a toothy smile.

Luckily they didn't have long to wait. A pack of filthy mortals that stank of sulfur moved into the mouth of the alley. There were cars speeding past on the busy cross street, honking as their lights flashed by behind them.

These beings felt… oily. Sickness bled from them, and she didn't even want her male to touch the tainted creatures. She'd never seen anything like them and was happy for that fact.

Pothos didn't want her to use wind tunnels, so when the pack split, she allowed several of them a moment to get closer. She noted that Pothos had already gotten one of his raging mortals in restraints and stuck him behind a large metal container that stank nearly as much as the three black-eyed mortals in front of her. Her maðr had been so fast, she hadn't even seen what he had done. And then her male placed himself in the middle of the alley, apparently planning to leave her with nothing to do as the disturbing beings spit violent curses at him as they brandished daggers. Some launched at him all at once as he ported easily away.

She shook her head at the protective male, but there were too many for him to keep from her as he covertly picked them off one by one.

One sped by her male, tilting his bald head shining with grease, and his black eyes took her in with a sinister leer she found offensive. The male's clothes were different, more fine than some of the others. She kept glancing to her male to see what he was doing. Two more were sitting in the heap now, seeming to be held down by some power that only fueled the outraged words. She mentally growled at not having seen Pothos put them there.

The bald possessed circled to the side of her. Another had come from the other side of the alley, forcing her to turn and watch them both. The other had pale powder on his face and metal sticking out from his lip and eyebrows. “What is this? Not a Guardian…” Their tones had an odd cadence that displeased her ears. The pale one grabbed his shaft crudely. “We have time to play with her. Fuck her.”

Pothos snarled as he fought the others, not seeing this one’s display, but likely feeling her disgust.

She decided she’d had enough. She couldn’t listen to them speak for another moment. Gefn would secure them her way. With a flick of her wrist she sent power to the muddied elements of the filthy city and pinned both beings to the muck-coated wall. Papers and debris were caught in the wind, so she made use of it, sending the materials into the sputtering maws of the foul beings.

P turned from securing the last male to see what she’d done, but she knew for a fact he’d been tracking her the entire time. “You said no wind tunnels,” she pointed out with a smile.

He chuckled. “Would you care to gag the others as you’ve so conveniently done with yours, *thea mou*?”

She beamed a smile at him and happily obliged her male as suddenly dozens more rushed in from both sides of the alley. Before she could do anything, she felt Pothos unleash power in a beautifully controlled wave, enthralling them all into eerie stillness. All of the possessed seemed almost as if they were set in stone, yet cars kept passing unaffected. She felt Pothos’ relief and pleasure through the bond. This was a proof he needed that his ability was completely in his control.

With a turn she noticed that even those she’d caught were contained by his power. A few steps and she was gazing up at her male with a smile, her hand sliding into his.

Her smile fell after a moment. “Now what will we do with them? The beings are evil? A scourge on your civilization?”

"They are, and my father and Sacha have a way of dealing with them. There are too many to teleport out of here, so we'll wait for one of the others to finish and help transport them. This is a ridiculous amount to find in one place."

She watched the cars pass and humans hasten by the alley. "No one will think this is suspicious?"

"Sadly, no. Most humans do not see what they don't want to. Especially in dark disgusting alleys."

*****

Hades and Sacha didn't have long to wait in the dark alley in Paris. Possessed were drawn to him, or more accurately their masters enjoyed using them like puppets to taunt him.

There were six, several in suits, the others in dirty pants with rotted teeth. One of the suit-wearing males stepped forward, and Hades watched his eyes light with flames as the eerie sinister echo of Deimos' voice came from the male's lips. It was the Tria reaching out from their prison in hell again. "Hades, you have to feel it now." The human turned from pale to gray in seconds, and when the body dropped, dead from being the demon's conduit, a second male stepped forward to take its place. "You will want to release us. We will help."

"You're boring me, Deimos."

Outraged shrieks from Than and Phobos could be heard mixing with Deimos as their human mouthpiece dropped dead. Another stepped forward. "You have been warned. We will rip your female piece by piece in front of you, and we will feast on her screams."

Rage filled Hades like a rolling force, and he ripped the souls from the remaining fiends before he could hear any more. Sacha put her hand on his back. He flexed the muscle, feeling bare when his wings were retracted to blend into the human Realm. He only wished he had more souls to rip free of fiends.

Draken, we are done here. What is the next location? he growled.

His nephew answered in a second with a visual of another dark alley. This time Hades wouldn't listen to them first.

"We need to tell Drake they were taunting you again. Especially now that we know that there is a darkness coming to the world."

He shook his head. "They've given us no information. They just want to play a game. Soon Pothos and his female will have real answers." The Thulians might well be able to provide him with reasons why the Tria were so active. Hades had thought it was his presence back in Earth, but now he wondered if the demon spawn sensed the darkness coming to this world. He was tempted to go to the bowels of hell to pay the Tria a visit.

"Not without me." Sacha's determined words gave him cold chills.

"That will never happen, my love. You will never breathe the same filthy air as those fiends."

Chapter 28

Pothos and Gefn's Home, Tetartos Realm

P and Gefn reformed back at his home after finally getting rid of the dozens of possessed they'd been babysitting. He couldn't believe how a power that he'd battled for control of for his entire life could be so easily manipulated now. He lifted his female into his arms, at a loss for words, because *she* had done this for him. Her long sexy legs wrapped around his waist as he carried her.

She set her soft fingers to his lips and whispered, "You were magnificent out there."

He nipped and then licked the pads of her delicate fingers before they moved away so she could slide her palms over his stubbled cheeks and then into his short hair. Her touch was like fuel to him. "Fuck, I love your hands on me."

A quick stop by the spare room showed the cats sprawled out on the bed. Golden eyes glittered back at them, but neither moved.

He ported his female into the bathroom and she giggled. "In a hurry?"

"Always." He smiled down at her before taking her lips in a quick kiss. In record time they were both stripped of clothes that still held the stench of sulfur and alley grime.

He needed to cleanse her of it, and with a thought, the water was on and filling the stone walls and mirror with steam. He carried her in through the glass door and kissed her before scrubbing every inch of her clean as she lathered his hot flesh. He groaned, making sure to take extra care with her full gorgeous tits.

Her soft moans drove him as she pushed those sexy mounds into his palms, demanding more. He sent the spray over her skin and began replacing his hands with his tongue while her fingers gripped his head. *So greedy.* His lips curved against her nipple. *Relax and enjoy what I do to you,* thea mou.

She bit off a curse when he moved lower and wrapped one of her long, toned legs over his shoulder to devour her up against the shower wall. Water slid over his back as he ate at her relentlessly. *Come on my tongue, my sexy girl.*

He growled as he sucked her sweet little clit and loved how she cried out, convulsing against him. His cock throbbed with the need to be inside her as he slipped out from under her leg and lifted her slack form into his arms.

He had plans for her tonight. She smiled up at him. "I like your determination."

Carrying her into his bedroom, he followed her down on their bed with a languid kiss that had her writhing against his body.

His cock was aching against the cradle of her sweet, wet pussy. He lifted from her, he wanted to look at her, but she tried to pull him back down. "Let me look at you," he said as his fingers grazed one tight nipple and then the other. "So tight, let's see how much I can make them ache." She groaned for him and he smiled.

He sent power out and a bowl with ice came to sit beside him. She stilled; his curious female was studying the frozen cube he lifted up. Leaning on one forearm, he used his other hand to circle the cold chip around one tight bud and then slowly over the tip as her back arched. “My naughty Goddess likes that. Let’s see what else you like.” He slid it between the deep cavern of her tits to roll over the other tight tip while sucking the one he’d already tormented, warming the cold he’d caused.

When he lifted up, her eyes were flashing wildly as she mewled for him not to stop. He languidly moved the ice up to her throat as it melted against her hot skin, sending water sliding down to her cleavage before making its way over her sides and then down to her belly button. Her head angled, making room for his mouth. He kissed and nipped her throat before sucking on the other cool peak and making his way lower as she wriggled and gasped for him. “Spread wide,” he commanded. “Show me how hot that pussy gets for me.” He lifted another cube and slid it over her mound.

Her shaking thighs spread as he set his tongue to her belly button. She was getting more and more frantic as he placed the cold cube onto her clit and then rubbed it down her hot slit before pushing it in a fraction and then running it up again. “That’s it. So fucking hot it’s melting all over these pretty lips.” He leaned down and licked up the juices mixed with cool water as he let the chip slide lower. “Tilt your hips for me. Show me everything.” When she did, he moved the nearly melted cube to her tiny ass. He groaned at the sight of her all spread out for him. He trailed his fingers into the water before pushing them inside her cool pussy. “It looks like I need to warm my mate.”

When he moved up her body, he slid her ankles over his shoulders before positioning his cock at her slick pussy.

He smiled into her lust-hazed eyes as he slowly pushed inside, stretching her inch by inch until she tried to move to meet him. He kissed the arch of one tiny foot as he thrust inside her. Her juices were already sliding around his cock.

God, she felt good.

That's it, take every inch. It's all for you, thea mou. *Everything I have is yours,* he whispered in her mind as he gazed down at the beautiful creature who would be his for all eternity.

He saw in her eyes that she understood, and he watched her throat as she swallowed. Beautiful. He stayed that way, watching every reaction flash across her face as he took her. Making love to her nice and easy even though she pushed and grabbed at his ass, begging him to take her harder, faster.

"Pothos, please."

He finally gave in and slammed his hips, loving the way her tits bounced with every hard thrust. He sent tendrils of power to toy with her nipples and clit until her eyes rolled and she shouted her release, clenching down on his cock like she'd never let him go.

He came hard, still thrusting as if he'd die if she didn't suck down every last drop, and then he wrapped her legs around his waist and leaned down to kiss her. His arms were shaking as he held himself up, but he didn't want to leave her body. He never did. Every time he had her, he was tempted to stay wrapped inside her warmth forever.

"You can give me your weight," she said as she pulled him against her. "I won't break."

He smiled. No, his Goddess wouldn't break, but he wanted to talk to her about something. He lifted up to look at her. She had a cute crease between her eyebrows. "What is it?"

"Are there traditions for our joining that you missed?"

She laughed a little. "I am the first God of Thule to be joined.

There are no traditions for this."

"We're making our own, then?"

Her smile was beautiful when she looked up at him. "The bond I have with you is the most beautiful of traditions. But I would like a marking like that of your people. And I would like nothing more than to have a place on your skin like the rest of your family."

"You don't want to do it at the celebration in your world?"

"No. It's something I want for myself. And I'm not sure when we will have time to deal with some big event." He loved the way she wrinkled her nose.

"You don't want a big display? A pretty dress?"

She shook her head. "I'm a Goddess. I can wear a pretty dress whenever I choose to." Her laughter was music to him. "The celebration will be for Thule. All I need is my place in your soul."

He groaned and kissed her.

"Then mark me, *thea mou*."

"Show me how." Her need was so strong it nearly brought him to his knees.

"Gladly." He demonstrated how to use the warm power as he set her hand against his chest. He groaned deep at the sensation of her marking him as hers. When she finished, she telepathically sent the image of her symbol spanning the entire width of his chest. The twin dragons were entwined with her name in the old language just as he'd wanted.

She stared at it for long moments before trailing her fingers over the curves. "It's beautiful. Does it hurt?"

He lifted her fingers to his lips. "It doesn't hurt. It feels like your warm palms are still on my skin, *thea mou*." Her soft hands were fucking heaven to him.

"Then can I have your mark there?"

"On your palms?"

She smiled. "Yes. So that my touch belongs to you."

He groaned deep and kissed her fingers and her palms. "I love you, Gefn."

"And I love you."

Chapter 29

Guardian Manor, Tetartos Realm

Sirena met with Drake and Era outside the hallway to Alyssa and Gregoire's new room. "They're all fine, but we are now missing another chunk out of the manor. We'll be lucky to have any rooms left by the time the baby comes." And she was very worried about it.

Smoke filtered from the dragon's lips. "When is the baby due?"

Alyssa's stomach had gone from flat to round in no time. Sirena felt her hands shaking when she answered, "Weeks. Maybe sooner if the little one surges in power again."

He shook his head, and she could feel the tension radiating from the dragon. "And you're certain this is not harming either baby or mother?"

"They're healthy, but that baby is incredibly powerful. Scarily so."

"I thought maybe the babe was getting more agitated because of the activity with Thule, but it could be the Tria," Era said. Her beautiful face was framed by black cherry hair, and Sirena could almost feel the power she was sending to calm her mate. Era was wearing a dark tank top showing the dragon marking on the female's bare shoulder. It moved and seemed to settle after a moment, the tattoo was a unique and entrancing manifestation of her bond with

Drake's beast.

Sirena took her eyes off the other female's skin and answered, "This time it felt linked to the Tria for sure. What are they doing?" Frustration welled.

Drake shook his head. "I don't know. But I will figure it out."

"How?"

"I don't know yet." Drake growled, frustrated. But she could feel his determination to find out. Era's golden eyes went stormy and a hint of her dragon smoke filtered from her lips. She was incredibly protective of her male. It was one of the things Sirena loved about the once feral female. She also appreciated how Era was thriving as a new healer, her eyes brightening whenever she was able to help use her deadly power for something good.

It was hard for Sirena to accept assistance because she'd always been so bent on taking care of everything herself, but right now the stress of Alyssa's baby and the fact that she was hiding something from her family was turning her inside out. "Alyssa and Gregoire would probably be grateful if you checked on her, Era." Sirena caught the way the female's eyes shone, and it both warmed her and made her feel out of sorts. Healing was her life. She shook it off. "Would you mind watching over things for a couple of hours while I grab some sleep?"

"I would be happy to," Era said with a beautiful smile that made Drake's features smooth as he gazed down at her.

"Call if you need me sooner," Sirena said as she headed down the long hallway to the suite of rooms she'd taken to be close in case Alyssa needed her. She was lost in her own world the second the door clicked shut behind her. Her head fell back against it, and she felt numb, hollow. She'd never thought to find a mate, Immortal females didn't generally mate a male less powerful than themselves, and that meant there were no compatible males in Earth. All the powerful males were related to her. The second she'd felt Hroarr's power, she'd been paralyzed with the knowledge of what he was to her. He hadn't touched her, so they were free, but the memory of his power licking at her skin, filling her senses, had ruined her. She hadn't even seen the male; all she'd known was the sensations wrought by wild tendrils of his ability and that deep seductive voice, a voice that caused shivers of desire to run through her body even now. It was one thing to know she'd never find a mate; it was an entirely different matter to know that her mate was some autocratic, asshole warlord God of another world. She would never leave her duties, her world, or her family.

She couldn't. She banged her head against the wood.

Slipping out of her high heels, she took a deep breath and started removing her clothes. That done, she tugged the tie from her hair while mentally turning on the shower. The warm water was just what she needed to relax her tight muscles.

After washing, she stayed under the spray until she felt her skin wrinkle. Sleep was a necessity, a deep sleep that wasn't invaded by imagining dirty words growled in a deep, seductive voice.

When she opened the shower door, she jolted at the sight of Gefn's cats staring back at her and barely contained her power before stopping their hearts. She'd heard they'd teleported to Vane, but they had to stop doing this or someone would harm them. She shook her head as they purred at her. "What are you two doing? I'm happy to see you're feeling better." When she stepped out to reach for a towel, she felt herself breaking apart.

She was shocked and then panicked when she couldn't stop herself from teleporting away, and in moments she knew exactly where they were taking her and fought against it hard, to no avail.

She reformed in a dark bathing room filled with steam and an intoxicating masculine scent she shouldn't know. Without looking, she knew the cats had gone, leaving her at the shadowed end of a small pool. She sucked in a breath at the sight of the massive male standing in profile under the spray of an open shower a couple dozen feet away. His black hair clung to muscled shoulders; a strand slid lovingly over his bearded cheek.

Sirena nearly moaned aloud at the sight of what he was doing to himself. One heavily muscled arm was braced against the wall as a tanned hand worked a massive cock. Harsh grunts issued from his lips as he violently thrust into his own palm. Every heavy muscle lining his body strained in the God's quest for completion.

She braced her back and hands against the wall, unable to move or to take her eyes from him as she fought the need to touch herself. His scent was drugging her. She could see the line of his jaw as it clenched under the short beard.

Her nipples were tight peaks as the steam caressed her overheated flesh, yet she was incapable of doing anything as she grew wetter with each animalistic noise that issued from him, clenching the lines of his stomach, his ass down to his thick thighs. He was made for a female's eyes. Every line, every dip, including the one that angled from his hip, directed her to that long, thick cock.

His bicep bunched with each hard pull against his flesh as he moved faster until finally throwing his head back on a harsh roar. She was completely mesmerized as his cock jetted streams of hot come against the wall; she'd never seen anything like it. Suddenly, he stilled. She hadn't realized she'd been holding her breath until his head snapped in her direction and she was captured in the emerald gaze of the most ruggedly gorgeous male she'd ever seen. Warrior

God.

He stalked from the water, growling a demand. "Who. Are. You?"

And then it was as if he were an animal scenting the air; his massive, muscled chest expanded. "Healer?" His tone changed from angry to that of a primal male as his hand moved back to his already re-hardening cock. "Have you come for payment?" Those emerald eyes flashed with so much blatant heat she nearly dropped to her knees.

But the sexual implication of what he'd said hit her like an anvil. If he touched her, it was over.

She teleported, but instead of going to Tetartos, she reformed back in his bathing room with a curse. He narrowed his eyes at her. His massive cock was getting heavier with every second that passed, and her traitorous eyes wouldn't stop staring at it.

The God growled, "What game is this?" He moved so fast she didn't see him. His arms caged her against the wall; he towered over her. She could feel his warmth, and the compulsion to touch was almost uncontrollable.

Someone hammered at the door before it was thrown open and his massive back was in front of her, shielding her. "Get out, Dagur."

She only heard the other male say, "It's urgent," before she found the will to move. She broke apart and reformed in the room where she'd healed the cats. It was empty of all but the two infuriating beasts.

She stared them down, her voice shaking. "You owe me. Take me home now, or I call Gefn and Pothos to get me." It was the last thing she wanted to do. If Pothos or the others found out her secret, it was all over. They would be the ones telling her that there was no outrunning fate.

She heard bellowing in the hallway. And was closing her eyes, getting ready to call for P when she was porting again. If the beasts took her back to Hroarr, she would have their fur for rugs.

When she touched down in her bathroom, she grabbed a towel, and one beast purred for her like they hadn't just nearly destroyed her life. "Don't think I will forget this," she snapped, pointing at them, and then they were gone.

There was no sleep in her future. She'd have to be on constant guard against matchmaking cats and now potentially marauding warrior Gods.

Her skin ached with need, and she was shaking with how close she'd come to the mating frenzy. That male was a force far beyond the males she was used to dealing with. There was no give, no compromise in him. He was not someone to be mated to. She groaned and collapsed in the chair by her bed, aching with desire she'd never be able to fulfill on her own. His scent was in her lungs, and she couldn't take a breath without having him inside her.

And now he knew who she was.

Chapter 30

Pothos' Home, Tetartos Realm

Gefn moaned as she woke with her male's mouth between her legs. Morning light slid through the balcony door as her back arched when Pothos ruthlessly sucked her clit. It wasn't long before she was gasping and mewling for release. *It's time to give your male his breakfast*, whispered into her mind. She writhed against his mouth until she cried out, coming against his relentless tongue. Her eyes were hooded as she watched him climb up her body with a wicked smile.

She was still catching her breath when he leaned down to kiss her.

Drake's voice in their minds broke his kiss and brought a string of curse words to his lips. "Everyone in. We have more fucking Tria issues."

She put a hand to her lips to still the laughter. "I know it's not funny... We can be fast," she offered.

He scowled and then groaned, "Not that fast."

He was upright and looking pained when they both felt something. The air charged, signaling that a strong portal was opening into Earth, to that mystical lake. She shot up and started to dress beside him, knowing it had to be her brothers.

Drake's voice was no less pleased when he added, "P, go see what your fucking in-laws want. Hades and I will both meet you there in case they have news about the darkness." Pothos had already warned his father and Drake that Gefn left instructions for her brothers to open a portal if she was needed. Even if she and Pothos had been in Thule, his Guardian family would have felt the disturbance of a portal and informed them telepathically. It was the best way she could think to communicate with her family.

So this could just be them checking on her, but in her gut it felt like something more ominous as she listened to Pothos answer Drake. "We're on it."

*****

P was cursing the confines of his fucking jeans and the fact that he was forced to meet his female's brothers with a hard-on when the door opened to their bedroom, displaying their furry entourage. The cats either now had opposable thumbs or had developed an ability with telekinesis.

"They could always do that," his Goddess answered offhandedly as she slid on her boots.

He shook his head and hoped to hell he wasn't about to get bad news, but the feeling in the pit of his gut told him this wasn't going to be good.

Within moments he, his Goddess, and the cats were at the lake.

Dagur and Hroarr both stepped through at the same time. Hroarr gazed around with ruthless intent, and P tensed, wondering what had set him off. Power emanated from him in relentless, furious waves.

Gefn tensed and was already anxiously demanding, "What is

it?”

His father, Sacha, Drake and Era all appeared at their side, alert to the dangerous tension in the air. It was nearly electric.

Dagur bit out, “You have a serious problem in this world.”

Those words filled P with dread, and his female gripped his hand tighter.

Gefn snapped, “What did you find?”

“Something exists in this world that is calling the darkness here.”

“How long do we have?” nearly all demanded at once.

Dagur was shaking his head and ground out, “A year at most, if you are blessed with luck. And that is if we cut off what is calling it here.”

Curses rang out from his father. “The Tria.”

“You know the cause?” Hroarr demanded.

“Yes,” P said as Gefn shook her head in shock.

Everything inside him pulled tight with the need to protect her, all of them.

His female started sharing the details of the Tria with her brothers as Drake bit out to Hades and P, “We need to get them into a more secure prison.”

P growled, “If we release three Gods, we can put them in the sleeping units.”

Son of a bitch, this was his worst nightmare. Apollo’s unit was broken, so they were going to put the bastard in Hades’ old unit. That meant they still needed three more. "Have we made any progress on creating more of the units?"

Smoke filtered into the sky from Drake's lips. "No. They were made with Creator power."

"We might be able to fit two of the Tria in one of the couple units," P bit out, thinking of the two larger units holding Aphrodite and Ladon or Athena and Niall.

"They must be separated. Have we learned nothing from what they are putting us through from their prison now? They are too powerful to be contained together," his father dismissed. Hades' furious power mixed with that of Hroarr's.

Hroarr's voice cleaved the air. "You will need more than you have to survive this." The male was shaking his head. "We can provide the prisons that will help your world, but I demand something in return."

Gefn growled, "Hroarr!"

Hades narrowed his eyes while flexing his wings. "What do you want?"

The warrior God's arrogant lips curled. "Your healer."

*****

The air had no sooner charged than Sirena was hit with a wave of panicked emotion. She used air currents to dry her hair and threw on clothes, knowing a portal was opening. Hroarr was coming. Would he seek her out? Demand answers as to why and how she had trespassed in his bathing room?

And then everything happened at once. Era informed Sirena that she and Drake were meeting the Thulians at the lake, and seconds later the entire manor rocked with the force of another explosion.

Sirena quickly answered Gregoire's urgent, bellowed summons and ported to Alyssa. He was beside her on the bed, his arms wrapped around his female, who was wincing in pain, her pale green eyes flashing with it. Gregoire was roaring for Sirena to do something and snarled at his mate's mother and father as they charged into the room. The sheer force of the power that rushed over the area was beautiful and wild. She put her hands to Alyssa's raised stomach at the same time the small female cried out.

The baby was coming whether they were ready or not.

She focused fully on her task as she infused her voice with enough power to soothe them all. "You're about to meet your baby girl."

Series Glossary of Terms and Characters - For Reference Only:

Agnarr – God of the world Thule, long ago ally of Hades

Ailouros – Immortal race of half felines, known as the warrior class, strong and fast

Akanthodis – Hell creature with spines all over its body and four eyes

Aletheia – Immortal race with enhanced mental abilities and power within their fluids, can take blood memories, strong telepathy, the race that spawned the vampire myth

Alex – AKA Alexandra, Demi-Goddess daughter of Athena, sister to Vane and Erik, mate to Uri

Alyssa – Hippeus (half warhorse), daughter of Adras and Ava, mate to Gregoire

Aphrodite – Sleeping Goddess, one of the three good Deities, mother to Drake

Apollo – God who experimented with the Immortal races, adding animal DNA to create the perfect army against his siblings

Ares – Sleeping God and father of the evil Tria who are imprisoned in Hell Realm

Artemis – Sleeping Goddess and mother of the evil Tria who are imprisoned in Hell Realm

Athena – Sleeping Goddess – One of only three Gods that were good and didn't feed off dark energies and become mad, mother of Alex,

Vane and Erik, mate to Niall

Bastian – AKA Sebastian, Kairos (teleporter), Guardian of the Realms, diplomat for the Guardians within Tetartos Realm, mated to Natasha (Tasha)

Brianne – Geraki (half ancient bird of prey), Guardian of the Realms, hybrid, mated to Vane

Charybdis – Immortal abused by Poseidon and then sold and experimented on in Apollo's labs, she gave a portion of her life force to create the mating spell, aka mating curse, so that no Immortal could breed with any other than their destined mate.

Conn – Lykos (half wolf), Guardian of the Realms, mated to Dacia

Creators – Almighty beings that travel worlds sowing the seeds of an ancient race, creating Immortals and giving birth to Gods

Cyril – Demi-God son of Apollo, Siren/healer, dead bad guy

Dacia – Lykos, mated to Conn

Dagur – God of Thule

Deleastis Rod – A spelled artifact that was used by Apollo to lure Immortals to him

Demeter – Sleeping Goddess

Demi-Gods or Goddesses – Those born to a God or Goddess

Dorian – Nereid, Guardian of the Realms, mated to Rain

Drake – AKA Draken, Demi-God dragon, leader of the Guardians of the Realms, son of Aphrodite and her Immortal dragon mate Ladon

Efcharistisi – City in Tetartos Realm

Eir – Long dead priestess of Thule, P's mother

Elizabeth – Aletheia – evil female who found a way to free Apollo

Emfanisi – Yearly, week-long event where Immortals and Mageia of age go to find mates

Era – AKA Delia, powerful female experimented on by Cyril, mated to Drake

Erik – Demi-God son of Athena, Ailouros (half-lion), Vane's twin, Alex's younger brother, mated to Sam

Fólkvangr – Realm of Thule

Gefn – Goddess of Thule

Geiravor – Priestess of Thule, bonded to Hroarr

Geraki – Immortal race of half bird of prey, power with air

Gregoire – Hippeus (half warhorse), Guardian of the Realms, mate to Alyssa

Guardians – Twelve warriors of different Immortal races chosen by the Creators to watch over the four Realms of the world.

Hades – One of the three good Gods, father to P (Pothos)

Havoc – Uri and Alex's pet hellhound that was rescued as a pup and bonded to Uri

Healers – AKA Sirens, Immortal race, power over the body, ability with their voices

Hellhounds – Massive black hounds blood bonded to the Tria in Hell Realm

Hephaistos – Sleeping God

Hera – Sleeping Goddess

Hermes – Sleeping God and Apollo's partner in the experimentation and breeding of Immortals for their army

Hippeus – Immortal race of half warhorses, power over earth

Hroarr – Ruling God of Thule

Ileana – Ailouros (liger), Jax's mate

Jax – AKA Ajax, Ailouros (half tiger), Guardian of the Realms

Kairos – Immortal race whose primary power is teleportation

Kara – Goddess of Thule, imprisoned by the Guardians after her attempt to take Hades

Ladon – Immortal dragon, mate to Aphrodite, father of Drake, friend of Jax

Laire – Guard of the Goddess Gefn of Thule

Limni – City in Tetartos Realm

Lofodes – City in Tetartos Realm

Lykos – Immortal half wolf with the power of telekinesis

Mageia – Evolved humans, mortals compatible to be an Immortal's mate, have abilities with one of the four elements; air, fire, water, or earth.

Mates – Each Immortal has a rare and destined mate, their powers meld and they become stronger pairs that are able to procreate, usually after a decade.

Mating Curse – A spell cast in Apollo's Immortal breeding labs that ensured the God wouldn't be able to use them to continue creating his army. Charybdis cast the spell using a portion of her life force and now Immortals can only procreate with their destined mates.

Mating Frenzy – Starts when an Immortal comes into contact with their destined mate, a sexual frenzy that continues through to the bonding/mating ceremonies.

Mist – Immortal priestess of Thule, bonded to the God Hroarr

Nastia – AKA Chaos, Immortal created by Apollo, twin to Natasha

Natasha – AKA Tasha and Nemesis, Immortal created by Apollo, Nastia's twin

Nereid – Immortal race of mercreatures, power over water

Ofioeidis – Huge serpent hell beasts, hardest to kill out of all the hell creatures

Ophiotaurus – Hell beast with the head of a bull and tail of a snake

Ouranos – City in Tetartos Realm

P – AKA Pothos, Guardian of the Realms, Son of Hades, second to Drake

Phoenix – Immortal race with ability over fire

Poseidon – Sleeping God

Þrír – Thulian priestesses or Immortal three who are bonded to a God or Goddess of Thule

Rain – Mageia, destined mate to Dorian, best friend of Alyssa

Realms – Four Realms of Earth; Earth - where humanity exists,

Heaven - where good and neutral souls go to be reincarnated, Hell - where the Tria were banished and evil souls are sent, Tetartos – Realm of beasts – where the Immortals were exiled by the Creators

Reginleif – Immortal priestess of Thule, bonded to the God Hroarr

Sacha – Kairos (teleporter), Guardian of the Realms, diplomat for the Guardians within Tetartos Realm, Bastian's mother

Sam – AKA Samantha Palmer, mated to Erik, power over metal, Mageia/Ailouros

Sander – Phoenix, Guardian of the Realms

Sirena – Siren (healer), Guardian of the Realms, primarily works to find mates for Immortals in Tetartos

Spa – Massive black lynx looking cat gifted to the Goddess Gefn at her birth, one of the two Guardians of Thule

Tetartos Realm – The Immortal exile Realm, once known as the Realm of Beasts

Thalassa – City in Tetartos Realm, where the Lykos clans live

Thule – Once thought a mythical land to the north, it is a world where Hades long ago found allies in God's birthed by different Creators

Tria – Evil Triplets spawned from incestuous coupling of Ares and Artemis; Deimos, Phobos and Than

Tsouximo – Hell beast resembling a giant scorpion

Tyr – Evil God of Thule

Uri – AKA Urian, Aletheia, interrogator, Guardian of the Realms, mate to Alex

Vane – Demi-God son of Athena, Ailouros (half-lion), Erik's twin, Alex's younger brother, Brianne's mate

Velspar – Massive black lynx looking cat gifted to the Goddess Gefn at her birth, one of the two Guardians of Thule

Zeus – Sleeping God

COMING SOON!

New Releases

Subscribe to Setta Jay's newsletter for:

book release dates

exclusive excerpts

giveaways

http://www.settajay.com/

About The Author:

Setta Jay is the author of the popular Guardians of the Realms Series. She's garnered attention and rave reviews in the paranormal romance world for writing smart, slightly innocent heroines and intense alpha males. She loves writing stories that incorporate a strong plot with a heavy dose of heat. Her influences include Judith McNaught who she feels writes a smart heroine to perfection, Gena Showalter, Maya Banks and Lora Leigh. You can often find her writing compared to JR Ward, but if you are a fan of the Black Dagger Brotherhood be warned that Setta Jay's novels are more erotic in nature.

Born a California girl, she currently resides in Idaho with her husband of ten plus years who she describes as incredibly sexy and supportive.

She loves to hear from readers so feel free to ask her questions on social media or send her an email, she will happily reply.

Where you can find her:

http://www.settajay.com/

https://www.facebook.com/settajayauthor

https://twitter.com/SETTAJAY_

https://www.goodreads.com/author/show/7778856.Setta_Jay

CPSIA information can be obtained
at www.ICGtesting.com
Printed in the USA
FSHW02n2017140818
51449FS